THE ONE
SPECIES INTERVENTION
#6609

J.K. Accinni

EK Publishing
Lakewood Ranch, FL

This is a work of fiction. Names, characters, places and incidents are either the product of the author's imagination or are used fictitiously, and any resemblance to actual persons, living or dead, business establishments, events, or locales is entirely coincidental.

THE ONE
SPECIES INTERVENTION #6609
J.K. Accinni

An EK Publishing book published in arrangement with the author, Lakewood Ranch, FL.

Other Books by J.K. Accinni:

Baby (Species Intervention #6609, Book 1)

Echo (Species Intervention #6609, Book 2)

Armageddon Cometh (Species Intervention #6609, Book 3)

Hive (Species Intervention #6609 Book 4)

Evil Among Us (Species Intervention #6609, Book 5)

Dedication

This book is dedicated to the memory of my grandfather, Sherly Burrow. He was born in 1898 and his farm is the setting for the Hive.

As a child, I played on the granite rocks in the woods that guard the Hive. To this day, I still have dreams in my sleep of the private moments I dreamed of fairies, curled in the very depression on the rock where Scotty fell asleep on as a boy in *Echo*.

But this is a tribute to Bunka, my grandfather, who got up to work before sunrise to tend the farm. He worked long and hard along with my grandmother, and later my mom. In the summers, he would move my mom and aunt into the dining room so they could make some extra money by renting out their room to young men who came from Germany to Sussex County for the summer. They were part of a large group called the Hitler Youth. Yes, that Hitler.

My mom has wonderful memories of her life on the farm. Even though the sometimes backbreaking work was never over, she did it with a father she adored. A father that sat with his children on the front porch during thunderstorms so they could enjoy the lightning. A father who taught his children the ethic of hard work and responsibility; of telling the truth and never cheating; of kindness to others and respect for the land and the creatures who thrive on it.

They never knew they were poor because they had the farm and each other.

A few years before he died, he sat me down and spoke of things he had seen in his lifetime. The first plane, the first car, the first radio, the cure for polio that had inflicted my mother . . .

I'm very thankful for the time in which he lived. For if he could see the world as it is now, he would cry.

Chapter 1

2058 AD

The library resonated to echoes of their footsteps on the dusty rock floor as they made their way through the silent makeshift stacks of books; the classics rubbing spines with zombie and vampire paperbacks from 2013.

Jose and Wil carried the treasured seed in two crocks, while Abby and Netty guided Baby and Echo to the back of the library.

"It's just off the tunnel that was used to get the books here."

Netty opened the door to Daisy's classroom, where they quickly passed the artifacts from other planets. Planets that existed in other solar systems, in other galaxies.

"Ah, the possibilities." Netty spoke low, and Abby smiled and nodded as if she herself had been thinking the same thing.

"As Daisy becomes more proficient, I have great hopes she'll convince her mother to let her have the procedure. I think we can leave it in her hands. There's no point in trying to persuade Ginger Mae ourselves. She'd only fight us. Besides, there will come a time when Daisy is an adult and can make her own decisions. Even though she'll still look like a child, her mother will not be able to interfere," Netty announced.

As the Elders reached the back of the room, Netty swept away the camouflaging debris that masked a diminutive opening into the beginnings of an endless tunnel.

Baby and Echo entered first, accepting the containers of seed as Wil and Jose knelt to squeeze themselves through the opening. After wrenching their prodigious wings painfully through the hole in the wall, they stood, smoothed their bent feathers and healed the unfortunate broken ones.

"Are the two of you all set?" Netty's voice carried from the other side. Abby's heart tripped as she weighed their risk. Auras calmed her mind as the minions reassured her.

"Sister Abby, fear not. We have a big task, but we will be back safely. And we will destroy the tunnel behind us when we are clear. Brother Wil and Brother Jose will depart as soon as they have secured the seed. Trust and have faith. The Womb is with us."

"The Womb be with you," Abby and Netty murmured together.

The foursome didn't have to wait long before they found the tunnel branching off in the direction of their destination.

Turning south, they started the walk that would take them most of the night. Wil and Jose found they could make better time if they carried Baby and Echo. Unfortunately, the tunnel wasn't large enough to allow them to fly.

The fact that they had never been there before was an additional handicap; they could only will themselves there if they could encapsulate themselves with their wings and envision a location they had once visited.

Using their luminous eyes to light their way, they walked throughout the night. Arriving at their destination, they stood before a dead end. Jose approached the wall.

"This is it?"

"Yeah, we should be able to kick it in." Instructing Baby and Echo to stand back, they set aside the casks of seeds and began kicking.

Little by little, a hole developed in the wall. They worked hard to widen it until it was big enough to allow them to slip into a large cavern, similar to the one they had gathered in on the survivors' first evening in the Hive, almost a year ago.

Helping Baby and Echo scramble through the hole, they set down the seed casks and decided to do some exploring first.

"We must proceed carefully, Jose. If we are discovered it could be the end of our own safety and comfortable existence in the Hive. The Womb will not tolerate any possible threat to the animals. There is no telling what would happen."

"Yeah, yeah, I know. We'll just be a few minutes. Echo, you and Baby stay here and get started. You remember where everything goes?"

"Brother Jose, this is not our first time. Did you not see the growing field that Brother Scotty and Brother Kane are so proud of?"

Jose grimaced. "Sorry, guys. I forgot. I know you'll do a good job. We'll be back in a while."

Wil and Jose crept quietly out of the cavern. Weaving their way around obstructions on the dirt floor, they found a tunnel leading away from the cavern. Signs of long-forgotten mining abounded; old-fashioned timbers still shored up the walls and ceiling, although some had dropped to the ground.

"Do you think we need to make this safer, Wil?"

Tripping over a fallen brace, Wil steadied himself. "I guess I could have the Kreyven check it out."

The two Elders poked around some more, wondering how far off the beaten path they were.

After thirty minutes of exploring, they picked up the smell of smoke. Following the acrid scent, they were led to a fire pit in a small cavern not far from where Baby and Echo worked. Piles of debris had been swept to the side to create a clearing. Burnt-out torches lined the walls. Bowls sat on the floor alongside hand-hewn beams which had been placed around the fire, perhaps to serve as a place to sit.

Wil picked up a bowl and sniffed, upending it to have liquid drip to the dirt floor. A rudimentary spit was suspended over the blackened fire.

"Looks like someone's been cooking here. And not too long ago."

Jose kicked around the debris pile, his foot hitting something with a crunch. He bent down to investigate, freezing as the round shapes came into focus.

"You better come here, Wil," he said, swallowing tightly.

Wil made his way to the debris pile as Jose pushed one of the objects with a toe.

"Oh, good Lord. It's true. We'd better get out of here. Come on, Jose. There's no telling how often they use this fire."

Wil and Jose hurried back to Echo and Baby, leaving behind the evidence of boiled human skulls from the most vulnerable in all species: the newborns.

Echo finished digging in the newly-arrived fertile soil. As she dug a hole, Baby would drop in a seed and lightly cover it over.

The Kreyven worked hard and fast, filling the cavern with the smell of sulfur as it carved more efficiently than a modern-day steam shovel. The basin for the waterway began to fill with water that trickled down the wall of the cavern from the new hole the Kreyven had punched in the ceiling. Before long, the trickle had turned into a nice, steady flow, having been directed from an underground spring through a new pathway created by the Kreyven through solid rock.

Wil and Jose appeared, watching as the minions and the Kreyven finished their miraculous creation: a brand new and productive growing field.

Once Baby and Echo had emptied half the caskets, Wil and Jose joined in the planting. The Kreyven sent solid ribbons from its body along the freshly-planted rows to create trenches, which the trickles of water sought out hungrily, bringing lifeblood to the waiting miracle seeds.

After laboring long and hard, the two Elders and golden minions made their way back to the small hole Wil and Jose had kicked through the wall. They turned back to the new growing field to watch the Kreyven conclude the life-giving construction.

"This is taking longer than I thought, Wil. We need to get out of here." Jose's anxious whispers made them all jittery.

"Calm down. We're almost done. If someone shows up, the Kreyven will take care of it."

"But Wil, we can't have that. They would never return to discover the new groves."

"Look, Jose. We're almost done. Relax, would you?"

The Kreyven hovered over the new field from its position in the cavern wall. They watched as it appeared to puff itself up, increasing its monstrous size. The odor of fresh organic loam combined with sulfur to make the air unbreathable.

They backed away as the Kreyven let loose with a black substance, spraying it over the new soil. It then began to shoot a mucky flesh-colored substance onto the walls of the great cavern. As the substance hit the walls, it spread, changing color and lighting the cave with ultraviolet light that would, in time, take on all the properties of the wondrous membrane that lined the walls of the Hive.

The Kreyven turned to the hole in the wall where the foursome huddled. It slowly descended from the heights of the cavern to suspend itself in front of the opening.

Echo wobbled out from behind Wil and Jose to peer at the creature. The Kreyven swayed to the left and to the right, appearing to assess the minion.

"Echo, I think you need to back away." Jose slipped himself in front of the little creature. The Kreyven jerked back up to the highest point of the cavern. Echo's aura pricked Jose's mind.

"It is not necessary, Brother Jose. The Kreyven is just curious. It is in the service of the Womb. It is time for us to go. It needs to seal up this hole and remove all traces of our visit."

They backed away just in time as the Kreyven gathered itself to attack the hole, leaving the growing field silent but charged with miraculous activity under the blanket of extraordinary earth.

Chapter 2

Ginger Mae and Daisy finished breakfast, the remains of Netty's delicious purplewort loaf lying in crumbs on their plates.

It had been three months since Seth's justified death by the Kreyven. From the looks of the rest of the survivors, that was now a distant memory; camaraderie was back in boisterous force.

They ducked as flying food sailed over their heads from another table, accompanied by hoots and sniggers.

Ginger Mae breathed a grateful sigh as she realized most of her confidence regarding their safety sat firmly back in place.

"Momma, it's time for me to begin my lessons. I'll have Kimir accompany me to my lab."

"Oh, you will, will you?" She smiled at her seven-year-old precocious daughter. "Since when is it your lab?"

"Silly you, Momma, you know I alone use the lab, hence the possessive pronoun."

Ginger Mae rolled her eyes at Daisy. Her daughter dribbled water from her mouth onto her plate, watching it splatter. She stuck a finger to her tongue and sucked, watching her mother from the corner of her eye, a suggestion of mirth tugging at her lips.

"Don't put your fingers in your mouth, Daisy."

She slapped the finger away from her child's lips. Her head swam with the realization that Daisy's powerful mind was robbing her of the joys normal children experienced.

Yes, the Hive did present limitations to a child's growth, but they truly had everything they needed for productive childrearing. Trees to climb in the growing fields while the pollinators slept, water to splash in the bathing caves, corridors upon corridors to play in, creatures to further the development of responsible compassion, a huge and diverse family of caring adults to model after, healthy and unusual foodstuffs to delight the most finicky child, and a first-rate library to expand the mind.

Ginger Mae tapped her work-reddened finger on her smooth cheek as her eyes tracked Netty and Abby's figures, wings tightly molding their backs, tawny tails flexing naturally as they moved around the sink washing bowls.

She couldn't help but wonder what exactly they had planned to do to Daisy if she had been willing to relent and give permission for this procedure they wanted her to have so badly.

She glanced again at her unusual daughter, assessing the likelihood that she would eventually demand the procedure herself.

Daisy's hair hung thin and lank, no matter what she did to it. Her pale skin shined with an unblemished translucence, giving her a fragile appearance. But her light-gray eyes; they sparkled with unbridled curiosity and intelligence. She could identify a spark of raw determination that had not been there a mere year ago.

And how was it that Daisy had miraculously learned to speak upon her first meeting with Abby?

"Sorry." Ginger Mae nodded hello as Peter and Bonnie squeezed by in their perpetual hurry to assist with the animals. Sighing over the mystery of her daughter, she rose to carry their dirty plates to the sink so her day could begin.

First up, bathing the stranger; then off to start the daily census. Parking Daisy in a chair, she crossed back to Abby to question her.

"Will she be with you all day?"

Abby gave her a gentle smile. "If that's okay with you. I have work to do in the library, and Netty will set up her lessons."

"You mean hook her up to those weird contraptions."

The young Elder ran her hand up and down Ginger Mae's arm, the warmth of her golden touch soothing her.

"I'm sorry. I know she's only learning things. It's just that she's my only child. The only child in the Hive if you don't count Kimir. That makes her the youngest."

"You can trust me, Ginger Mae. She's in good hands. And she's so happy. We all want that for her. I know you do too. Even if her path is meant to be different."

Ginger Mae nodded, giving Abby the suggestion of a smile.

"Let's just make sure it's not *too* different, okay?"

With her firm tone, she had made it clear to Abby that she was the one in charge. Waving to Daisy and picking up her clipboard, towels and small bucket of hot water, she said goodbye and left the homey seductiveness of the kitchen.

Lumbering along the stone corridors, careful not to slosh her hot water, she unexpectedly caught a glimpse of Gloria and Billy sneaking into the sleeping caves. *Hmmm, bet I know what they're up to.*

"Hi, Ginger Mae." Captain Cobby and Karen passed her in the corridor, hand in hand, Cobby nodding as Karen gave her a blissful beam.

What, I'm the only one working today? Smiling back, Ginger Mae turned and entered the chamber that held the man called Hudson.

Dipping her cloth back into the cooling water, she finished rinsing Hudson's now dense, long, dark hair. She contemplated a haircut but decided, why bother? Except for the occasional visit from Netty, she was the only one who ever saw him. She suspected that most in the Hive barely remembered he was here.

As she dressed the now healed and reasonably fit man, she surveyed his body for signs that might prevent him from regaining consciousness.

A few months ago, she had gathered from Netty that the man was in his late fifties. He certainly didn't look that old to her now. Maybe forty five? She had come to accept that most in the Hive no longer looked their exact age due to the health benefits from the nightly tendrils.

She brushed up against the one that disappeared into Hudson's ear; watching it ripple as if to say excuse me. He was obviously responding well to the effects of the tendrils, yet still remained in a coma.

Brushing the wrinkles out of his new, clean smock, she slipped it over his head, lifting him to brace his upper body with her shoulder as she smoothed it down over his naked healthy form.

Hudson let out a sigh. She raised an eyebrow as she hadn't heard such a sound from him before, only groans.

Now it was her turn to sigh as she laid him back down, dropped her cloth into her bucket and lowered herself to the hard floor, overcome by a sudden wave of loneliness.

Sitting cross-legged, she took her face into her wet hands and held her head. An unexpected tear coursed down her cheek as the memory of the two couples in the corridor flitted across her mind.

By no means was she jealous, but she couldn't shake the unexpected feeling that had just blindsided her. *Since when have I ever felt so lonely, except for the time I waited for Daisy to be born? And even then, it had felt different than it does now.* She lifted her hands to rub them hard into her scalp, then massaged the bridge of her nose while her mind searched for the source of her discomfort and loneliness.

"Can I give you a hand with something, miss?" Ginger Mae's heart missed a beat as she looked up to see the man she had been nursing for so long sitting upright, his feet over the side of his dais, all traces of the tendrils evaporated, and with a kind smile on his rugged face.

She slowly rose to her feet, not taking her eyes off the man. Her mouth dropped open, astonishment muddling her senses.

The man struggled to stand, finding himself very unsteady. She rushed to his side, slipping his arm over her shoulder as he became aware of the uniqueness of his surroundings. It was his turn to open his mouth to speak, but he became overwhelmed with the sensory strangeness.

"What . . . I . . . miss, who . . . I don't . . ."

"Shh . . . it's okay, sir. Please, why don't you just lie back down?" She eased him back onto the dais, where he remained in a sitting position, bewilderment his sole expression.

"I don't understand. Where am I? Who are you?"

His hands roamed over his body, he flexed his extremities and found himself sound. "Why am I not dead? I don't feel . . . pain." His eyes closed tightly. Waiting a beat, he opened them to expose her to the agony that lurked on the surface.

"Where's the angel? I remember a beautiful angel." His eyes roamed over her face and body.

"You're the angel, aren't you? But your wings . . . where are they?"

His eyes rested on her forehead. "No, I guess not. She was golden with horns . . . she had horns that sparkled in the dark. Please . . . can you not speak to me? Miss? Can you tell me your name?"

"Oh, yes . . . I'm so sorry. I just don't know where to start." They stared at each other as the seconds ticked away. He slowly extended his hand.

"Well then, lovely lady, let me start first. My name is Hudson. My friends call me Hud."

She rose to take his hand, finding it warm and strong despite his weakened condition. She looked into his eyes as a feeling tickled the back of her stomach.

"I'm pleased to meet you, Mr. Hudson. My name is Ginger Mae Shrute."

News of Hudson's awakening raced through the Hive. Some were frightened, all were curious. Most of all, Netty was forced to come to terms with the finality of her former life resurfacing in the form of the cowardly sheriff who had failed to honor his badge and prevent her greedy, psychotic and unrepentant ex-husband from having them all killed.

As much she had been touched by his plea for forgiveness when he became aware of her identity the night they had discovered Baby's brand of retribution, she planned to weigh his every move in the Hive.

As life would have it, Ginger Mae wouldn't take her eyes off Hudson for months to come as he slowly integrated himself into the Hive, after first coming to terms with the fact that he was still alive and his own family long dead.

He retained no memory of the decades Baby had held him hostage in the tiny cavern with the other two men. And he apparently no longer recognized Netty, Wil or Baby. To him, they were the rulers of the underground sanctuary where he found himself after being awakened from the dead.

All of the survivors, with the consent of the Elders, agreed to let the past remain the past until Hudson himself felt the compulsion to inquire.

Loading the recovered man up with just the facts of the war above, the current year of his existence, the life in the Hive, an explanation for Baby, Echo, the Elders and a huge tiger that skulked in the background without eating anyone was more than any one mind could ever hope to process.

Even the existence of the Womb was held in abeyance until Wil decided Hudson could handle the facts.

The dishonored sheriff naturally chose Ginger Mae to attach himself to; joining her at meals, helping her with the census, and taking delight in her daughter.

Daisy and Hudson fast became buddies as he professed an interest in her studies at the library, joining her from time to time and gaining a growing awareness of the insignificance of man and his planet.

The tall, quiet gentleman of wisdom and firm voice became someone to rely on as he took turns helping everyone with their projects, including a stint in the growing fields, yet always coming back to Ginger Mae and her creatures.

It was no surprise to anyone when Hudson and Ginger Mae fell in love . . . except to them of course.

It was only one year later that Ginger Mae and Hudson, now called Hud by all, were married in the first official wedding held in the Hive.

At the lovely ceremony, Ginger Mae was given away by a somber Dezi. The best man was none other than Wil, who had incongruously developed a great friendship with Hud. The ceremony was officiated with all necessary gravitas by a benevolent Netty. The two flower children, who preceded the beautiful bride and her handsome groom down the makeshift aisle in the great cavern of the survivors' beginnings, as well as a few sad endings, was none other than Daisy, hand in hand with Baby tottering alongside.

Baby considered it a great honor as he continued to be mesmerized by Ginger Mae's position of mother to the wondrous Daisy. Privately, it was astonishing to all the survivors that Baby's bloodthirsty streak of revenge no longer deviled him, allowing him to peacefully accept Hudson's presence in his life.

Behind them minced baby Tobi, adorned in a wreath of fragrant greenery picked and woven by Kenya and Chloe. Tobi stole the show as she ran from guest to guest glad-handing or, shall we say, glad-trunking?

Crystal's mother pig, Tulip, attended, adorned with made-over fragments of her long-discarded tutu. Caesar melted into the background with the dog posse, never taking his eyes off Scotty, who stood stoically while Chloe cast pensive eyes from her beau to the bride and groom.

Only the Womb could tell how many women cast wishful musings toward the men whose arms they clung to as Netty pronounced the happy couple, man and wife.

Needless to say, a great time was had by all as the festivities carried on merrily into the night.

Chapter 3

2066 AD

Suzy carefully ran the clippers through ten-year-old Tandy's hair, relieved to find lice. She knew some of the men in the vast camp were not above checking through the mass of discarded hair in the dirt to confirm their presence, trying to catch her in a lie to discredit her with Doc Benjamin.

When she was lucky enough to find lice in one head, she found she could get away with claiming a dozen. The men were so squeamish about the bugs, no one checked further. She found it a great advantage in her efforts to keep the younger girls safe as long as possible from the sexual advances of the men who owned them.

"There you go, Tandy. You might want to mention you've come down with scabies if you're bothered again. I'll speak to Doc Benjamin for you. He needs to know the men aren't honoring his laws about the age of consent. I'm sorry they tried to force themselves on you. This should help. You have a good three years yet before you have to submit."

Suzy lowered her voice as a group of grungy men trudged by, their boots clanging loudly on the boards that lay on the floor of the cave, lifting them a few inches off the cold, muddy floor.

She kept her glance conciliatory and vague, forcing her natural intelligence and bitter resentment to stay well concealed.

She was fully aware of the festering anger against her as she insidiously influenced Doc Benjamin to the benefit of the women in camp, even at her budding age of fourteen. For her, it was all about surviving until she could find a way to escape.

Her and Liz's idea to shave off the hair of the younger and most vulnerable of the female children was showing encouraging progress. Little girls hardly look seductive with shaved heads, discussions of lice, nasty clothes, and surreptitious applications of feces to their shoes and the backs of their leggings.

Whatever it took to keep the little ones safe from the perverted sexual advances of their common enemy was a necessity. The fact that she herself would be at risk if not for the occasional protection of Doc Benjamin made her more determined to give the others every edge she could dream up.

Little Tandy scampered off after a timid hug for Suzy, looking like an emaciated scarecrow. She had felt Tandy's bones protruding under her layers of rags, her skin shuddering with the perpetual chill of their makeshift temporary home.

She set the heavy clippers down, shutting off the electrical connection that Avery maintained for her on Doc's orders. She dropped her aching arm down across her lap to rest as she struggled to massage the tired muscles. Tandy was her fifteenth cut today. Not all new shaves, some just touch ups, but holding the heavy metal razor was very tiring nonetheless.

She breathed in heavily, feeling a hitch in her chest even as she sucked in the too-common stench of feces and sweet, ripe sweat.

Most of the tribe only bathed occasionally. There was only so much you could do with one bucket of water per person each day for cooking and cleaning. At least Doc Benjamin had decreed drinking water would be limitless.

Straightening up, she quickly packed up her precious razor. It had taken her months to wheedle it away from Doc Benjamin. Her constant complaints of lice in her own hair had finally worn him down, but she knew she couldn't take her eye off it or it would disappear. Slipping it into its box, she tamped it down to the bottom of her worn backpack for safe keeping. Her fingers searched, reassuringly patting the pilfered medications she needed to deliver to the other side of camp.

Scanning the makeshift construction of hodgepodge tiny hovels strewn around the main cave, she waited for the right moment to begin her difficult errand of tracking down Liz. She unfortunately lived in one of the other caves reserved for the men held in less esteem by Doc Benjamin.

Liz was in her late twenties. The only reason she hadn't been discarded by her man was because she was so smart and funny. Their lives were so tragic that anyone who could maintain a gentle humor was valued. To have the ability to make one of the men laugh was priceless. Her man kept her in his hovel with the other females he bedded simply because she made him feel good in a different way. She was an Insider.

The discarded women typically slept outside with what comfort they could fashion from cast-off and surplus materials. They were the Outsiders.

Of course, nighttime was dangerous. That was when the weaker of the men prowled the discards of the stronger. Many of the women were claimed and dragged to the front of the cave where the undesirables slept, exposed to the unspecified dangers of the cold winds which blew through the opening to the entrance of their home; low in status, lower in wealth.

Yes, wealth. Females were coin. To be traded, awarded, loaned or sold.

Females did 70 percent of the work in the camps and all of the cooking and cleaning. They never stopped, not even at night. And lo, to be the lucky man with plenty of females. Remember the old expression, the rich get richer? The old practice of barefoot and pregnant now took on a more useful meaning. And if what Liz and the older woman suspected was true, a very sinister one indeed.

Her squinty brown eyes, alert as a bird of prey's, watched for her chance to cross through the council square in the middle of the cavern, with the huts ringing the clearing based on Doc's own private ranking system.

She was haunted by the verbose claims as the men congregated in the square after dinner with Doc Benjamin to scream about what they would do if they managed to find the lost shelter of Suzy's grandfather.

The current wisdom was that it was filled with all the gold from the U.S. Treasury. Suzy wondered what gold looked like and what one would do with it. To her mind, the only thing of value she could recognize was freedom. *Or maybe a fresh juicy peach,* she thought wistfully.

She retained little memory of her old family. Just two names, Lorna and Seth. He had either been a friend or relative; no one seemed to be clear anymore. She thought she remembered having a sister, but she wasn't sure. Frankly, she didn't have much time to think about it as her life was consumed by frantic plots and subterfuge, all meant to keep her safe.

Liz was the center of the well-guarded subversion the women tried to keep alive in their ranks. But they had to be careful. There were spies everywhere. Some of the women would sell out their sisters to curry favor with the man that owned them. Especially the older ones as their looks faded quickly in their new, unhealthy environment.

The sickness in the air from the war nine years ago had robbed everyone of their vitality. Oddly, it had taken a bigger toll on the women. It shouldn't be a surprise that some would turn on their friends, hoping for an extra morsel at dinner; their only real meal, if you could call it that. But it was more nourishing than the unleavened flatbread dispersed by the communal kitchen every morning.

Suzy had once overheard Doc and Avery whispering about the fact that their flour supplies were dangerously low. It forced her to wonder why most of Doc's inner circle looked so much heftier than everyone else. The only tribe members who ate extra rations were the myriad of expecting women and the scouts. Doc was forced to bribe the scouts with extra grub to motivate them to do their jobs.

Facing the winds, pregnant with an assortment of hot bugs, came at great risk to anyone's health. Unfortunately, someone had to do the nasty job of combing the countryside for anything left alive that could be eaten.

They labored to locate vacant grocery stores which might have something left in their cellars or storerooms, even breaking into homes to salvage what may have been left behind. And pharmacies. Not that much was ever found.

They usually had better luck with medicine cabinets in the vacant homes. When you're fleeing for your life, you just don't think about what's in your medicine cabinet. Although other thugs and marauders had usually picked the houses clean from the year of the bombs, they hit jackpots often enough to keep Doc supplied and make the risk acceptable. Everyone knew that if they ran out of the critical medicines scavenged by the scouts, many would sicken further and die.

The fact that all of the original members of the scouting teams were now dead, failed to discourage the younger members of the new teams. No doubt, the extra rations and periodic borrowing of the camp women to help them relax and enjoy their week's rotation off, served to obscure most thoughts regarding their probable early demise.

She looked down on her own frame, poking her bones under their layers of rags and salvaged clothing retrieved by the scouts. She felt her tender skin stretched taut over bony ridges that stood out in deep relief. Her bald head sprouted scabs all over its sallow surface.

She was lucky that Doc Benjamin shared his creams and medicine with her, or her sores would weep and stink like the rest. She never failed to catch the resentful glances at her dry head. Doc's favoritism did not go unnoticed.

Now that she was no longer a child, the men thought she should integrate into the community like the rest of them. She knew she was referred to as Doc's house pet, even though she did her share of work around camp.

But the truth of the designation made her very useful to Liz and her group of defiant women. And that was the only thing that mattered to her. She vowed to do all she could to participate in the growing female insurrection, with the fervent hope that it could somehow lead to her freedom.

You see, Suzy Calloway had a secret. Years ago, as Doc Benjamin treated her with inexplicable kindness, she had re-emerged from the distant, deep blackness her mind had chosen to hide itself in. Her psyche slowly sparked; a tiny ember that flickered in the shadows, desperate for the nourishment that would allow it to burst into a tangible flame capable of sustaining itself and allowing the traumatized child to live again.

It had taken a few years, but Suzy's mind had healed. She wasn't quite as good as new, but better. They say if life doesn't break you, you grow stronger. Regrettably, Suzy had been broken. The sweet, innocent and sheltered child from a happy prosperous home with doting grandparents was forever gone.

Funny how nature sometime hands you exactly the tools you need to survive as circumstances blindside you. Some fail to adjust and perish, while others discover a buried capability.

For, in the place of the naïve victim of a brutal kidnapping, a cunning and secretive creature had emerged, wise beyond her years in the art of manipulation. Her education had been fast-tracked over the days and months she had studied everyone in camp as her recovery afforded her the unexpected opportunity. From Doc Benjamin's elite hovel, she watched, absorbing everything. Her survivor's mind calculated who had the power; both real and perceived.

She marveled in her cunning virgin's mind as the men fashioned a makeshift town of bastardized abodes, using the paraphernalia looted from so many small towns and cities, purloined from the cold hands of so many murdered folks.

And then the time came to mutely witness tribe members sickening and disappearing, her thoughts refusing to accept the silent ride on their death trolley as one of the men wheeled it down the deep burial tunnel to dispose of. Oh, no. That was not going to happen to her.

Over time, she celebrated silently with the rest of the boisterous tribe members as Avery harnessed the mystery of their water source alongside the western wall of the enormous cavern.

It rose a dozen stories to the pinnacle of the astonishing launch of their life-saving waterfall. The fall dropped powerfully past the floor of their cavern to disappear deep within the serpentine faults of the mineral-laden boulders and walls of their ancient refuge. It allowed them to fill their buckets with a system of lines rigged by the ingenious Avery.

The mist from the thunderous falls drenched the surfaces of the rock walls and cold floor, intensifying the bitter cold and creating a dangerously slippery environment. Therefore, Doc restricted the water gathering to the necessities. Baths were not considered necessary, of course.

The women managed the best they could. Liz drummed it into them all that a clean body was a healthy body. Their bodies were the only currency they could attempt to control. If they were to obtain their freedom, above all, they must stay healthy.

Eventually, the tribe obtained fully-functioning electricity, thanks to the mechanical genius behind Avery's huge ugly mug and their lifesaving waterfall. Candles no longer burned to add smoke to the widening cloud of pollution that gathered high in the cavern ceiling like a malignant tumor from the numerous individual fires that burned for warmth and cooking.

As the pollution cloud increased, Doc's council members wisely decided a central cooking arrangement would be of great benefit. Preferably in an unexplored tunnel they could test for a possible ventilation source to remove the deadly smoke.

A location was selected and the demands on the woman increased as they staffed a huge cooking facility created to feed the several hundred members of the tribe.

Before long, under Avery's direction, the men rigged up enough kerosene and gas heaters to make the perennially-chilly cavern livable. Suzy shut her eyes tightly, willing her mind not to remember the flames and agonizing screams of the dead tribe members, mostly women who had catastrophically fallen victim to a poorly-built gasoline heater in the dead of night. The explosion hadn't been huge, but the sound still echoed in her nightmares to this day.

Funerals were considered a waste of time and energy. No one complained as the tribe was only together out of necessity. It wasn't like they were family, after all. No opinions were ever solicited from the women who mourned their sisters' deaths in silence. Swift memorial words were said with all in attendance, crushed tightly, as close as they could around the Council Center. The mess was disposed of and life went on.

Suzy's thoughts of her earlier metamorphosis tapered off as she revisited the nugget that kept her warm at night and fueled her determination to flee. Her secret. One that was so dangerous, she refused to share it even with Liz until she knew the time was right.

For Suzy knew exactly where her grandfather and his wondrous shelter was located.

Her Grandma Lorna's words had inexplicably flowered in her mind when she had emerged from the pit of devastation brought on by her frightful kidnapping.

How she might determine the correct time was far beyond her ability to calculate. That part she had failed to work out. Yet. The monumental task of escaping with a hundred women and children in various stages of weakness and pregnancy loomed on her limited horizon like an approaching cyclone determined to bear down on her. At this moment, she just couldn't locate a safe path around the deadly obstacle.

"Psss . . . Suzy." A hunched-over young woman stepped close to the doorway of the hovel, dropped a folded note, then scurried away. Suzy scrambled over to the doorway to snatch up the note. Reading slowly, she sounded out the words, identifying the author as her friend Liz who begged for her presence.

Ripping the note into bits, she stuck the tiny pieces inside the pillow on her messy bunk. It wouldn't do to let Doc find the pieces. Women were forbidden to communicate amongst themselves except when sharing a task. Male eyes watched every move they made, making organized insurrection difficult to get off the ground.

She shivered with the knowledge of what would happen to both of them if the note were to be discovered. It didn't take too many hammered and mangled fingers of the women around camp who had been disciplined, for the rest of them to fear the risk. The note must be very urgent.

Checking to make sure her backpack looked innocuous with its load of purloined drugs, she made a dash across the council square, well aware she was being watched as men of all ages dropped what they were doing to observe Doc's house pet and wonder what she was up to.

Dodging nimbly around piles of garbage, serpentine aisles of hovels, bastardized bedrolls of the Outsiders and pathetic children all under the age of five, she made her way like a darting lizard toward the passageway leading to a smaller cave that housed the lower-ranked men and their women.

She stopped in her tracks as a female child of around three squatted in her path to move her bowels, naked as the day God made her. Snot ran from the girl's nose to mix with the food from her last meal that had dribbled from a mouth she was unable to close. Her acute hair lip, one of the common deformities of most of the newborns since the war, assured the poor girl a life of misery. What man would want that at his table?

Most of the mothers learned quickly to keep them out of the way of the men who raged at the sight of them. The toddler flashed an arm from behind her back, displaying further evidence of the damage done to her mother's DNA from the fallout of the bombs that had spread on the cold virulent winds before they had found their present shelter.

Eying the distorted limb with its missing hand and flattened forearm, she cringed. Suzy had heard unconfirmed whispers that the men found these babies such liabilities that a movement was underfoot not to waste resources on them.

Oddly enough, the male babies born with abnormalities were hailed a success, no different than an unmarked one. Her resentment simmered at the unfairness of it, but the women were powerless to do anything except attempt to hide the little girls from sight.

Sighing, she squatted in front of the child, removed a rag from her backpack and cleaned her off as she scanned the women in the area for the missing mother. Worried about the time, she tugged the child up into her arms.

The toddler's enormous eyes stared at her unblinkingly. As Suzy watched, the child screwed up her face and let out a wail. Spewed mucus and saliva splattered the teen's face as she ducked down with the child, trying to hush her.

"What do you think you're doing with that kid?" From out of the crowd of milling tribe members, shot Avery's hunk of a hand.

The giant's ugly face leered down at her, his shaved head with its knobby protrusions, blocking her escape. He wrenched the toddler from her arms as she frantically tried to twist away. Her voice growled back at him.

"Get your hands off me, you piece of garbage."

He laughed, tossing the toddler to the ground. Craning his neck over his massive shoulder, he shouted to another man.

"Get this worthless meat out of here. It shouldn't have been allowed to get this old. Go find out who it belongs to and report it to Doc. I want the mother to be made an example of at council tonight. We can't be having these monstrosities draining us anymore. You know what to do."

Avery's henchman bent to retrieve the child, distaste evident on his dour, scabby face as he held her by one callused hand, dangling the frightened toddler by her good arm.

Suzy watched the women from the crowd surrounding the spectacle quickly cast their eyes down in an effort to hide their burning hatred and frustration at their own impotence. Not a one dare come to the defense of the toddler as she quickly disappeared from sight, her fate unimaginable.

Avery turned his attention back to her. His hand on her upper arm tightened as he fumbled at the layers of rags on her chest. Squeezing a young breast, his eyes glazed feverishly.

"This should belong to me, bitch. Don't you even think I've forgotten. Doc can't protect you forever. He owes me."

Avery leaned in, his rancid breath a menace of its own. Trying hard not to cry or scream, she kept her face neutral.

All predators needed to see was one sign of weakness to know they had you. Summoning up the nerve, she spat in his face. Avery recoiled in surprise, titters from the crowd inflaming him.

Suzy didn't see the fist coming until it sank into her abdomen, the pain robbing her of the ability to speak as it forced up what was left of her last meal. Avery dropped her to the ground and turned to scream at the crowd, his thick meaty cheeks throbbing with indignation.

"What the fuck you all lookin' at? Move on before I give you something you wish hadn't asked for."

Avery wiped the spit from his face, distracted enough by the crowd to allow Suzy to crawl on her elbows and melt away. She heard the giant roar his anger as he discovered her escape.

Quickly, she hobbled the rest of the way to Liz's hut, grateful that Avery hadn't noticed her backpack. That would have been the end of her. Doc wouldn't have been able to save her had the contents been discovered. She realized that, sooner or later, the situation with Avery would explode. She chafed at her powerlessness, dispirited by the inequities of her miserable life.

The lingering nausea from Avery's punch swept over her in waves, acerbated by the heavier collection of unwashed bodies and slop buckets that awaited collection in Liz's section of the tribe's quarters. In her own cavern they had several locations to relieve themselves. Doc insisted on strict sanitary conditions. But the further away from the main cavern you traveled, the laxer the sanitation became.

Approaching her friend's hovel, she found Liz sitting, her enormous belly laden down with her own pregnancy; nothing new, since over half the women were pregnant at one time or another. Liz struggled to rise as she approached, getting assistance from two other young women that stood nearby, their expressions of frantic anxiety telegraphing the urgency of Liz's note.

"For heaven's sake, Suzy. What took you so long?" Liz hissed as she stood, her hand pressed hard to her back to message the aching muscles that invariably accompanied pregnancy and hard work. Thick clumps of coarse, dark hair escaped the elastic that swept the rest of her long mop back from her appealing face.

Signs of Outsider women, relegated and out of favor with Liz's owner, littered the surrounds with their scavenged mattresses. Liz's generous lips tightened as she swept them all into the relative privacy of the ramshackle quarters she shared with the man that owned her with his other two women.

The women helped lower Liz onto her bed, her delivery only a few weeks away.

"Well, did you get it?" Liz shook her hands with impatience, panic seeping into her expression to mirror that of the other women. They suddenly heard the sounds of a wounded animal not far away. Deep ragged coughing, a choke that morphed into a guttural scream filled with long agony. Suzy's heart almost stopped.

"Oh my God. Is that her?" Liz closed her eyes and silently nodded.

Suzy dove into her backpack, extracting her critical cargo. She unwrapped the towel that hid the lifesaving box of antibiotics and pain pills filched from Doc Benjamin's cache.

Rarely did any women have access to the drugs that often saved the life of a man felled by a formerly common infection. Infections that could now spell death if allowed to come into contact with any of the unknown microbes that strayed into their shelter on the dangerous winds that harbored them from as far away as New York City.

Dense suburbs of the onetime financial center were known to have spawned several outbreaks of diseases unseen in this country in centuries.

Suzy's shaking hands withdrew syringes from her pack. She noted the expiration date on the box of antibiotics, but said nothing, knowing that most medication viability lasted long after the recorded expiration date. *Here's hoping it's the same with liquids.* Her fingers absorbed the vital coolness of the antibiotics. For once, she thanked the chilly temperatures found in the mines. The medicine had been in her backpack and out of their refrigerated storage for well over twenty four hours.

"You know, if it's more than an infection, this won't help."

"I know, I know. But it's not like we have a doctor to take her to. And if it's a virus, wouldn't others have caught it by now?"

Suzy tried to reassure Liz. "I don't know. She's had this for almost two weeks now. I don't know how long viruses take to incubate. I think it varies. I don't even know what she has. But if the men find out, you know what they'd do." One of the other women stifled a sob.

"And Janie's overdue. What will this do to the baby?" Another coughing scream filled the air. The four women froze, blood draining from their faces as they heard men shouting.

"Oh, my God. I have to get over there." Suzy was close to panic. Liz clutched her arm.

"No. You can't go, Suzy. You'll draw too much attention. You know we can't have that. It may be too late as it is." They listened as male voices carried into the shelter, well into the throes of discussion.

"Kimmey, you and Liselle get over there. Now! Take this. Don't get caught with it, no matter what. There's no telling what would happen if the men find out. Give her a double shot. And try to muffle that noise the best you can."

Suzy passed the medicine to the other women and watched as Liselle stuffed it under her rags, failing to obscure the telltale bulge. Kimmey reach over and readjusted Liselle's layers and they hurried off.

Suzy sank to the ground and rested her throbbing head on Liz's comforting leg. The older girl reached down to stroke Suzy's bald head.

"It's okay, hon. We wouldn't stand a chance without all you've done to help these last few years." Liz turned Suzy's face toward her with a worn hand. "You all right? Something happen?"

Suzy's mouth turned down. "It's just Avery again. He cornered me on the way here. But not before he had a chance to remind me of how he feels." She rubbed her stomach, not needing to explain further. Liz sighed.

"I don't know how much longer some of the women can go on like this. We seem to get weaker and weaker as the men still look fit. The only thing we have in common is the sores that devil me so. Uurr." Liz picked at a particularly evil one on her arm that refused to heal.

"Let me put a bandage on that, Liz. You need to keep it clean."

"And just where will I say I got the bandage when he sees it tonight?" Suzy reached for her backpack to pull out an adhesive bandage for Liz.

"Don't worry, I can tie a rag over it. He won't even know there's a bandage underneath."

Nodding, Liz held out her arm.

"Did you hear Deborah, the redhead over in the next area to this one, killed herself yesterday?"

Suzy stopped working in surprise, a hint of fear budding in her already delicate stomach. She lowered her voice as she continued to bandage Liz's arm.

"I guess she never really recovered after her last was born . . . God, I can't even think about what the poor thing must have looked like without a skull. Does it seem to you that the younger girls have more babies born with defects that the older girls?"

"Ummm . . . I've noticed the same thing. It must have something to do with the damage done by radiation at a more tender age. Most of the girls that deliver the worst of the babies were captured at an early age." Liz's voice faltered. "Just like you were."

"There . . . you're done." Suzy acted like she hadn't heard Liz, stashing her scissors back in her pack.

Liz continued. 'You were such a sweet, little girl. Lucky too. You might be dead by now if it wasn't for Doc. I can almost see the person you would have been if this hadn't happened." Suzy picked up her pack and slammed it down, startling her friend.

"What the heck is the point to all this? I'm not that little girl. I'm a different person. I care about only one thing." Her face lit up with a ferocious determination. She grabbed both of Liz's hands in hers. "Come with me, Liz. We need to get out of here. You can't have your baby near a bunch of sick bastards like this. We can just walk out. Together."

Liz stared, stone faced, her voice flat and empty. "And where exactly would we go? With me ready to deliver in a couple of weeks?" She shook her head slowly. "I'm surprised at you, Suzy. You know I can't just walk out on the other women and leave them at the mercy of the men. What do you think would happen to them if we disappeared? I wouldn't give some of them more than a day with Avery's machete always itching for a chance to teach someone a lesson."

At the strange look on Suzy's face she stopped. Suzy noticed and turned away.

"Hey, what's really wrong with you? This is too out of character."

Silence.

"You gunna talk to me or do I have to drag it out of you?"

Suzy moved restlessly, not knowing where to start. "It's Doc."

"What do you mean, it's Doc? Something wrong with him? Is he sick or something?"

"No, no, nothing like that." She swallowed, suddenly shy and embarrassed with the attention on her. This was something she had hoped to avoid even as she knew it was impossible. "Eh . . . Doc . . . has been . . . eh . . . looking at me."

"Looking at you? What the heck are you talking about, girl? He's been like a father to you."

Suzy cast her eyes down and mumbled, "That's what everyone thinks. But he only cares to make me remember where my grandfather's shelter is. He's convinced I'll remember someday . . ." Her voice trailed off.

"Well, that's no big deal. It's not like he raped you."

As Suzy sat unmoving, the silence thickened.

"Oh . . . my sweet, little Suzy girl. Come here and sit next to me, hon. He did rape you, didn't he?" Her horrified voice reduced Suzy to tears and she quickly moved to the bed to be swept up in the capable hands of her best friend, mentor and surrogate mother. Her hot unshed tears finally emerged to gush unchecked onto the flannel smock of the only one in the whole tribe that could give her the kind of comfort she so desperately needed.

Two weeks passed in the Franklin Mines. Suzy managed to elude Avery, but her evenings became a nightmare. Even though she always knew the time was bound to come, she was revolted by the sick expressions dancing across Doc's face now every time he looked at her.

Often, they would sit outside their hovel to share the food she brought from the master kitchen. Suzy could always tell from the look on his face when she was in for another bad night, another assault. That's what she called it. That's what it was.

During the moments he demanded she disrobe, she could feel her spirit slip back into her secret black hole, piece by piece, as he caressed her barely-developed breasts and moved on to his beastly satisfaction.

She felt branded by the initiation. Branded and humiliated, positive everyone could see and mock her. No longer did she venture out into the cavern on her mercy errands, Doc's trove of medicines now safe from her sticky fingers. She missed her moments with Liz, but couldn't risk the exposure, and who had the strength anyway?

The last time Liz had sent someone to get her, she lay flaccid, unwilling to listen to the summons for help that was sure to bring more stress and pain at a time she overflowed with horrors of her own.

That's where she lay today. On the same shabby altar Doc Benjamin had first used when he raped her. Wondering why he had waited this long to do it, she could only imagine that he must have given up on the hope she would reveal the whereabouts of her grandfather's bomb shelter.

As she lay drifting in and out of her fugue, she suddenly felt the jarring of her bed. Opening her eyes, she realized Doc was back.

"Are you just going to lie there all day, missy? I'm not going to put up with much more of your prima donna conduct. You know I can't afford to let the tribe see you disrespect me like this. You're my woman now."

Suzy weighed the merits of rising, but was unable to rouse the energy. She watched Doc as he paced, his long, greasy hair tied back like the rest of the men, unable to disguise his now receding hairline. His once-straight legs had a decided bow to them, shortening his stature. Between his scabs, the blisters in his face, and the tooth loss they all suffered, he no longer retained the aura of a confident able leader she had once thought he was.

No. He just looked like a common man with an evil core; the core of a slave owner who abused his slave.

And now that she was a woman, Doc was treating her the same way the rest of the camp women were treated.

From inside Suzy's dark space, a burst of bitter bile illuminated her pain, crystalizing a shred of reality. She slowly lowered her feet to the floor of the hut.

"That's better. Now go get me something to eat, woman."

Fourteen-year-old Suzy stood, eyeing Doc's machete that lay in the corner of the hut. The bile from her dark space began to rise, tentative and unsure. She let her eyes again flicker to the machete. Smoothing down her tattered clothes and reaching for a cloth, she rubbed down her bald head as if preparing to leave.

Her feet slowly inched closer to the machete, sweat trickling down from under her arms in the coolness of the hut. Her right hand made contact with the handle of the machete as she continued to slowly and methodically rub her scalp.

They heard a commotion outside the hut. Doc moved to the entrance, peeling back the privacy blanket.

"Ladies? To what do I owe the honor of this unusual visit?" His voice thrummed with the message that served to remind the visitors their presence clearly was not an honor.

Two women belonging to Liz's man ducked inside, tears and red faces on fire as they gushed out the news.

"Please, Doc. Please. You must come. They're dying." Kimmey sank to her knees to blubber her entreaties while Liselle sidled up to Suzy with a low hiss.

"Suzy, you must come quick. It's Liz. Where've you been? There's blood everywhere. It's the baby."

As if emerging from underwater, Liselle's dire news pushed Suzy through to the land of the miserable living as her spark was released from where it hid and shocked her into action. Her eyes regained focus.

"Liz?"

"Yes. Now get us some help!"

Suzy moved to a chest filled with freshly-rolled bandages, reaching in to pass them to Kimmey and Liselle as Doc Benjamin laughed.

"Just what the hell do you women think you're doing?"

Suzy stopped, turning her bald head to Doc. She motioned to the women.

"Go . . . I'm right behind you."

Doc laughed again; scorn his flavor of the moment. "I don't recall giving you permission to go anywhere." He stood with his arms crossed, relaxed and appearing not to take her intentions seriously. Looking him in the eye, Suzy demanded the keys to the medicine cooler.

"You must be joking, dear girl."

She moved in closer, her face a mask of heinous intention and something else . . . something snake-like that flickered across her face. Something new that she understood frightened them both. "One more time. The keys." The intonations of her voice promised nameless misery as Doc removed the keys from his chain. His unexpected capitulation emboldened her.

"You're coming too." Wordlessly, with a shove from Suzy, they were out the door and on their way to Liz. Doc's medical bag with an assortment of chilled vials and capsules from the locked cooler stayed clutched in her white-knuckled hands.

The screams could be heard the second they stepped into the cavern, cutting through the thickening miasma of stench.

Hurrying, they followed the sounds of commotion until they reached the large crowd around Liz's hovel. Men and women surrounded the entrance, fear and terror in the posture of the women as they hung on to each other, praying for the woman who meant so much to their sanity.

Suzy fought her way through the crowd, which finally parted as they realized Doc was with her. Ominously, the screams stopped.

Suzy crept up to Liz's blood-soaked bed, struck dumb by the copious amount that couldn't possibly have come from one boney pregnant young woman. *Not my Liz.*

Casting her terrified eyes around the crowded hut, she watched Kimmey sobbing softly, curled up in the corner. Liselle stood motionless, her eyes wide and unseeing. Liz's man, Surrel, knelt at the side of the bed covered in blood as he tried to rub life back into the cooling hand of his favorite woman. Outside women clustered meekly at the foot of the bed, one holding a bundle in her arms.

Doc sized up the situation, before ducking back out of the room to return with three other men who began to roll up their sleeves.

"She died." The words dropped like stone . . . cold venom filling the room. Liselle turned to face Suzy. "She died. And where were you when she needed you, little girl?" Liselle launched herself at Suzy, arms flailing, blows landing ineffectually on the teen's head and shoulders.

Surrel stood up as Doc and the other men subdued Liselle. She stood shaking, fear in her eyes as Surrel slapped her hard across the face.

"What the hell's gotten into you tonight? I said to bring Doc not his useless pet." A quick glance over at Doc. "Beg your pardon there, Doc, don't mean no offence, now."

"No offense taken, Surrel. Why don't you let the boys get her out of here so the women can clean up this stinking mess?" Doc's tone was dismissive and impatient. He reached out to liberate his bag from Suzy's limp hands.

"You've got five minutes. I'll be waiting outside." Doc's voice sounded sure and commanding, the momentary control achieved by Suzy long departed.

As Doc left the hut, the men pushed Surrel aside and began to wrap Liz in the bloody sheets and blankets.

No one even heard Suzy whisper as they lifted her spent body from the bed. "Noooo, please God, give her back. I beg you . . ."

"Move aside there now, girl." Surrel began to take control of his hut and his women. "Kimmey, for Christ's sake, stop your sniveling and get off the floor. She's gone. It's not like she's not replaceable. Now get this place cleaned up. I want my dinner."

The Outside women brightened noticeably at Surrel's words, hoping one of them might be the lucky replacement, enabling them to sleep safely inside, well removed from the nightly marauders.

As Suzy numbly turned to leave, she heard the unmistakable sound of a newborn cry. Turning back to the Outside women, all eyes fastened on the bundle held in the arms of one of them.

The tallest man carrying Liz out the door stopped.

"You want to throw it in with this, Surrel? Or you gunna keep it?"

Surrel scratched his head, looking at the dirty floor. "I don't rightly know, boys. I'm of a mind to let you take it. I have enough little ones running around right now. His eyes lit up with a feral gleam of cunning.

"Don't suppose any of you boys might trade me for it?"

"Is it a boy or a girl?"

Surrel turned on the salesmanship. "It's a boy. And not in bad shape. The foot looks a bit turned, but no bad lip. Cauliflower ear, but that ain't nothing." The men looked at each other, a silent message flowing between them.

"Na, we'll take a pass. He won't be good for much with a turned leg. He'll just be a gimp. Doc don't want no more resources spent on unproductive outcomes. Ya know what that means. If it had a been a girl, we coulda worked something out."

Suzy watched everyone nod their heads as if they understood; the women all agreeing while Suzy could see they were plainly paralyzed with fear and horror at the new policy.

"Okay, just throw it on top here and we'll be getting out of the way." Surrel took the baby bundle from the woman and dropped it on top of the rubbish that was no longer Liz.

Weak cries came from the bundle as the infant hit the dead body of his mother. The men lifted the pile, moving out the door; just another disposal job to finish so they could get on with dinner and some relaxation.

"Wait," Suzy shouted after the men, running after them and out the door. She scooped the infant up from Liz's lifeless body, holding it against her chest, her heart thumping violently.

As one of the men tried to pull the bundle from her arms, the infant's cries increased.

"Suzy, what the hell's going on here? Let the men do their job." Doc pulled on her arm as the baby was wrenched away from her.

"Please." Suzy made a pitiful meow. Her face shriveled with emotions, panic paralyzing her. She cast a quick glance at the men with Liz's body and her baby, feeling that her essence lay under the bloody sheets with them.

Her life was over. All hope of freedom had died with Liz. Her love for the young woman that had protected, nurtured and educated her in the subtlety of patience, threatened to tear her in two. *And what of the other women in the tribe? What of their hopes of freedom and safety for their children, far from the brutality of Doc and his men? How could they replace Liz?*

Sure that her own strength came from the spirit of Liz, she knew she had to save the baby. Liz's baby. It was a sign. A glimmer of a lifeline. A wisp of hope.

She felt strength of purpose galvanize her into action. She threw herself at Doc's feet, wrapping her skinny arms around his legs.

"Please, Doc. The baby. I'll do anything. I'll take good care of him and keep him out of the way." Her beseeching words, so uncharacteristic, made Doc pause. Suzy noticed and pressed her advantage.

"I promise. I'll do anything." Jumping up, she ran to the men and made another grab for the infant.

"Hey. Doc said . . ."

Doc raised his hand silently, waving the men off. With resignation, they shrugged, mumbling under their breaths and moved off through the crowds with Liz's body.

Suzy walked slowly back to Doc, his expression unreadable. His silence made her nervous as she began to stumble and rush the words she hoped would persuade him.

"How will you feed it?"

Suzy's heart missed a beat. "I can get the milk he needs from any number of women in the tribe. Some have had their babies . . . eh . . .

taken." Might as well call it with the truth. "They'll be happy to allow the baby to nurse."

Doc's expression remained unreadable, but Suzy could see calculations behind his eyes. She held her breath.

"If I let you have this babe, I don't want to see any more sulking. You will take your proper place in the tribe like any other woman. You will come to my bed when I call and you will do it eagerly. Is that clear?"

The innocent child in Suzy was stung, her face drained of blood. Her thoughts warred with themselves as she considered the evenings of pain and humiliation it would take to save the baby. Her voice was a whisper. "Noooo. I cannot."

Doc moved forward to take the baby, his face darkening with anger. The infant suddenly calmed in her arms, a sweet musical squeak that muffled its way to her ears.

"Wait, wait." Sometimes pain can be bearable when done for the sake of love. Suzy didn't know this, but she did know she loved Liz's baby. Without it she would die anyway.

As Doc placed his hands on the bundle in her arms, she reached out to place her fingers on his arm, his sweaty maleness invading her nostrils. She pressed down on his arm, sliding her fingers up to his shoulder in an attempt at a caress. "Okay, I agree."

Doc looked stoically in her eyes. The seconds ticked. Then his broken smile declared his acceptance; possessive and knowing as he slipped his arm around her. "All right now. Let's go home. And no more nonsense."

Anxious over the deal she had just committed herself to, Suzy followed Doc through the stinking mess that Liz had called home.

Approaching their own cavern, they could hear screams of laughter and cheering. Suzy wondered at the sounds, unusual in their nature for they included the sounds of women's voices. As they followed the boisterous clatter, it became clear that something was occurring in the Council Center.

Weaving their way through the deafening crowd, Doc pulled her and the baby to the center where some of the men stood dancing.

Their faces were smeared with fruit juices and flakes of crusty green bits. The tribe members around them squatted in supplication, hands reaching out to beg as everyone stared at the impossibility of the giant fruit and vegetables piled high near the fire, the flames turning the healthy vibrant colors to jewels.

Stunned, Doc and Suzy approached. Doc reached down to pick up a three-pound peach, heavy with ripe juices. The fragrant smell of freshness made Suzy dizzy. Doc took a sniff, his eyes still unbelieving. He held the peach out to her, inviting a bite. She looked around at the cheering crowd then down at the bundle in her arms. She hesitantly bit down into the soft juicy meat of the mythical fruit, liquid running down her chin.

And Suzy smiled.

Chapter 4

2086 AD

Kenya's droopy eyelids fought with the calming sensation of Baby's leather hands as they stroked her huge abdomen. The warmth of Netty's cooking fire stroked tendrils of heat over her body, helping to suffuse her with the natural pheromones of relaxation that had kept her calm at meals for the last twenty nine years, thanks to Baby. She could feel the limbs of her unborn infant relax as Baby worked his magic with his auras on the unborn child.

"Does the baby talk back to you, Baby?"

"Sister, don't you know the baby can't talk?"

"You sound like a wise guy now, Mr. Furburger."

"I am very wise, Sister, but my fur is not of the burger kind. It is quite ordinary."

Abby laughed as she overheard the discussion. Bending down, the two women exchanged a warm hug. Abby's wings lay shimmering down her back, following the natural curves of her slender figure, the lethal emulsion in her delicate crystal-like horns reflecting prisms on the walls from the light of the fire.

"I can see the two of you are discussing serious affairs again this evening. Don't let me interrupt." Patting Baby on the head she moved on, tossing a wave to Echo who sat curled up with Barney on his straw mat near the fireplace.

The boisterous voices from the other tables thickened as the survivors sat down to await one of Dezi's supreme culinary confections, his talent as head chef now unmatched by anyone in the Hive.

"I don't know how many times I need to tell you, Johno. Tobi and her herd of sixty nine will be invaluable for lugging the material out of the Hive when we need to build."

Johno grimaced as Jose made his case. "I don't want my elephants to be exploited. Haven't they been through enough in their lifetime? Especially Tobi. Do you think she forgets, my friend?"

Jose assumed his most persuasive voice. "I'm just bringing it up now so they can get used to what we'll need. We can practice with them. We have plenty of time."

"Then why do you keep bringing it up if we have so much time? Let them live and enjoy their new calves and their freedom in the growing fields with the dogs and piglets. There'll be plenty of time to fight over the exploitation of Tobi and the herd. Miss Netty said we have another seventy years or so."

They both glanced up as a screech of laughter sounded from the entrance to the kitchen. Scotty, Kane and Chloe entered with their arms around each other; radiating youth, perfect health, and not looking a day older than when they had entered the Hive twenty nine years ago. Kane threw his perennial pregnant bride a wide kiss as Echo stood from her perch next to Barney to take to the air, her wings propelling her to Scotty's arms, the curly, white-haired dog trotting along on the floor.

"Whoa, girl. How about a warning?" Scotty beamed at Echo as he disentangled himself from his wife and best friend to catch the creature that understood him the best; his muse, his soul mate, his co-conspirator, his number one buddy. Auras reached out to caress his mind, steeping him in joy and pleasure.

"I missed you, Brother."

Scotty slipped a hand down to pet Barney. "I know, Echo. I missed you too. But we're back now. It didn't take as long as I thought it would. If you could have wormed out of your daily jaunt with Netty and Wil and their food truck, you could have come with us."

"Yes, Brother. But I could not. Now that my Brother Baby must devote his time to Sister Kenya, I must assume some of his duties. I pray that the chore will soon come to an end as Brother Wil is rethinking the situation and Sister Netty needs a break from the pressure." Scotty could hear Echo actually sigh in his mind.

"The time is getting close, Brother."

"If you insist on being so cryptic over the reason for these daily food deliveries, I'm not going to fill you in on our day."

Echo hung her head.

Chloe reached out to stroke her back. "Cheer up, Echo. It can't be that bad."

The creature's aura included her. "You understand, don't you, Sister?"

Chloe reached out to claim the creature from Scotty, settling her on her lap as she chose the table they would enjoy their dinner from. "Scotty's just yanking your chain."

"My chain? Is that like your chain?" Echo reached out to Chloe's neck with a single leather finger, slipping it under the platinum chain that held the gold coin Scotty had given her on her sixteenth birthday.

"No, I mean he's just teasing you. You know our guy. He loves to do that. And I certainly do understand, sweetie. That's why we girls must stick together." She rocked Echo softly in her lap as if she were a baby, leaning in to coo over the tolerant creature's perceived hurt feelings.

"Don't worry, we'll fill you in. Scotty and Kane have some good ideas."

As Kane and Scotty made themselves comfortable at the table, Kane stacked the dishes out of the way so Scotty could lay out the paper map of the growing field and the caverns beyond. Turning to Echo, he explained, "We located a spot that would work for the expansion of the habitat for the cats and bears. If you and Wil, with Hud's help, can work with the Kreyven, I think we can break through to their existing space. We can make a tunnel that would be about half a mile long from one to the other. It would be fantastic for them. Give them a sense of bigger territory. Now that we're up over two hundred, they need the space."

Scotty spoke up. "I think we'll need to continue all the feeding in the existing space, though. How are we going to lug all that food if they're fed in both locations?"

Chloe set Echo on the table. She stood to examine the map. "It won't kill us to lug the food. We can use Wil and Netty's wagon. We only have two hundred now, but how many do you think we'll have in another ten years? We need to keep them calm. It's not fair to still have the implants regulate their behavior. And if they're used to feeding in one spot, won't problems develop as it gets more crowded?"

Scotty examined the distance to the new cavern. It was even longer through the corridors they had traversed to find it. At least they had yet to see signs of food aggression in any of the species. By now, they were all used to an unending supply of protein-rich green pods and all the greens, seeds, fruit and berries the bears could ever dream of. Food aggression was of little concern.

"Since food isn't the problem it was on the surface, maybe they have no need to be aggressive about food. Especially those that were born in the Hive. They've never known hunger like the original creatures who once lived in the wild or the nasty roadside carnivals where some of them were rescued from."

Echo inched over to the map on her butt. Her long, slender leather fingers traced the outline of the growing field. Her aura questioned them all. "Tobi's big herd and the dogs' birthing beds are growing. The piglets are increasing too. Sister Chloe and I found our new plantings trampled last week. And it was not my friend Tobi or her herd. They know better. I think it was last year's batch of juvenile pit bulls. They do not have any sense in their heads yet. I think we need to ask the Kreyven to carve out some more space on the other side of the stream."

Chloe leaned in, excitement in her voice. "Great idea, E! We can create a bridge over the stream to contain the dogs at night. Buffering the new side with rocks so the dogs don't try to swim across should be considered too. While we're at it, I think we need to dredge the stream and increase the flow. I don't think we're getting enough moisture in the new field, do you, Echo?" They all turned to Echo as she remained silent.

Chloe was first to voice to notice. "E? What's up? You don't like my idea?"

Echo squirmed. "Your idea is first rate, Sister Chloe. But you called me E."

The three friends burst out with laughter, drawing the attention of the other survivors. Dezi hollered from the sink. "Pipe down, you hooligans. I need to concentrate on my masterpiece."

Everyone lowered their voices, not wanting to disturb the master at work. No one held the true power as Dezi did. These days, the happiness of the Hive rose and fell in direct proportion to the delectability of Chef Dezi's creations. A position Salina was more than happy to retire from since her life had changed after the deaths in the Time of Seth.

Turning back to Echo, Scotty whispered an explanation. "I think Chloe was giving you an ultimate compliment, Echo."

"A compliment, Brother Scotty?"

Chloe chimed in, her face full of love and . . . shyness? Scotty's heart swelled with pride over the long path his wife and Echo had walked and stumbled for years as they struggled to share his attention and find their rightful twin place in his heart. "E is just a more familiar form of your name. A nickname, if you will, shared only between those that love you the most. It just slipped out. I hope you don't mind." Chloe's words slowed, careful of overstepping with the mysterious creature as she often used to. Looking up, she tossed Scotty a quick wink, relaxing them all.

Echo's aura swished around their minds as she stood on the table to touch Chloe's face. She traced the bones of the young girl's face that held all the acquired wisdom of her now forty four years in her prudent intelligent eyes, all traces of the lazy, petulant, self-centered teen gone.

"You are part of me, Sister. Sometimes I believe it is more than the part of me that belongs to my Brother Scotty. I am honored that you call me E."

Scotty jerked his head back in surprise. "Well . . . I guess you told me."

"No, Brother Scotty. It is different—much different with Sister. You are my heart and my soul. But Sister is my future."

Chloe and Scotty met each other's puzzled eyes. Understanding signaled between them. The unusual remarks by Echo must be set aside for another day after they had first talked among themselves and analyzed the ominous overtone.

Chloe changed the subject with a half-hearted nervous laugh. "Well . . . ahem . . . now that we know that, I think we can solve the next problem. Can we please have your opinion on the expansion of the growing field, Echo?"

As Echo's auras began to swirl again, Kane rose from the table. "I'm on board with anything you all decide. I agree the dogs are just too numerous. Who knew Teddy would finally discover that ears were non-reproductive? I'm surprised little Molly stands still for your monster, Chloe. She's had close to a litter a year now. I love all the little rug rats, but, counting the others, we're well over one hundred new dogs if you count the pitties and Penny and Honda's pups. The fox cubs are no trouble at all, they behave just like the dogs. You might want to think about separating Teddy and Molly for a while, though."

Kane gave a hearty stretch, his eyes on Kenya. "I'll be back in a while. I want to see if Kenya is up to eating with us over here. I guess that means Baby, too. I'll swing by Wil and Hud on my way back to fill them in."

As Kane sauntered off, the remaining threesome put their heads together and returned to their map.

At the end of the table, Ginger Mae leaned over Peter's back, her arms resting around his neck as he glanced up and shared the laughter of a comment Bonnie made. Bonnie mock charged them both, enveloping them in her own brand of merriment.

"I give up, I give up," Peter shouted as Bonnie piled her full one hundred thirty five pounds on them both. "Ginger Mae, help. Can you get this child bride of mine off us?"

"Child bride? After fifteen years of marriage I hardly think that applies."

Ginger Mae disentangled herself while Peter and Bonnie bantered. "You two are too much. Why don't you meet Hud and me after dinner for a swim? We could really use a soak."

Peter and Bonnie nodded as they grinned to themselves like happy fools. Live sparks danced in their eyes as they contemplated a relaxing soak. Peter, no longer the shy bemused outsider, but a confident friend and generous helpmate who had blossomed into an ardent husband for the woman he loved so deeply, answered for them both. "You have yourself a deal. Is this for just old married couples or open to all?"

Ginger Mae leaned in to answer, her soft-brown, pixie-cut bob swinging with her, low whispers indicating her desire to keep the swim private. "If we go a bit later than normal, I bet we'll have the place to ourselves. Daisy and Kimir plan to go to bed early—some new test in her lab. She's training Kimir to assist her, finally. Sound good?"

"Sounds great," they both agreed. Ginger Mae moved away to join her husband and Wil at their table, brushing past a patient Netty, who struggled laboriously with Gloria's long thick hair.

"You almost done, Netty? Just tie it off, she looks fine," red-headed Billy commented, watching the ordeal.

"Now, Billy, I know it doesn't matter to you. You'd love her if she was bald. But it matters to Gloria."

Gloria surveyed her husband of nineteen years. Rolling her eyes, she commented, "Babe, these French braids take a while, but it's worth it. And Netty does such a nice job."

Netty sighed. "Not much for me to do these days now that Dezi's running the kitchen. He doesn't like me to interfere, you know?"

The women looked up at Billy as they felt him examining them. "Hmmm, can you imagine what our babies would look like with Gloria's lush hair and my fire-engine-red color? Her darker skin would sure be a bonus. I don't want no kids a mine saddled with this ghostly white skin that came with my hair."

Gloria's shoulders drooped. "Let's not bring that up tonight, babe. You know what a sore spot it is. And the other women don't need to be reminded either." She lowered her voice. "Especially Bonnie. You know how hard they've been trying, with Salina the way she is. A grandbaby is just what Salina and Clyde need to help them mend over the scars they carry from the Time of Seth." They all tried to avoid mentioning Emma's name for fear of picking at a scab that refused to heal and constantly leaked drops of blood.

Christening the early time in the Hive the 'Time of Seth' reminded them to call evil what it was, so they'd be ready next time; prepared to recognize it.

Netty sighed long and heavily.

"I know. You never get over losing a child. I thought Jennifer would help, but it's not the same." Gloria turned her head around to look at Netty. "You okay, Netty?"

Netty dropped the hair she was braiding. "I don't know . . . maybe it's time."

"Time? Time for what?" Billy spoke up, concern on his face; Netty had sounded far, far away. "Netty?" She didn't answer. Gloria turned to meet his eyes. They both looked back at the strangely-acting Elder who appeared to be in a trance.

Gloria stood up to take Netty by the shoulders, her downy wings crushed under Gloria's hands. "Netty."

"I'm fine, Gloria. Sorry . . . I spaced out for a spell there. I just have a few things on my mind."

"I understand, Netty. I'm sure it's getting to you too."

Netty appeared startled. "Getting to me?"

"Well, yeah. I know how much you love Wil. I'm sure you want to have his children as much as we all want them, too."

A single tear slipped down Netty's golden cheek. Gloria took her into her comforting arms, clearly assuming they suffered from the same longing to have a child that all the married female survivors bore.

Netty's eyes dried, but she had clearly mentally left the room as her head rested on Gloria's shapely and sympathetic shoulder.

"Okay, gang. Dinner is served." Dezi's voice rang out as Salina and Karen delivered platters of steaming crisp confections of various colors and shapes, then returned to their seats next to Clyde and Cobby.

Netty hurried to grab the teapot, giving Wil a glance, well-laden with meaning. As Wil gazed at his beloved, his pensive yet knowing eyes followed her as she served tea to the survivors that now counted as their beloved and irreplaceable family.

From across the room, Scotty caught the subtle exchange, knowing without a doubt that something bad was blowing their way.

Chapter 5

The two couples lazed by the edge of the water, exhausted by the spirited swimming and overwhelmed by the beauty of their effervescent and jeweled bathing cavern that refused to get old.

Ginger Mae's laughter echoed off the stalactites and stalagmites, a delightful contrast to the sometimes spooky atmosphere with its flickering shadows that enticed memories of trysts held by most of the couples in the Hive.

"Hud, I think we all know how you feel. What do you think, Bonnie? Two or three hundred times?"

Bonnie snorted. "I lost count after the first five years."

Hud looked fondly at his wife. "I know, babe. It's just the beauty of this cave. It's still hard to accept how the Womb shined so much luck down on me. Every day since I woke up to your adorable face twenty eight years ago, I've pinched myself. I can't help reflecting on my life here. It's just so darn surreal. Here it is 2086. I was born in 1881. I was in my fifties when I . . . died. You all mourn the loss of the life you knew with its conveniences and foibles. Yet half the time, I don't even know what you're talking about. And when the Earth heals and we surface? We'll be setting the clock back to before I was born. To the country as it was before man settled here." Hud's amazement plastered itself all over his face. "Do you see the irony of that? For me? It's really hard to absorb all of this even though I've had years to work on it. That's why I keep saying I'm so lucky."

"My . . . you sure are introspective this evening." Peter's observation came with a warm smile that quickly sobered. "Do you think your mood has anything to do with the announcement Netty made after dinner?"

"Maybe. Anyone have any idea what this meeting after breakfast is all about?" Bonnie piped up; her cheerful face still that of a teen, but her maturity reflecting the full forty four years of her life.

"Maybe it's about the new plans to expand the habitats for the wildlife. Scotty and the gang have been working pretty hard on it," remarked Ginger Mae as she nestled closer to Hud.

"I could sure use some extra help with the count. I don't have time for anything else during the day with two decades of newborns to account for. I still think it odd they can reproduce, but none of us girls have been able to conceive." She reached out to grasp Bonnie's cold hand as her friend's face fell.

"I'm so sorry, Bonnie. I know the subject is painful for the two of you. Billy and Gloria aren't much better off. They're dying to have a baby. And I know Karen is plain old desperate." She kept her long-held opinion about Cobby's longing for Abby to herself since Cobby had broken down under pressure and actually married Karen ten years ago.

Bonnie's words were slow and painful. "So you think this meeting is about more room for the animals? Netty looked awful somber for that to be what this is about. Did you notice how she was hanging on to Wil? Neither one of them looked too happy."

Hud let out a loud sigh as he used his hands to slick back his long dark hair, not a trace of gray among the thick strands he twisted into a pony tail to hang down his back to dry.

"I'm afraid you're right, Bonnie. I was with Wil most of the night and he seemed fine until Dezi was ready with dinner. Then they both got quiet. I've never seen them like that before."

"We have." Ginger Mae sounded defiant. "I know you and Wil are big buddies, Hud, but it wasn't always like this. In the beginning there were secrets. Netty was under a lot of stress. Whenever they felt pushed to disclose bad news, they got like this. Just like they were tonight after dinner." Her hand flew to her mouth, her questioning eyes on Peter. "Do you think?"

He shrugged his shoulders. "Do I think what? That Wil and Netty are hiding something again? That they're going to dump some bad news on us in the morning?" Peter compressed his lips, his smile tight. "Maybe. But whatever it is, I know we're all strong enough to handle it."

He stood up, holding his arms out to Bonnie. He pulled her to her feet, then rubbed his hands up and down her back, bringing a smile to her lips, the sparkle back to her eyes.

"Come on, child bride of mine. Time to hit the hay." Both couples rose and fondly bid each other goodnight, leaving the unanswered questions behind. Morning would come to the Hive soon enough.

The next morning, Sheriff Hudson and Ginger Mae strolled through the corridors arm in arm. They were in no hurry to join everyone in Netty's kitchen for the mysterious meeting. Ginger Mae leaned her head briefly on Hudson's broad shoulder; pensive and thoughtful.

"Hud, how come we've never discussed why I seem to be having trouble conceiving?"

Hud looked down at his wife, permitting Ginger Mae an opportunity to relish the tiny flip her heart did every time she studied his world-weary, ruggedly-dear face. She knew every laugh line and wrinkle by heart. Who knew that life would bring this compassionate and wise man to her bed? With him behind her, she knew she could climb mountains.

Ruefully, she conceded the Hive failed to offer many mountains to conquer these days. But she knew she could count on his stalwart strength when the time came to reclaim the world above.

"I don't know, babe. I just assumed we must be too old." He reached out to cup her head in his large hand, giving it an affectionate tousle.

"Now Hud, you know very well the Hive repairs anything in our bodies that goes awry. We're all perfectly fit and healthy."

"What brought this up now, babe? If it's meant to be, it'll happen. We have lots of time. Before long, this place will be filled with urchins that have your beauty and my . . . hmmm . . . my what?"

Ginger Mae heard an underlying note in his voice which disturbed her. She stopped in her tracks in the middle of the corridor that would bring them close to the kitchen. She didn't want to have this conversation where anyone could hear; especially not their best friends. Peter and Bonnie would be so hurt. "How about your inability to lie to me? You're going to start now?"

Hud evaded her perceptive eyes, his tone tender. "I can't bear to see you hurt, babe. Don't you know I feel every pain, every sadness, you have?"

Puzzlement creased her brow. "But I'm not sad, Hud. I've never been happier. My life is complete. Well, except for wanting your child. All of us are happier than we've ever been."

Her voice slowed, a thoughtful dawning intruding with its presence. "Except for all of us not being able to conceive." She stopped speaking, her silence making Hud squirm.

"Ginger Mae?" She cocked her head to consider a thought, and then continued to hold her lovely face still.

"Okay babe, you got me." Hud pulled her from the center of the corridor to perch her on a small boulder that clung to the side of the wall, the membrane of the Hive quiet and ignored. Goose bumps on her pale arms testified to the alarm she was beginning to feel.

Hudson sighed loudly, pacing in fits and starts in front of her, his hands wringing with helpless gestures.

"For Pete's sake, love. Just spit it out." She held her breath.

"I don't know why you can't see it. It's obvious. Maybe you're all subconsciously denying it so as not to rock the boat? Understandable in light of what was going on here around the time you all found out what Baby was up to." He glanced quickly away. "With me and all. That was so long ago, yet just like yesterday. I feel—"

She reached out her hand to grab his arm. "We've talked and talked that subject to death. We both have pasts we're not proud of. They're behind us and what matters is our today and our tomorrows, Hud. That means our children. They're our chance to do it right this time. Daisy's all grown up and way out of reach. I no longer even know what she does in that so-called lab of hers with Netty and Abby." Studying her lap, she whispered, "I want our baby. I know you do too."

"You don't need to worry about Daisy. She's marked for otherworldly pursuits. It's what she wants. We can't hold a special child like her back. She's not even a child anymore. I know it's creepy, looking like a six-year-old but she's what . . . thirty nine, forty?"

"Thirty five. But this isn't about Daisy. It's about us."

Hud knelt down before her, taking her hands in his. She could identify many emotions in his eyes. She winced inwardly as she admitted pity took precedence.

Hud's words were low and soft. "I don't think the Hive wants any of you ladies to get pregnant."

Ginger Mae sprang to her feet, sending Hud sprawling back on his butt. "What? No, no . . . they wouldn't do that to us. That doesn't make any sense. And how? I mean . . . really . . .?" Hud climbed to his feet, picking off dried scat that had adhered to his butt; droppings from one of the animals that had passed through the corridor and been overlooked.

"I don't know how, babe. Maybe you and I can swing some time alone with Netty and Wil, and bring it up together?"

"But Hud, Wil's your best friend. Can't you just wring it out of him?"

He shook his head. "No . . . we never talk about the Hive, the Womb or the weird stuff. You have to remember, Wil and I lived in the same time, long ago. He's from the next county where I lived with my family. We talk about home, carpentry, advances that have been made since we . . . died. I really can't share that kind of stuff with anyone but Wil. He's a good kid. Well, not a kid. I mean a good guy. I just wish I'd known him before Netty's ex got ahold of him. I might have been able to do something . . ." His enhanced memory illuminated the pain from his past; the faraway dullness in his eyes fading as he snapped back to the present, "Let me work on it, babe. I'll try to talk to him today if the right moment comes up." He took her arm, tucking it into his and bent down to kiss her oh so softly, savoring the promise their lips exchanged.

"Do we want to be the last to arrive?" She gave her head a tiny shake no.

"Well then, let's go. I'm starved." The beautiful reformed ex-prostitute and the handsome dishonored ex-sheriff turned the bend in the corridor to join the rest of the Hive family for breakfast and Netty's meeting.

*

Ginger Mae noticed a subdued atmosphere in the kitchen as they entered, even as Netty presented platters of steaming hot purple and black cake-like fritters that featured a spicy, salty-sweet bite on the tables; one of her most popular dishes, usually reserved for special occasions.

Glancing at the counter by the sink, she could see an assortment of fruit pies that must have kept Dezi baking into the night. Chance snuffled at Dezi's feet as he rolled out the dough for another pie. *Hmm, wonder what this means?*

As she and Hud made their way back to their waiting seats with Bonnie and Peter, they exchanged quick, quiet greetings with the others, a wave here and a smile there.

Ginger Mae didn't fail to notice how jumpy Netty appeared; nervous almost. She startled as Netty herself slipped around their seats to put down a platter, the hot steaming breakfast cakes wafting their enticing spices along the wooden table.

Hud spoke up. "Morning Netty. Where's Wil?" Ginger Mae hadn't noticed his absence.

Netty gave Hud a dreamy, goofy smile. "He'll be back by the time we finish breakfast." She appeared to sober, her happy expression flashing back to nervous and jumpy.

Murmurings circulated the tables as the survivors gossiped in discreet undertones, Netty's uncharacteristic behavior and particular breakfast a puzzle.

Baby and Echo lounged silently and unconcerned at the fireplace with Barney and Chloe's Teddy, both dogs alert and jumpy as they sensed the change in atmosphere.

No one uttered a word as Netty kept glancing at the entrance to the kitchen while Salina and Karen cleared the empty plates and Shirley poured the tea. The tension in the room increased while Dezi sliced into a walnut raspberry cobbler.

Clyde's granddaughter, Jennifer, quickly dispensed the treat as Netty rose from her chair at her private table to pick up a smaller version of her own chair that had sat unnoticed along the wall, before ceremoniously depositing it at her and Wil's table.

She returned to stand and face them all, stealing another quick, nervous glance at the door.

Ginger Mae scanned the crowd, observing the expectant faces and curious minds calmly and innocently awaiting Netty's announcement.

Netty bowed her head. She fidgeted with a wing, her tail tightly wound around her waist as if holding her together. Her face lifted to reveal an odd coupling of pride and a sudden flash of . . . *Was that fright?* Ginger Mae wondered.

Netty cleared her throat and gave them a weak smile. "I don't actually know where to begin."

The crowd stirred and exchanged looks.

Netty intercepted some of the looks, causing her to stiffen her spine. She began. "There are two parts to this meeting. First, I need you all to understand something important. We . . . the Womb, the Kreyven, the minions, and Wil and I planned for many years to institute the intervention that Baby should have begun upon arrival on Earth. You all know the story well by now, but we needed to keep a few things to ourselves for a very good reason. Until the right time. I think the right time has come."

The room filled with groans and exclamations of surprise, Clyde's being the loudest protest as usual.

Netty held up her hands, her voice soft and gentle. "Please . . . hear me out. This has not been easy for us either. As you know, Baby's mission did not originally plan for the need of the Hive. The Womb had originally made the decision to intervene in a more catastrophic way. It would have left no humans on the planet to interfere with the lives of any remaining species, or new ones for that matter."

Her hands rose to cut off objections, her expression hardening as she became absorbed in the telling.

"As Baby and I met so very long ago, we began a productive life together. Then Wil entered our lives. The Womb decided to take a wait-and-see attitude as Echo stayed in the Hive to gauge the new developments. Then came the interference from my ex-husband and our brutal deaths.

"I'm sure you've all heard that, even as we are immortal, that doesn't mean we can't die. Luckily, Echo convinced the Womb to send the Kreyven to rescue us for what you call cloning and what we also know as mind transference.

"What most of you don't know, is that we were not all able to be rescued." Netty's voice stumbled, great pain coming up from deep within her.

"Wil and I had a baby."

Gasps of sadness came from the entranced survivors as they sat spellbound, watching the stunning Elder they had all come to admire and love.

"Without going into detail, please accept that my baby died before Wil and I even had a chance to name her." Netty rubbed her temples, her pain clear to all. She took a deep breath and straightened.

"Our adjustment to our rebirth, the Hive, knowledge of how the millions and millions of solar systems worked and our new role in it, took us a very long time. Decades passed as we fought to come to terms with our new lives.

"Humans are not meant to be Elders. Only minions. Yes, we have descended from minions, which made it all possible, but we have many traits and limitations given to us by evolution. They needed to be . . . modified. And some things needed to be enhanced." She ran her hands from the top of her head, sweeping down to rest at her side.

"And this is what we got." She smiled and nodded to herself. "Not too shabby, right?"

"As time wore on, we also began to realize our plans for the planet needed to be altered. Echo became attached to the family who discovered her, and we realized we had more Elders on our hands. You know their story.

"Just as the decision was made to change our plans, we learned of an element in your population who planned mass destruction without our intervention. We needed to quickly ready Abby for her part of the mission."

Ginger Mae watched Abby and Netty's eyes meet, the hero worship from Abby plain as the crystal horns on their heads.

Clyde stood up, impatience in his voice.

"We already know most of this. Why don't you get to the point?"

The crowd shushed him as Salina pulled him back down to his chair. "Let her tell it her way, for gosh sakes, Clyde. Can't you see how painful this is?"

Resuming, Netty's voice added a defensive note. "You must understand. We did not have plans for anyone other than Scotty, Chloe, Abby and Jose."

"Why Chloe? What's so special about her?" A resentful-sounding shout from the crowd.

"You all know about The One. Someday, you may be very grateful. The needs of The One must always be considered."

Ginger Mae peered around Hud's shoulders as Chloe muttered, "Needs?" with an arched eyebrow. Scotty slipped a kiss on her forehead as he squeezed her tight.

"My needs," he whispered.

"There was no way to rescue all the wildlife before the bombs dropped. We're lucky Abby rescued what she did. That includes all of you, too." She swept her hand to include the room.

"Unfortunately, we had no way to know in advance that events would unfold this way. We were forced to improvise as Abby accumulated you all along the way." She smiled. "I'm sure you've noticed the disarray in the storage room and library. These items were obtained as it became apparent Abby was planning to rescue people too." This time she smiled brightly at Daisy.

"We are ever so happy you've adjusted so well. I'm sure Wil and I don't need to tell you how fond we are of all our survivors."

Netty was now grinning from ear to ear. A clatter sounded from the hallway where Caesar kept his vigil. Ginger Mae craned her neck. Was that the sound of Netty's food wagon?

A high scream was heard. A grinning Wil entered the kitchen behind the most amazing sight. A whirling dervish of a handful; all three feet four inches of a three-year-old Elder toddler. She ran screaming to Netty, who scooped her up in the air, swinging her around and holding her tight. She deposited her on the counter after showering her with kisses. Netty turned to face the stunned and speechless survivors with tears glittering in her eyes.

"My daughter, Maya."

The crowd sat speechless. Ginger Mae glanced at Hud and looked around the room. Mouths hung open, puzzlement entering eyes. As Ginger Mae tried to make sense of it, she caught flashes of hurt in the eyes of some of the women. Tentative smiles tugged at compressed lips as the natural beauty of an innocent child tugged at hearts. A groundswell of emotional voices swept the room within seconds.

"Your daughter?"

"When did this happen?"

"Why did ya hide her, Netty?"

"Yeah, what's the deal here?" The voices escalated. The child, Maya, curled into Netty's chest, the noise from the astonished survivors frightening her.

Netty held up her hand to quiet the crowd, her face dark. "Wil, can you please take Maya?" She scanned the room, quickly locating the minions.

"Baby, Echo? Can I ask you to go with Wil and stay with Maya? You can take Barney with you. Hurry back, Wil."

The two minions wobbled over to the kitchen door where Wil waited, Maya blowing kisses to Baby and Barney. As they disappeared through the door, Netty turned back to the confused survivors.

"All right . . . all right." Netty held up both hands. "I know you have questions. I'm not finished."

"Oh, Netty, she's wonderful." Abby's voice brokered some agreement in the crowd as they recognized their rude behavior toward the child. Chagrined voices added their compliments as everyone settled back down.

"Well, at least someone was able to get pregnant." Crystal's wry voice cut deep. Ginger Mae recognized the pain in the expressions of many of the women in the kitchen. Pain and longing. *I know how they feel.*

She turned her attention from her fellow survivors back to Netty, who now stood quietly, her face expressionless, waiting until she had all of their attention. Ginger Mae could feel the crowd becoming restless.

"Maya was born three years before the bombs came. She's still mentally a toddler. I asked the Womb if she could remain so, unlike the rest of us."

Hushed expectation greeted Netty's words. Tension again filled the room as they all realized the true reason for the meeting was about to be revealed.

"Wil and I quickly understood our daughter's presence would be a problem once I was forced to inform you that the surviving women here in this room would never be capable of bearing children."

The gasp from the crowd made Netty flinch. Angry voices assailed the homey kitchen. Ginger Mae felt Hud's strong hands reach out to hold her as she failed to stop a desperate tear escaping her eye.

She raised her face to peer at her sister survivors, who sat stunned at the news, faces scared and wet with tears. The outspoken Clyde was the first to respond, calm yet incredulous. "Are you trying to tell us that we'll be the last of our race? And just how is it that you know that exactly?"

Netty held her head up to take the brunt of the anger that seeped into the consciousness of the gathering.

"It's the food isn't it? Or the tendrils? The fucking tendrils. You throw us a bone while you rob us in our sleep." Billy the trucker cradled his shocked wife in his arms, bitterness getting the best of him.

"No, it's not the food or the tendrils." Netty began to meet anger with anger. The room filled with simmering resentment. "You're alive are you not?"

Cobby stood to face his fellow survivors. Karen's stricken face turned to watch as he attempted to calm everyone down. "Come on, gang. Let's hear her out. She's one of us."

From the keeper's table came a determined voice. "No, sir. Miss Netty is not one of us. She's an angel of the Womb. We're only alive by mistake. I'm grateful and well understand my place in the Hive. I would not be making any demands on Miss Netty." The keeper's big round eyes trailed the walls where the membrane breathed, his protruding white orbs a contrast to his awed dark face.

"Thank you, Johno. Now perhaps I can continue?" Grumblings and tears swept through the survivors, calming only as Cobby shushed them.

Netty took a deep breath, visibly settling herself. "The decision to end your species came from the Womb. The original Elders were your makers . . . your creators, but we're always at the beck of the Womb in all its infinite wisdom." She gestured toward the membrane.

"Most of you are aware that our necessary light source comes from the membranes that support our life here. The light contains a high-frequency light spectrum that destroys the enzyme needed to procreate. It's the same enzyme that is destroyed by the sun in areas close to the equator.

"As your species evolved, skin darkened to protect that enzyme. Now, the Womb merely introduced a different light spectrum not found in the sun, but lethal to this necessary enzyme. It is temporary. When you resurface, you will no longer come into contact with the spectrum."

The crowd buzzed, some relief evident in their grumbling.

"I'm sorry to say . . . the Womb will then introduce something into your environment to produce the same result."

A bitter shout came from an angry face. "All except you. You get to have your child. And probably Princess Abby will be able to have them too, won't she?"

Ginger Mae spotted the stung expression on Abby's face, her hand reaching back to Jose.

Netty began to stroll as she spoke, her eyes again flicking to the kitchen door. "If Abby wants to have children, she can undergo a process that will allow that to happen. She's an Elder. She will decide together with the Womb when that should happen."

"Don't I get a say in the matter?" Jose placed his chin on his hand, resting his elbow on the table as his emotions expressed themselves in the abrupt twitching of his tail.

"No, not really. You know you are a consort for Abby, Jose. That's why male Elders don't grow horns. Our society is a matriarch one. Before minions lost their immortality, only females had antlers. Now they all do. One small concession for their loss. Baby is the first immortal male to ever have antlers. And the last, I imagine."

Moving on, the issue dismissed as far as Netty was concerned, she continued. "Under these circumstances, when it was discovered Abby was recruiting unexpected guests, our plans were altered for your comfort. We knew the time would come where pressures would necessitate explanations. It was believed the women would accept the news better if my own child was not here to stoke resentment. So . . . so I . . ." Netty swallowed. "So I was forced to send her into exile. My own baby . . ."

The group remained silent as Netty pulled herself together. "She has been here in the Hive. I go to see her every day for a few hours. But it is not nearly the same."

A movement caught Ginger Mae's eye. From her seat next to Peter, Bonnie rose. "I'm very sorry for all you've gone through, Netty, and I'm very grateful to be alive. But Peter and I love one another, just as you love Wil. We can't help that we yearn to share our love the same way you have—with a child." She ran her hand up the roots of her hair, grasping and pulling down to assuage her pain. "I don't know what to say . . . I know I can't go on feeling this way." She turned as Peter rose, burying herself in his arms to cry.

Ginger Mae took inventory of the other stricken women, watching as Salina ran over to her remaining daughter. Bonnie threw herself into her mother's arms, sobbing deeply as Salina's bitter cold tears made their quiet way down her long-suffering face.

Suddenly, Wil appeared at the doorway. "Are you ready yet, Netty?"

All attention swiveled back to Netty, her expression now hesitant. "Yes, Wil. I think now is the time. Can you please bring the father in?"

To the astonishment of the survivors, Netty's food wagon emerged from outside, propelled by a large figure draped in a clergyman's robe. All they could see inside the hood that covered his large head was the rich, dark color of his wide and bushy beard. From around his neck hung a heavy cross of an unidentifiable metal.

He was assisted by a young woman in her twenties, her round face a complement to her cocoa complexion and her thick, shiny ebony hair pulled back in a ribbon that flowed down her stout back. She wore a light-brown cotton smock with a similar cross, although smaller in size.

Together, they ushered the wagon into the center of the kitchen to complete silence from the incredulous survivors.

"I would like to introduce you to Father Garcia and Madeline Perez."

As Madeline and Father Garcia stepped over to Netty, a squeak was heard from inside a huge basket that sat on the wagon.

Father Garcia smiled at the crowd, removing his hood to reveal a man in his late sixties, his watery-blue eyes a clear palette of weariness. Madeline hung shyly behind him.

"Come along dear . . . they won't bite, now will they, Netty?"

Wil hurriedly removed his chair from their table to rush it to Father Garcia. "Please, Father, sit." As he clapped Wil on the shoulder, Father Garcia eased his large body down onto the chair, Madeline standing by.

"Thank you, my boy. These old knees of mine still insist on warring with the tendrils. I think my knees are winning." He looked brightly around the room, his measuring eyes lingering on every face.

Netty waited respectfully until Father Garcia was satisfied. He gave her a slight nod, and she began again.

"I understand you're all curious. I can see the heartache my information has stirred. So." She nodded to Father Garcia. "With Father Garcia's permission, I'm going to do something I have long awaited. Then we will continue this story."

Walking over to the large basket on the food wagon, she placed her hand on the edge facing the dining tables. "May I please ask that Ginger Mae, Karen, Bonnie and Gloria join me?"

The four women glanced at their husbands, their confusion clear as they searched for support in the faces of their sister survivors. Slowly, each woman stood to join Netty near the wagon.

She reached out to guide them to the wagon where they looked down into the basket. Sudden gasps brought hands to mouths as tender expressions, fragile and hopeful, searched the basket, then back up to Netty's face.

Ginger Mae bit her knuckle painfully as hopeful tears dropped hot and painful. For there in the basket, nestled in their blankets, lay three infants who stared straight up at her, unblinking. Tiny feet kicked and buckled under their covers, the only sign they knew they were the center of attention. One white- and two dark-skinned infants looking like satisfied kittens.

Bonnie turned to the tables, her smile fighting through fresh tears. "Peter. Come look."

Peter hurried to her side where she threw her arms around his neck, slowing down his anxious attempt to peer into the basket. Soon, everyone milled around the infants.

Ginger Mae's heart froze as she realized three infants didn't go far with four desperate women who would never conceive. With a heavy heart, she led Hud back to the table and quietly sat down, ignoring the questions in his eyes.

It didn't take long before the sweet surprise wore off, fostering the return of suspicion and betrayal. Ginger Mae watched as Father Garcia sent a subtle nod to Netty.

Making her way through the crowd at the wagon, she directed the survivors back to their seats. Karen spoke up first as the spell of the infants wore off.

"Are the babies for us, Netty? Where did they come from? Where did Father Garcia come from? Were you up top, sir? Are there other survivors?" At the mention of the possibility, a roar sounded; hope springing desperately, just like a baby bird's mother as she pushed her fledgling from the nest to take his first flight.

But just as the mother bird's hopes are dashed when the fledgling crashes to the ground, so Netty crushed theirs.

"No . . . I'm sorry. Father Garcia has been here in the Hive as long as you have. There is no one . . . nothing . . . left above."

Bonnie's small voice cut through the din, the whisper pointed and forlorn. "The babies."

"Let me explain, if you haven't already figured it out." She helped Father Garcia from his seat as she spoke. "As I mentioned, Maya has been with Father Garcia since your arrival. But I knew the time would come when I could no longer bear to hide her. I needed a way to make it safe to welcome her into our family, which includes women who would be resentful and bitter about their inability to conceive." She turned toward Abby.

"My wonderful, Abby. You gave me the solution." The two Elders' faces gleamed with the pride that comes from two women who hold each other in the highest regard. Netty inclined her head, encouragement for Abby to speak. Slowly, falteringly . . . Abby voice gained strength as she found the answer.

"The innocent babies. All of them. It killed me to leave them behind along with the rest of the creatures I failed to rescue. You knew?"

Netty nodded. "Of course, my dear. The implants. We knew your every thought." Abby blushed deeply as Ginger Mae swore she saw her glance guiltily toward Cobby from under her veiled golden eyes. *That's interesting.*

Netty resumed. "We had hoped to rescue more, but the time—it just plain ran out. It was only a few hours before you got here that the Kreyven returned from a tinderbox called Newark. Its proximity to New York City and abundance of ramshackle buildings, which had been shortchanged during construction by corrupt town officials and greedy building inspectors, all but guaranteed its collapse."

Father Garcia spoke up. "It just happened to be in one of those exact buildings that the church housed the homeless and surrendered children. We had been there for forty five years. Many a child called it their first and last home."

He took out a yellow handkerchief and swabbed his dry brow, attempting to wipe away the memories.

"When the Kreyven came, we were moving the older children to the basement. We had lost all electricity and had no way of knowing about the bombs, other than the first one in Vegas." Father Garcia shook his head mournfully.

"I knew there'd be more. As sure as water is wet, I knew the politicians would muck everything up. And we have no one to blame but ourselves. We gave them the power and turned our lives over to them for a few pieces of silver." Father Garcia scrutinized everyone in the room, one by one. The silence weighed heavy as they waited for him to continue.

"Was that pittance the value of our children?" He closed his eyes, appearing to be in pain. His words came out slow and soft. "We made a deal with the Devil and sold out our children's future. Then the Devil came calling again.

"Netty Capaccino is as fine a woman as I've ever met. She did this for you. I just wish we could have saved more than three. We felt the bomb hit. I was running back upstairs from the basement to help Maddy bring down the babies. We no sooner had them in our arms, then the Kreyven busted in and wrapped us in its body and took us underground. We felt . . . the ground shudder."

Father Garcia's voice faltered, his eyelids closed tight as of to fight off the chaos of the memory. Madeline knelt at his feet and squeezed his hands tightly. Tiredly, he continued. "That's all we had. Three. The rest were all left behind." He sighed fast and deep, pushing away the painful memory. "Well . . . that was a long time ago. Let's hope you place a greater value on these children. It appears they are the last of their kind."

With those words, he rose to his feet, lifting Madeline from her knees.

"Come, my dear, we have a long walk home." Turning to Netty and Wil, he bid them good day. "I trust we will see you in the morning again? We'll bring the babes." With nods from the Elders, and a perfunctory goodnight to the survivors, Father Garcia and

Madeline wheeled the wagon back out to the hallway and disappeared with the infants.

Ginger Mae's head swam. The unexpected promise of the infants was overshadowed by the knowledge that they'd been hidden here all this time. With two grown adults. Why hadn't they challenged Netty or Wil about the food wagon? She massaged her temples, the answer obvious.

In the beginning, they had feared Netty and Wil. The mental trauma caused from fleeing the bombs, the deaths from the Time of Seth, the discovery of the Kreyven, Baby's hidden revenge on the men from Netty's past, and the revelation of the tendrils and length of time they would live in the Hive had given them all enough to deal with. And she herself had had to cope with her disfigured face, the animosity from Peter, her pressures from the daily count, her jealousy over the amount of time Daisy spent with the Elders and her head-over-heels romance with Hud.

"Are you okay, babe?" Hud leaned over to massage her shoulders. She smiled gratefully as her head swirled with the emotions generated from so much chaos. She leaned back until her head rested on Hud's chest.

"Three . . . only three babies." All around her, the other couples conferred, somber yet hopeful.

"Okay, everyone. I'd like everyone with an interest in the infants to arrive for breakfast an hour early tomorrow. Now . . . let's get on with our duties."

The crowd buzzed as everyone filtered out to begin their day, several stopping to congratulate Netty and Wil on the birth of their lovely little girl. Bonnie and Ginger Mae linked arms and funneled out with their apprehensive husbands bringing up the rear.

Chapter 6

Ginger Mae rushed Hud as he dressed the next morning.

"I'm going as fast as I can, babe. Take a deep breath. I know you're anxious. But they won't open the envelopes until we're all there."

Ginger Mae looked at the envelope clenched tightly in her hand, wrinkled and creased from the attention they had given it since Netty had stood before her after dinner last night.

Each woman had drawn their envelope from the small box in Netty's hand. Four white envelopes with yellow squares inside. Three with the letter B, one blank.

Her stomach contracted painfully, her nerves fragile and frayed.

Hud tipped her face up to his, slowly planting soft lip caresses like whispers of promises on her face.

"I love you, Ginger Mae Hudson. No matter what happens, we have each other. If we're lucky enough to get a baby, great. I can't think of anything more perfect than that. But we need to be prepared for the worst."

"Nooo. I can't. This is our only chance, Hud. I feel good about it. I'm scared, but I know there's a B inside this envelope."

Hud wrapped her up in his strong arms, expelling his breath loudly.

"Okay, babe. Let's go get our baby."

Karen, Gloria, Bonnie and Ginger Mae sat at the table in front of the room. Cobby, Billy, Peter and Hud stood behind their wives. Salina and Clyde hovered nervously by the fireplace where Baby lurked, refusing to accept that the grandparents should not be there.

Ginger Mae could see their presence only served to make Bonnie more nervous. The best friends held hands tightly . . . painfully, the now sweat-stained envelopes plastered flat on the table.

Everyone glanced up as Father Garcia and Madeline wheeled the food cart in with its precious cargo.

"Good morning ladies . . . gentlemen. Wil, Netty, nice to see you so early in the morning for a change. I must say that Maddy and I are so pleased we can now integrate with the rest of the Hive family." Maddy gave them all a shy smile as Father Garcia placed the wagon in front of the table. He turned to take his sizable bulk to a chair to watch where he was joined by Maddy.

Netty approached the table. "One unfortunately, will not get a baby. I know of no other way to handle this. Do any of you want to step aside?" Her question met terse silence. "Okay. I'm going to pick up a baby. It will go to the first couple who opens their envelope and gets in line with it. Go."

Thus the scramble started with little warning. The women tore at the envelopes. All eyes focused on the beautiful letter Bs found inside. Ginger Mae and Hud broke out in glorious glee, hugging and jumping up to join the line at the wagon. Chairs fell on the floor as the women tripped over themselves to see the babies. Ginger Mae was third in line to receive her tiny bundle.

"It's a boy." Netty placed the infant in her arms as she smiled into Hud's surprised eyes. The baby looked back at them with clear colorless eyes in his dusky skin.

"He's so wonderful," breathed Ginger Mae.

Squeals and laughter filled the room. The men clapped each other on the back and shook hands. Father Garcia and Maddy beamed with joy.

Wil entered the kitchen with Netty's Maya in his arms. She squirmed to get down and ran laughing to her mother's arms.

The sudden slam of a chair made them all look up. Ginger Mae gasped in horror. Bonnie stood at the table, her envelope crumpled on the floor, tears coursing down her face as Peter held her back. "I never ask for anything." That was all she said as she ran from the room, a distraught Peter letting his eyes linger on the infants as he left behind her. Salina and Clyde pushed through the bunch around the wagon, the pain on their faces contrasting with the blissful relief of the new moms. Relieved it was Bonnie and not them.

Except for Ginger Mae and Hud, that is. She looked to her husband then the baby. "Oh, no. It can't be Bonnie. Oh, Hud . . ." Hud's stricken expression matched hers. They pulled away from the celebrating crowd and stared at one another. The baby kicked gently against Ginger Mae's arms as he smiled for the first time. Ginger Mae examined the baby's face. "He's perfect, Hud."

"I know, babe."

"We could really love him."

Hud's sadness intensified. He spoke softly. "We sure could." They stared at each other again, moisture in Ginger Mae's eyes. Together they said goodbye to the other celebrants and left the kitchen with their baby.

Peter comforted Bonnie as she cried face down on the dais they shared together in the private quarters they had moved to once they were married. Salina knelt at her daughter's side as Clyde paced frantically, wringing his hands near the back of the tiny cavern, careful to avoid the drape of the membrane on the walls.

Peter's anguish knew no bounds as his attempts to comfort the best and sweetest person he had ever had the pleasure of calling his friend, let alone his wife, met with no success.

It left him ill prepared to handle his own deep disappointment over being the losing couple. Jealousy gripped his senses as his dream of being a father lay as broken as his old eyeglasses from twenty nine years ago. He exhaled with futility.

"Peter, Bonnie?" Peter jumped off the dais to confront Hud and Ginger Mae.

"Oh, guys . . . I'm sorry." He wiped quickly at his damp cheeks and straightened his shirt. He held out his hand to Hud.

"Honey . . . look who's here. Congratulations, you two. Congratulations on your baby."

Bonnie slipped off the dais, her cheeks creased and red. She tried to smile and failed.

Ginger Mae handed the tiny bundle to Hud as she softly kissed his forehead. Hud leaned in to hug the three of them together. Straightening up he walked over to Peter. "No . . . your baby, Peter."

Bonnie gasped. Salina began to wail, stepping woodenly toward Ginger Mae, arms outstretched to wrap her in a shaking embrace.

Peter stood dumbfounded as Hud placed the infant in his arms. His knees knocked as he felt the lightness of the bundle. Bonnie walked as if in a trance, her mouth wide open in astonishment. Peter watched the rise of hope and disbelief war across her face.

Hud reached out to take his wife's hand. Squeezing tightly, they cleaved together for strength as they watched their best friends, new grandparents and all, welcome their new son.

The excitement over the babies settled down as the lucky survivors put their infants to bed for the first time.

The couples were all surprised to discover a miniature stone dais at the foot of their own beds. The walls curved up for safety, creating a comfortable nest for the baby, well within sight of the new, proud parents.

In one chamber reserved for married couples, exhausted sobbing could be heard. Ginger Mae's red and blotchy face rested on Hudson's strong arm as they lay on their soft dais.

She hiccupped as she made him a tearful vow. "I'm sorry, Hud. I know we did the right thing. It's just that it still hurts. I'll be fine in the morning. Promise . . ."

"I know you will, babe. There's no one stronger than you. We'll be fine," he lied.

Her sobs tapered off as his gentle rocking and soft, heartbroken kisses lulled her to sleep.

The corridors of the Hive lay silent as the wondrous tendrils of the night began their journey across stone floors and from under fertile soil to locate the survivors and animals that now depended on them to keep them healthy and young.

Even the still-diminutive Tobi, matriarch of the now significant herd, slept on her feet, safe and sound in the growing field with her beloved pigs and various dozens of dogs; chuffing and snorts filling the night air with comfortable unconscious creature noises.

The membrane-lined walls and ceilings had dimmed their human-enzyme-killing light hours ago. Temperate air flushed through the silent hallways, sweeping away the odors of the humans and their beloved animals. Peace settled deeply into the subconscious of all that lived and breathed.

From far away, the foreign sound of groaning rock fell on deaf ears; the sound preceded by pressure that had no one to feel it. No one except the Kreyven and the tiny package it sheltered.

Breaking through a far cavern wall, the gelatinous creature travelled the Hive hallways, lighting up the membrane walls as if greeting a well-known friend as it passed by.

The Kreyven reached the sleeping chambers, pausing to assess each opening, rejecting them all until it found the one it was looking for. It hovered at the open doorway, swelling and weaving, its mass undulating and flashing gold and emerald light. The smell of deep earth permeated the air as it hovered, hesitant. Suddenly, its flashing light stopped and the beast floated into the room.

It stopped at the foot of the dais where a couple slumbered, wrapped in each other's arms. A thick portion of the Kreyven's body separated and dropped to the floor. From the bowels of the beast, a stone object made its way to the head of the monster's extension until it was vomited to the floor to stand free and clear. The separated portion of the Kreyven returned to be reabsorbed into the main body.

The massive creature hovered over the deposited object as if to inspect it. Slowly the bulk lowered, separating two nubs of itself which appeared to shelter the tiny package it held protectively to its upper body near its head. The arms of the Kreyven dipped into the stone object to deposit its burden, then retracted as it continued to hover, silently . . . expectantly.

It suddenly moved to the side as Echo appeared, her wings beating quickly, slowing as she lowered herself to the floor. She looked into the miniature stone dais delivered by the Kreyven, her aura searching the mind of the beast commanded by Womb.

"There is damage . . . unfortunate. But that can be fixed." Echo turned to the Kreyven, golden eyes flashing.

"You have done well. Now all will be happy." Glancing once more at the sleeping couple, Echo and the Kreyven vanished as if nothing had happened. The only sign left behind was the pervasive musky odor of rich dirt and the stone dais with its fragile burden.

The next morning, Hud woke as if fighting the lingering effects of a painful hangover. Absently sniffing the air, he rolled over to Ginger Mae. "Hey pretty lady. Time to rise and shine."

"Eum." She waved him off without opening her eyes; not even a trace of a smile for his efforts.

"Come on, babe. If we don't show for breakfast, Peter and Bonnie will feel bad. You did a great thing. We don't want to dampen their joy. I'm sure they realize what the cost was for you. There's no point in making it any worse." He pulled her over to his big body. "I'm here for you, babe. We can bear this together."

Ginger Mae opened her eyes, flat and unresponsive. "I'm sorry, Hud. I know this affects you too." She put a hand to her mouth as a tiresome yawn got the best of her. "We might as well get up. I still need to start the count. That should cheer me up."

From the foot of the dais came a sound, freezing them both. Hud rose up to inspect the room for the source. He looked back at Ginger Mae, dumbstruck.

"What is it, Hud? What's wrong?" She swung her legs to the floor, not taking her eyes off her speechless husband. Rounding the foot of the dais, she was confronted by the Kreyven's mysterious delivery.

"What the heck?"

"Oh, my." Frozen, they stood staring at the tiny naked baby inside the stone dais. Its squinty eyes barely opened, its face so wrinkled and red, it was unaware it was even being watched. The infant made a sudden weak snort, its right hand twitching.

"Oh, the poor thing." Ginger Mae looked for reassurance from her husband as the infant's hand evinced palsied twitching of the claw that was its hand. The two last fingers were fused to the bone and curved in, like that of a dead bird. A purple splash of color around the infant's right thumb looked like the shape of a large half-moon.

The astonished couple glanced at each other, confusion and pity mixing to further complicate the matter. A squeal brought their attention back to the infant.

"She looks like a newborn. Like she was just delivered, Hud. Where could she have come from?" She skirted over to Hud to hold onto his arm as they examined the baby from above.

"I think I should pick her up. What do you think?"

"I don't see why not, babe."

Ginger Mae reached in to lift the baby as her eyes tried to open and focus. She gurgled as the pressure from Ginger Mae's arms delivered reassurance. "Do you think she came from Netty and Wil?"

"I don't know where else she could have come from."

"But why is she naked? Netty wouldn't leave her like that. And last night, no one said a word about another baby. Father Garcia said they only rescued three."

Hud appeared reflective. "And wouldn't the tendrils have healed her . . . her . . . hand by now? What about the redness of her skin? Wouldn't it have also been resolved by now? No one here was pregnant, so we can't have a newborn here."

Ginger Mae's hand shot to her mouth. "Oh, no . . . Kenya."

Hud slapped his thigh. "Of course! It must be Kenya's baby." He looked at Ginger Mae, his face screwed up in confusion. "But why is she here in our room? Where's Kenya?"

Ginger Mae's face drained of blood. "Hud, we better go find Netty."

They hurriedly dressed, wrapped the baby in a soft cloth and hurried to the kitchen where they found everyone already assembled.

Ginger Mae and Hud rushed up to Netty at the sink, whirling her around so fast her wings banged against the counter. Hud searched the room with his eyes, desperate to catch sight of the obstreperous Kenya.

Netty eyed the bundle in her hands. "But I thought Bonnie said—"

They couldn't help themselves as they all turned to Bonnie at the table.

Scooping up her baby, Bonnie hurried over to the sink, puzzlement mounting as she recognized the bundle in Ginger Mae's arms as being another baby. "Hi guys. What's up? Whose baby is that?"

Netty stroked the soft tender skin of the newborn, her tone of voice pensive and thoughtful. "Yes . . . where did this baby come from?" Netty hooked her finger around the baby's desiccated claw that should have been a hand. "Hmm, where would this baby have come from?"

Ginger Mae held the baby tight to her breast, rocking slowly. "Does anyone know where Kenya is? Could she have delivered her baby?"

Netty sighed loudly. "Highly unlikely, but it wouldn't surprise me since I seem to be out of the loop these days." The knot of survivors turned as they felt the presence of Echo, who fluttered high in the air.

Landing on the kitchen counter, Echo stared at Ginger Mae then the baby.

"Did you want something, Echo?" asked Netty.

Ginger Mae shrugged her shoulders. "Echo just does this sometimes. You know that, Netty," she said dismissively.

From across the room came a shout. "Don't you be jiving me so early in the morning, chickey. If I say I can help, then I mean it. This ole belly a mine don't stop me from doin' what I want ta do . . . ya got it?"

The cluster around the baby showed signs of anxiety as they recognized Kenya's voice. One possibility eliminated, the baby's parentage was still clearly a mystery. Ginger Mae spoke up. "Can I leave the baby with Father Garcia and Maddy while I work today?" Arrangements had been made for the new twosome to become the official baby minders while the survivors' schedules continued uninterrupted. The only change in plans was the thought that Netty's comfortable kitchen, center of all that was survivor harmony, should finally undergo a remodel with the addition of a nursery annex. A room that would open into the kitchen, but provide the babies the privacy they needed to be . . . well . . . babies. Squalling, yet close by for the mom and dads at every meal.

Rising from his comfortable chair at the end of the table with Johno and Shirley, Father Garcia left Maddy in their care and approached the new baby. "Well . . . what do we have here?" He traced the flanges of the deformed hand, muttering under his breath, then swept the baby from Ginger Mae's arms. Hud stepped up to stop him, pulling back just as quickly.

"Don't you worry none about this young one. She'll be in good hands until we solve the mystery. And if we can't?" His eyes twinkled his goodwill toward Ginger Mae and Hud. "Then I know a fine couple that just might make a willing momma and papa. See you at lunch. Come, my dear."

They both relaxed as Father Garcia beckoned over to Maddy and left the room with Bonnie's baby in Maddy's arms and the mystery babe with Father Garcia.

Two weeks passed as the new moms and dads in the Hive adjusted to the delights and responsibilities that come with infants. Hud and Ginger Mae assumed the roles of parents to the mystery baby, but refused to name her. Until the rightful parentage could be assessed, they both felt safer holding back a portion of the emotion that would enable them to fully accept the baby as theirs. All Ginger Mae could think of was the pain of giving up their rightful baby to Peter and Bonnie. It would be months before the ache went away. She had no wish to revive more baby pain, even as she knew in her heart they had done the right thing for Peter and Bonnie.

Hilarity was the tone as the new moms claimed the fireplace after dinner with their infants tucked passively in their arms.

"We let Kane name our new baby girl." Karen rocked smugly, her long legs stretched out before her. Confidence oozed from every pore as she knew her life was secure; a hard-fought patient battle for the man of her choice and a brand-new baby to cement them as a family.

"What did Kane name her?" asked Bonnie.

"Aurora. He said that was the name of Sleeping Beauty in a story his mother read to him as a child. He thought it was the most beautiful name for a girl." Her face saddened. "It's about all he remembers of his mother except the anger she was so filled with. That's not what I want for my baby. She's going to be loved by both parents at the same time. Always."

"We named our little boy, Taj. Billy says it reminds him of Caesar. He's never seen such a magnificent animal in his life. I didn't even know he noticed Caesar. Well . . . how can you miss him? But you know what I mean." Gloria laughingly rocked in her chair. "And our little Taj will grow up to be a big man . . . just like his dad . . . and just like Caesar."

"We named our little boy, Peter. After his dad." Bonnie looked up, her beatific expression telling them she was besotted with both her husband and her new baby. Dreamily, she turned to Ginger Mae. "I'm so happy your baby looks 100 percent healthy again, Ging. It didn't take long for the tendrils to do their job, did it?"

"No, it's amazing all right. Her tiny hand is straight and normal now with five fingers. That's a relief. Her birthmark is still there, though. That's fine. But it still doesn't answer the question of where the baby came from. Do you think anyone might have survived above ground?"

She catalogued the expressions of the other women. Karen's standing out the most as she spoke. "I think we'd know by now, don't you? Netty and Wil would have told us. I think you need to put that idea right out of your head, Ginger Mae. We have everything we need right here now. There's nothing but poisons above. We all know that. Stop rocking the boat and enjoy what you have."

Ginger Mae kept her mouth closed and continued rocking the baby, her eyes resting on Karen. *Yeah, I can see you wouldn't want the boat rocked. Maybe all is not as well in the Cobby family as we all assumed.* Aloud she remarked, half to herself, but clearly heard by all. "I just can't help but think of the pain the mother must be going through with her newborn missing. I wouldn't wish that on anyone."

Chapter 7

Suzy Calloway knew he was up to no good; Lafe hadn't turned up for lunch. He never missed a chance to gorge on the juicy fruits and confections the communal kitchen produced all day long. As a result, his physique was round and doughy, just like the rest of the men. Ever since he had been seven years old, and Doc had taken an odd shine to him, the lame son of her mentor, who she had raised with love as her own son, had turned into a disrespectful brat.

But now that he was twenty years old, she had noticed a developing manipulative sneaky side that he took great pains to hide. She again wondered why Doc let him pal around with him and the other men of the council. It wasn't like he was appealing with his slash of lips so distastefully distorted and puckered, his turned foot creating a disabling gait that slowed him down. His long, choppy, dark hair hung thickly in his face, concealing the clever glint in his shifty eyes that told her Lafe worked overtime devising ways to outwit and command the group of young thugs he ruled when Doc turned his back.

With a deep grunt, Suzy shifted on her chair as she considered going to hunt for him. The fact that she was almost nine months pregnant didn't daunt her one bit. But she had an appointment with Liselle.

"Suzy . . . you in there?"

"Come on in, Liselle." Suzy's second let herself in to the private room that had been added on to the hovel almost fifteen years ago. It had taken almost five years before the women (with Suzy's prompting at age eighteen) had organized themselves enough to begin to insidiously and cautiously influence their men; the formerly hard-bitten brutal monsters who had grown soft and lazy under the influence of their insatiable gluttony for the fruits and vegetables found mysteriously growing in a huge cavern deep in the mines.

As the previously skeletal men packed on the pounds, the scouts found their duties decreased as the perpetual hunt for food and other reusables outside in the nasty poisonous atmosphere no longer seemed as urgent as it had once been.

The men found they had more time on their hands. It wasn't that hard to convince them to clean up their living space and enlarge the hovels. Now all the women had room to sleep inside. No more Outside women.

Of course, that presented another problem for the men. Women had become more inaccessible—which only served to create a rise in furtive assaults. The women, under the guidance of Suzy and her own inner circle, had developed ways to protect themselves. Honed metal spikes became their weapon of choice, as they were easy to conceal among the layers of salvaged clothes they were still forced to wear in the chilly tunnels.

It became Suzy's law. Never, ever travel into another sleeping cavern or tunnel unless accompanied by your man or two of your sister wives.

Suzy peered up at her second. "How's he doing?"

"Not good. We don't think he'll last through the night. Kimmey's prepared." The two women broke out with huge grins.

"We're just lucky Avery only has one woman. She'll be easy to spirit away to Surrel's house. As long as Kimmey prepped him right, Surrel will just think he's manly enough to attract women. And at his age, there's not much harm going to come to her. Kimmey said he just likes to touch for a few minutes, then he's snoring away. The women make such a fuss over his prowess that he thinks he's still sexually active. He's so old now, he can't remember what he had for breakfast." The women laughed.

Liselle sobered. "If the men catch on to how we're shifting the women after the death of their man, we're going to have some trouble."

Suzy nodded her head thoughtfully. "We're running out of senile old men. They're all dying. We can't even get any more of the younger men to join the scouts anymore. Too many of them have died. Once you become a scout it seems you'll be dead within ten years. They all fight it now. Even the promise of women by Doc can't tempt them. As long as they still have access to the magic fruits and vegetables, no one cares."

The older Liselle picked at her worn hands, her clothes appearing shabbier than usual. "We'd better spread the word to take care of our resources. If we can't replenish from outside, I don't know how long this place will last." She swept her hand in the air.

"Don't worry, Liselle. I'll figure out something. We'll be fine for another ten years or so. The big thing is getting rid of Avery." They both relaxed again.

Relief from the brute that had terrorized Suzy and some of the other women for so many years bode an improvement in the quality of life for many. Suzy had lost count of the rapes and murders they knew Avery had been responsible for in the last twenty eight years. The only tears that would be shed would be Doc's. His unaccountable affection for the tiring monster was actually responsible for most of Suzy's safety. As Avery had fallen out of favor with the rest of the men, Doc was the only one left to champion the sick psycho. It wouldn't do for Avery to piss off his only benefactor by raping or harming his woman.

"How's Doc taking it?"

Suzy shut her eyes with relief. "Doc is so preoccupied with his own feeble health at the moment that he doesn't even think to notice Avery is missing from the Council Center. The rest of the men are so impressed with their own flatulence from the disgusting brew they cook to get drunk on, that they don't want to hear about anything else."

Liselle rose to her feet, pacing in the small space heaped with bits of board, fabric and odd pieces of metal that had caught Suzy's assessing eye for future use. "Do you realize most of Doc's original men are dead and dying? And we're down a few women from our inner circle, too."

Suzy rested her hand on her stomach, the baby restless. "I know, Liselle. Doc says it depends on how long you were exposed to the air after the bomb." She rubbed her hands on her eyes, sweeping back her dirty, ratty hair. "It's a good thing Doc finally had the men build the door over the mouth of the mine. At least the wind doesn't blow the soup in here any longer. I don't even notice the stink anymore, do you?"

Shaking her head in agreement, Liselle asked the question that sat heavily on both their minds. "How's Tom making out with Avery? And how responsive do you think he'll be?"

At the mention of Tom's name, Suzy gave a start and the baby jumped as if it knew the name of its real daddy. Speaking carefully, Suzy assured Liselle that Tom was ready to assume the critical duties that Avery attended. The waterwheel, the electric grid, and even the council's homemade still. "Tom's ready. Using him as an apprentice for Avery was a great idea. When I put the bug in Doc's ear, I didn't know who he would come up with. I wanted someone young and malleable, but with some maturity. He needed to be capable of learning quickly, but not quickly enough to let Avery catch on to the fact that we would supplant him. Tom's worked out perfectly." Suzy tried to conceal the blush that began a low creep up her cheeks.

"I know, Suzy." Liselle fixed a pointed stare on Suzy's hot cheeks.

"You know what?" Even to herself, Suzy's voice sounded defensive and guilty.

Liselle knelt down in front of Suzy's chair, taking her swollen hands and bringing them to her lips. "It's all right. God knows you've given so much to improve our lives. And Lafe's. If any of us are able to steal a little happiness in this hellhole, we deserve it. No one would begrudge you."

Suzy remained silent, unable to find the words to explain. Her face sagged with the heavy weight of her secret. "It just happened," she whispered. "He'd report to Doc every day and I'd be there. I wanted Doc to think this was his own idea so he would feel in control. He knew Avery was getting sick and old. Tom started to show up earlier and earlier. We . . . we got to talking . . ." Suzy bit down hard, her voice rising.

"I was so lonely. You have the other women, but I can't be seen hanging around other caverns. It would get back to Doc and he'd get suspicious. And Lafe, he's just out of control. He's picked up the attitude of the other men. He treats me like garbage."

She shook her head, discouragement in the downward slope of her strong chin. "I taught him better. I thought he'd be part of the first generation of men to treat women as equals. I thought we could help them change . . . be better human beings." She sighed deeply, a catch in her throat at the thought of how she had loved the orphaned infant, finding direction and solace in her new purpose. The decision to escape to her grandfather's refuge, buried deep and forgotten as she delighted in the raising of Liz's baby.

"Maybe we were just too close in age. Maybe it was my inability to overcome Doc's influence . . ."

"Suzy, is this baby Doc's?"

She gazed silently into Liselle's eyes, her negative shake barely discernible.

"Does Tom know?"

Another negative shake.

"You must never tell him. We need to let Doc think the baby is his. What do you think will happen when Doc dies? He's what . . . late sixties?"

Suzy rallied, Liselle had her full attention. "No, he's still in his fifties. He just looks like shit with that lard he's lugging around like the rest of them."

"I'm sure they all have compromised immune systems from the soup we all breathed in. The men got the worse of it."

Suzy suddenly brightened, a canny gleam surfacing as she did quick calculations. "With Avery dead and the other men in the council circle in bad shape, who'll be left when Doc dies? Hmm. I'm beginning to get the picture." She slowly stroked her huge abdomen.

Liselle clasped her hands. "You can do this. We've already made strides with subtle influence on our sons and some of the younger men. Plenty are in awe of you. You're the next direct link to Doc." She placed both her hands on Suzy's, caressing her abdomen.

Her face lit up in hope as Suzy contemplated the thought. "And if they don't accept me as a replacement for Doc, we have the baby."

Then Liselle groaned. "What about Lafe? He may try to claim the position. He's been awfully close to Doc. He hangs out with him at the Council Center and knows the others well. Technically, he's Doc's son."

"I don't think we'll have a problem. Most of the other men . . . the original ones with Doc . . . are at the end of their lives. Most of them have the sickness. They'll be replaced with younger men from the ranks that don't know Lafe except as the kid I raised. Besides, I don't think the men will be interested in listening to a snot nose brat with the kind of . . . well . . . infirmities that Lafe has."

Liselle stood. Suzy could see her head spinning with possibilities, just as hers was. "If we can garner the support needed to grant me the command temporarily . . . until the baby is of age . . ."

"I think we have a plan, Suzy."

The very pregnant Suzy struggled to her feet. Clasping Liselle as best she could with her belly fighting for room, the women hugged. "Let's put the word out to the Inner Circle. Get them to work harder on their sons and other men and women in their caverns. And keep your eye out for Lafe. He seems to be everywhere these days. We can't afford to have him discover our plans."

Liselle prepared to leave. "I saw Lafe near the tunnel to the crop field on my way over here. He was with some other boys." Her voice faltered. "They were watching the Janice twins. Looked like they were heading into the tunnel with their baskets."

"They were alone?"

"Suzy, they're in their teens. I'm sure they carry spikes. They'll be fine."

Saying goodbye at the door, Suzy leaned against the stalwart piece of wood as she remembered the look in Lafe's eye when he had departed a few hours ago, refusing to say where he was going. The usual nastiness had ensued.

"You're not my mother, bitch. I don't have to tell you shit."

She had rushed to the door as fast as a pregnant woman could. "You don't need to be so disrespectful, Lafe. I'm just worried about you."

He had turned to her with such an expression of indifference and contempt that her heart had shriveled, leaving her close to tears. "Get out of my way," he had said coldly, shoving her aside. She had cringed as his malevolent eyes and distorted lips dismissed her. He had slipped out the door without a backward glance.

Layering on a frayed jacket that failed to stretch across her abdomen, Suzy decided to visit the crop field for some of her favorite peaches. She could try to discover if the Janice twins had arrived safely. They were the children of one of the women in her inner circle. The twin girls had been brought up to be resourceful and brave, and Suzy had great hopes for them. But they knew better than to travel in the mines without an escort.

Grabbing a satchel and secreting her well-honed metal spike in the jacket pocket, she stepped outside the expanded hovel. Surveying the tiny and quiet pathways from hovel to hovel, she breathed a sigh of relief. Most of the women would either be inside or at the communal kitchen working on the prodigious tasks it took to produce the meals for the tribe. Even though their numbers were not as great as they had once been, the chores were relentless. And most of the men were undoubtedly already drunk on the disgusting brew they concocted.

She nodded to the occasional tribe member who crossed her path, the women getting one of her rare smiles as they shared a look of renewed confidence in their female role in the tribe.

Her mind idly wondered at the actual numbers of the tribe. Illness, flu and radiation poisoning had quickly killed off the weakest members. And in the early years before the crop fields, more than half of the infants had been taken away as they'd been born, deemed too defective. No one knew where they were taken, their fates unimaginable. Female infants were given a pass as long as the defect was tolerable in the eyes of the men. As a result, the tribe now numbered more women than men . . . a fact that warmed Suzy's heart. Although they were still owned by the men, her inner circle's plan to change the power structure in the mines would eventually succeed. She was sure of it. It was just a matter of time and patience.

Awkwardly ambling around the last dwelling in her cavern, she entered the tunnel filled with stray hovels that she needed to bypass to get to the tunnel which would take her to the crop fields. The walk would be a long one, but the deeper she went, the easier her navigation would be.

The tunnel was dimly lit by exposed wiring rigged so long ago by Avery. Their almost endless supply of light bulbs easily replaced the occasional broken bulb. Blowouts rarely occurred as the low wattage bulbs seemed to last forever.

She picked up her pace, the hard tunnel floor smooth and debris free from the decades of feet walking to the crop fields. Over time, the ceiling and walls had been reinforced with salvaged wood discovered by the scouts at a lumber supply company on Route 23 outside Franklin, a few miles from the mine. It had been this discovery which had enabled them to expand the hovels to something more fit for human beings to live in.

Suzy knew she was near the crop fields. Breathing deep, she sucked in the cleaner air. Soon the smell of fresh fruit and vegetables added their seductive fragrance to the air mixed with an undercurrent of foreign organicness.

Every once in a while, she passed an opening to another tunnel. Treading softly, she stopped to listen for voices at the mouth of a small cavern near the fields. The darkness inside taunted her. Was that a sound? Straining, she listened to the hushed, empty silence. If Lafe and his gang were in the tunnel, they were probably returning from the field and picking crops. The twins were probably long gone by now.

Moving on, she approached the opening to the field. Her heart began to hammer. She breathed deep, attempting to calm the cries from her body that begged not to go into the frightful place. Shutting her eyes, she forced herself to walk through the unexplained pocket of pressure she was forced to cross to gain entry. She shuddered as she cleared the pressure point, stopping to study the magnificence and horror of the magic field.

She scanned the massive cathedral, awed by the viscous skin that lined the ceiling and walls. The organic smell overwhelmed her with its rich loamy and musky textures. On the horizon, a dangerous cloud of lavender-blue creatures hovered, the alien protectors of the wondrous fruits and vegetables that they now lived on.

Many a careless tribe member had met an untimely death in the early days before they fully understood why the creatures were here. Some of the men rejoiced at the sight of so many trees and began to cut the groves down to use as firewood to generate warmth in their hovels. Warnings about preserving the trees for their fruits went unheeded in the face of so many. The reaction of the lavender-blue creatures was sudden and deadly. After the attack, six men were dead. No one had ever tried to cut down a tree again.

The large growths on the trees were carefully skirted as the tribe discovered the creatures' homes and realized they were necessary for the pollination of the trees' blossoms. No creatures—no food. It was an uneasy alliance as the tribe finally dismissed the idea of burning them out so they could gain access to the valuable wood. *The stupid men would find out just how valuable the trees were after they cut them down and they started to starve again,* thought a disgusted Suzy.

She made her way over to the men who were picking the crops, several women in line choosing specimens to take back to the communal kitchen. Their eyes lit up with suppressed determination as they spied Suzy.

"Ladies. How is your day going?"

The women answered her carefully, the men now listening. "Fine, as always, Suzy."

"That baby looks due any time now." Nice and innocuous. Suzy turned her back to the men as she selected a peach for her satchel.

"Lafe and his gang of thugs were seen entering the tunnels behind the Janice twins. Have any of you seen any sight of them?"

They shook their heads and spoke low. "That sounds like trouble to me, Suzy. Those two young ladies are both too brazen if you ask me. They know better, but refuse to listen. They're like a blood feast to a pack of wolves."

Another jumped in, hissing, "If I was their mama, I'd a tan their hides to teach them some sense."

"They're ripe for pluckin', that's for sure. But if Lafe and his boys think they're going to be the lucky ones, they can forget it. The girls are all spoken for."

Suzy agreed. "I know. Doc said they're to be handed over at the next council meeting. That's in a few days. I'm sure the men are chomping at the bit to get their hands on those girls. They won't be happy if they get messed with by one of the young gangs."

"Can I give any of you ladies a hand?" One of the men had dropped his work to come over and check on them. *Can't resist spying on us, can you?* Suzy backed away, the rest of the women shutting down. Without a word, Suzy turned and headed back to the tunnels with her peach.

Her quick walk became a slow waddle as she left the field. Unexpectedly, a glow appeared to emanate from the small cavern she had passed on her way in. Remembering the sound she thought she had heard, she realized Lafe and his gang were the likely source. She transferred her satchel with her peach to her left side, leaving her right hand free and feeling for her trusty spike hidden deep in her pocket, then crept into the cavern opening.

Rounding a jutting wall, she had no difficulty understanding the shocking scene, and emitted a small scream. She dashed to a mound of debris, flopping down hard to reduce her figure, praying they hadn't heard amid the sounds of low, raucous laughter and muffled screams.

Lafe and one of his hoodlums had one of the twins backed up against the wall, blood trailing from her nose, the front of her ragged shirt ripped down the middle, exposing her chest, while Lafe's buddy groped with his eager hand. Lafe's hand sat plastered over her mouth, preventing her screams from calling attention.

In the distance, four young men bent over the prostrate unmoving form of the other twin. Her nude body lay face down as one of the men rose off her to pull up his pants. The young girl didn't move.

Suzy began to sweat in the chilly cavern, cramps from her uncomfortable position sending pain through her abdomen. She hunkered down as flat to the ground as she could get, her nose inhaling the scent of cinders. A large rock ground painfully into her chest to increase her discomfort.

Sliding her hand under her chest, she inched the large rock out. As she eased it from underneath her chest, her distracted mind noted the round smoothness. Absently, she pushed it to the side near her head, forcibly relaxing as she tried to calm her harsh breaths.

With her eyes shut tight, she prayed they wouldn't discover her. Cautiously, she reached into her pocket to retrieve her well-honed iron spike. She berated herself for leaving the hovel in her condition. Another cramp made her wince and open her eyes. Just in time to identify the stone removed from under her chest; in time for her mind to register that the stone looked back at her with two empty eyes, a hole for a nose and a tiny toothless grimace.

Startled, she screamed and shot up, her head and shoulders emerging from behind the mound of what she now realized were more tiny skulls in the rubble of an old fire pit.

Lafe and his thugs whipped around at her scream, the foursome with the raped and motionless twin charging toward her.

She stood frozen in place as the dawning horror of the infant skulls overwhelmed her. The stench from the old fire pit made her woozy as she understood what it had been used for. The babies . . . so many lost babies. Her stomach turned as she remembered how Doc's men had always lacked that ferocious starving effect that the rest of the tribe wore.

"What the fuck do ya think you're doing, bitch?" She was grabbed roughly.

"Goddamn it. It's Doc's woman. Lafe, get over here." The raw smell of sex and semen mixed with the other odors taunted her. Without warning she spewed a choking vomit over the thugs who surrounded her.

"Christ."

"Fucker."

"Aww, for Christ sakes, bitch." Glittering hatred from arrogant, overfed, puffy faces stared at her. Signs of the worthless men they would become seeped from every pore, violence dancing on the verge of explosion.

"What the hell are you doing here, Suzy?" Lafe stared at her, murder in his eyes, his arm wrapped around the neck of the surviving Janice twin.

"Ha, ha, he calls his mother Suzy."

Lafe exploded. "She's not my mother, asshole."

From deep in her bowels, Suzy felt a rumble . . . a vibration. The small crowd of Lafe's men grew silent as they too grew aware of the vibration. It sounded as if it came from the back of the cavern; from the cavern wall.

Unexpectedly, Suzy felt a warm wet gush puddling on the rock floor. *My baby . . . oh please. Not now!*

Groaning and bending over, Suzy realized her cramps were actually contractions. Lafe nodded to one of his men, signaling him over to Suzy as the Janice twin began to struggle in his grip. Suzy tried to resist as Lafe's minion wrapped his arms around her, squeezing under her breasts.

"My baby's coming, you fool. Lay me down."

As Suzy wrestled with the thug, the Janice twin began to scream. A horrendous sound of rock rendering on rock filled the cavern. The thugs began to back up, Suzy getting free in the process. Glancing to the back of the cavern in time to watch a live gelatinous mass ooze into the room, Suzy could feel her bowels release, the young men joining her as the stench hit her nostrils.

The large mass rose high into the cavern, its rear disappearing into the rock wall it had just broken through. Flickers of light, emerald and white, flashed inside the translucent beast. It emanated a deep musky earthiness and sulfur which mixed with the cacophony of odors already assailing Suzy's senses.

Lafe dropped the Janice twin and began to back-peddle toward the entrance, his fellow thugs frozen in place.

"Hey . . . what the hell's going on in—holy shit." The men from the growing field appeared at the entrance, shoved further along by the appearance of the women Suzy had spoken to in the fields. Bloodless expressions testified to their shock.

One of the women reached out to call to her. "Suzy, don't move. I'm coming to get you."

"No. Jessica. Stay there." Suzy glanced at the pile of infant skulls. Hadn't Jessica had an infant taken from her? She checked the monstrous mass that wavered high in the air. It appeared it didn't know what to do as it clearly focused on her. Steeling herself, she knew she had better not show fear. Not to the thing or to the women. She was a leader. "I'll crawl over to you." A contraction hit hard. She bit down on her lip, feeling blood well.

"Ohhhh." Breathing hard, she tried to pull herself up, embers from the old fire pit staining her trembling fingers as they clawed deep.

"Suuuzyyyy . . ."

She raised her hand for silence, hoping no one would discover the remains in the nasty piles she lay behind. The monster suddenly took its attention off her as it dipped down to the supine Janice twin in the back of the cavern. It hovered over the body as if sniffing. The truncated head of the beast suddenly shifted to Lafe's gang members, who cowered together against the dank cavern wall.

It happened so fast it took a few seconds to actually register. The monster dipped down, wrapping its gelatinous mass around the four men like a rope. One minute they were there, pissing their pants, and the next they were absorbed into the beast. Suzy could distinguish the lumps their bodies made as they traveled deep into the mass and out of sight.

Screams from the women again drew her attention. Struggling through another contraction, she watched as the beast headed toward the crowd from the fields, backing them up against the wall where they cringed, the cowardly men shivering behind the shield of women.

The contractions were coming hard and fast.

"Oh my Goddddddddd . . ." Breathing heavily between screams, she attempted to pull herself further away from the pile of infant skulls. With her face pressed close to the rock floor she persevered, inch by inch.

Suddenly, she felt a presence behind her. She froze, afraid to look. From the bottom of her bare feet, she felt a pressure that slowly moved up her legs, lifting her off the cold floor. The pressure reached her head, cradling and flipping her over to stare into the eyeless face of the creature.

Spreading her hands to steady herself, she found she was suspended and supported by the body of the creature as it pulled its head back to watch her. Her hands failed to sink into the creature's flesh as she would have supposed. Instead, she felt solid warm support, surprisingly comfortable. Her nerves calmed and her breathing slowed. Unaccountably, she felt her limbs relax. As the unexpected relaxation took command of her body, she felt no terror or panic as she lay in the grip of the monster.

Silence from the terrorized crowd from the growing field allowed her to concentrate on her baby. She could feel its time and desire to be born. With a painful swoosh, the baby passed through her birth canal and lay between her upraised legs. She searched for her first sighting, but found she couldn't raise her head.

The infant was silent. Her heart began to trip as she listened for a sound. From up high, she watched as elongated protrusions descended from the creature's head to where the baby lay. She saw them lift the baby, turning it over. The baby mewled. The arms of the creature placed the baby alongside her as she felt a second rush of pain from between her legs. *The afterbirth?* A second sound came from between her legs as another gush told her something special had just occurred.

She felt her pulse quicken and then subside as unaccountable feelings of peace quelled her panic once more.

The creature lifted the second baby, hanging suspended over her while it weaved back and forth. Her second child cried as it nestled in the monster's care, the umbilical cord still attached to her. She waited for the creature to return her baby, feeling overcome by the hint of sulfur that mixed with all the other ungodly odors of the cavern, forcing her nausea to return.

She valiantly attempted to suppress the urge to vomit, and the creature dropped her second baby into her arms. As she marveled at the luck of two babies, the creature lowered her to the ground, withdrawing the support of its body, then turned and disappeared into the hole at the back of the cavern from which it came.

The suddenness of the creature's disappearance stunned them all. Suzy lay immobile on the cold rock floor of the cavern, her babies gripped in her arms alongside her flaccid, aching body.

Slowly, the women from the growing field crept toward her, the men fleeing out of the cave, deserting them.

"We need to get out of here, Suzy."

"Oh, look at the babies." Hushed murmurings drew her attention to the babies. She looked down in disappointment.

"Don't worry, Suzy. They're still beautiful. And twins . . . twice blessed."

One of the women stood tall and apart from the others; her face a cypher of accusations. "The beast didn't hurt you. It helped you with your birthing. What does this mean, Suzy?"

"I . . . I don't know, Grendel." Suzy's voice was surprised and wondering, her mind off Lafe, the Janice twins and her birthing for the first time all day.

The women huddled around Suzy, somber and in awe. Whispers sped around, murmurings of the benevolence of the monster and its fortuitous appearance just when Suzy had needed a savior.

More whisperings . . . the hiss of accusation, the murmurings of awe and fright.

From the entrance to the little cavern came hurried footsteps. The excited men entered, Doc Benjamin held up between two of his men. His hand held a piece of cloth that blotted at the blood dripping from his ears and his nose; one of the signs of the sickness. Suzy could tell from her still supine position on the ground that blood had begun to leak from his eyes. That was a bad sign. Doc didn't have long.

Suzy shuddered at the thought that he might turn over the leadership to one of his men before she had everything in place. It was unthinkable.

Doc's men lowered him gently to the floor until he was sitting comfortably at Suzy's side.

"Why don't you boys check the back wall where the beast seems to have disappeared." He waved the men to the back of the cavern.

"But, Doc. What if it comes back?" His men stood above him, loaded and weighed down with a large part of their personal arsenals, faces white and doughy with fear in the dim light of their lanterns.

"For Christ's sake, Jet. Shoot the damn thing. Can you manage to do that, or do I need to show you how?"

The men quickly slinked to the back of the cavern and Doc turned back to Suzy, his voice whispery and full of happy concern. "You had the baby. I guess I mean babies. Ha, ha." He leaned in to get a better look. "What? Oh no."

Suzy's face reflected all the love and hope she had for her babies. She stroked them softly. "I know. But everything else is fine. A boy and a girl. Isn't that perfect?"

"Yeah, yeah. That's great, Suzy. I was hoping for a boy. One that could take over the tribe."

Suzy's heart froze. "I thought we agreed I would take over."

Doc stroked his wispy beard, his eyes sly and glittery despite the smears of blood. "Well now, my girl. I don't rightly know. You sure are a mystery—a stubborn, pushy, secretive pain in my ass. Are you going to tell me what you know about this monstrous creature?"

Suzy's face was incredulous. "I don't know anything. What the heck are you saying, Doc?"

"Seems to me when a woman is about to be under assault by a bunch of thugs, she might need a bit of help. Interesting how the creature showed up just when you needed it. And then helps you with your birthing . . ."

Doc stared at the infants, emotions flickering across his face. "What am I to make of this, Suzy?"

And just like that, Suzy was struck by a lightning bolt, her conniving mind working overtime. "Make of it what you will. Perhaps it was just a coincidence."

"A coincidence you say? I would say that's unlikely." His voice rose, a bitter edge emerging, his brows knitted with unsuppressed anger. "Does this have anything to do with your grandfather? I remember Seth's claim of his shelter and growing food. Hmm . . . then we're surprised with our own field of food. Just like it was magic." His anger replaced itself with pensive wondering as he eyed the silent Suzy. "Still not talking, eh?"

"I could ask my beast to come back to answer your questions if you would prefer." She swallowed her trembling to spit out her outrageous claim, careful to stay as casual as she could.

As they locked eyes, Suzy watched hesitation and anger war in his expression, defeat coming when all that remained to declare her a victor was naked terror.

Scrambling up as the men returned from the back of the cavern, he said, "We need to get the three of you home." He turned to his men. "Well?"

"Nothin there, Doc. Just a highly-compacted round hole. The edges looked burnt or something. We could smell a funky odor and something like sulfur. Must be from the monster."

Doc shrugged with frustration. "All right. Let's get my women out of here. You can come back later and board over the hole. Although I don't know how much good it will do if she decided to call him again."

The men erupted. "What the fuck?"

"What do ya mean, Doc? You mean she can speak to the monster?"

Suzy closed her eyes to listen with satisfaction as Doc ordered the men not to repeat a word to anyone.

She knew it would circulate through the tribe within five minutes of her arrival back at the hovel. And, knowing the superstitious tribe members, she knew it wouldn't be the beast that would be the topic of conversation. It would be the fact that she could control it. Or so they would suspect.

Suzy suppressed her tired satisfaction as she felt herself lifted onto a wagon supplied by the arrival of more of Doc's men. As they wound through the tunnels, murmurs and whispers reached her alert ears.

Cupping her two tiny infants close, she rubbed her lips over their claw-like deformed hands. Kissing her little girl's right hand, she examined the birdlike extremity, its last two fingers fused into one, with a large birthmark in the shape of a half-moon. The infant waved her tiny, normal hand in the air.

"I think I'll name you Lorna, after my dear Grandmother Calloway."

Turning to her son, she placed her finger into the tightly-curled and emaciated claw of his left hand, the last two fingers fused just like Lorna's and sporting the same large purple half-moon wrapped around his left thumb.

"And the only name fit for my son, who will become a great support to you as I pass on the rule of the tribe, will be the only other name I remember from my past. You will grow to be a great man. I'll teach you how. You're destined to help your sister rise to rule this tribe and then the planet. I will change the course of this planet through your sister. She will be the one. And you will help her to attain her success."

Suzy cooed to the two infants, their futures seemingly assured through her plans of grit and determination.

"And won't you be sooo happy to help your sister. Yes, my little man." Suzy poked the infant's tummy, causing him to look straight at her. He stared unblinking and quiet.

"Hello, Seth. Welcome to your new world."

Chapter 8

News of Suzy's birthing and the return of the men from the cavern where the beast had helped deliver her babies traveled fast. A large crowd awaited them at their hovel.

Waving everyone aside, the men assisted Doc into his quarters while the crowd hovered around the newborns in the wooden wagon with Suzy. The men were respectful, befitting the reflected power held by Suzy as Doc's woman. The women of the tribe held their silence out of respect for their secret leader.

But Suzy could hear the faint whispers about the deformity. In the past, the boy would have been taken. The girl would be saved as she would be useful as a sexual plaything for the men of the tribe. Suzy's influence over the years had mandated the cardinal rule of no touching until the age of sixteen where all girls were given over to the next man in Doc's line.

Well, that's not going to happen to my baby, Lorna. As soon as the next council meeting convenes, I'll make damn sure Lafe gets what's coming to him for the death and assault on the Janice twin. The remaining twin will just have to suck it up and go to the man she's promised to.

Suzy caressed the top of Seth's soft head, grateful her boy would be spared the horrifying ending represented by the tiny skulls she had found near the old camp fire in the cavern. She idly wondered who of the remaining original men from Doc's inner council had been in on the cannibalism. Her nerves burned with bitter hatred for the greedy sick men. Pushing a germ of an idea to the back of her mind, she made ready to be eased out of the wagon.

*

Three hours later, with help from Liz and some of the other women, Suzy finished bathing. Her every bone ached with pains and exhaustion.

"We're all right now, Liselle. Why don't you and the rest go and have your dinner? I'll see you all in the morning. We can talk about our plans for the men's council meeting then." She fought to keep her eyes open and focused.

"We have a lot to go over. We must be prepared. Doc's really sick. It won't be much longer. We must see to it that I'm appointed in his place. We might have to let him think it's just temporary. Until Seth is of age. But it will be Lorna we prepare." Her eyelids lowered as her voice trickled off. "Check the babies once more, Liselle. Make sure they're snug and can't roll out."

"They're fine, Suzy, safe in their beds. We'll bring a proper bed for Seth in the morning. But he's fine now. Sleep." With that, Liselle and the women left the bedroom to take their leave, and Suzy drifted off to a deep exhausted slumber.

The next day, Suzy sat nursing Seth and Lorna as she tried to reason with Doc about the necessity of making her leader of the tribe.

"If you're going to continue yammering about this all day, Suzy, I'm going to leave. Can't we have one day without you plying your manipulations on me? I hear what you're saying. Now give me one of my babies." She blotted the weeping blood on his arm, wrapping precious gauze around the worst of his non-healing sores. She then placed Lorna in his arms, hoping to have him fall in love with her first.

Doc's scrawny body left little room to cuddle Lorna. Her claw-like hand tangled awkwardly in his long clumpy hair. As he became sick, he had stopped attending to his toilet and no longer bothered to sweep it back in a ponytail. Suzy cringed at the dirt and grime under his nails as he touched the baby.

"I saw them, you know," she informed him.

"You saw what?"

"The skulls. The infant skulls." Her mouth screwed up in distaste, her accusation skewering him with its venom. Suzy moaned with the thought of the pain the infants must have gone through in the hands of Doc and his brutal men as they readied them for the fire pits.

"You didn't see shit."

"I saw them."

"I don't know what you're talking about woman, and if you keep it up, I'm going to be forced to shut you up, you hear me?" Doc's eyes exploded with wildness, Suzy was too engrossed in her own revulsion to heed the warning signs.

"Ha, ha, ha. What can you do, old man? Look at you." She found herself unable to stop, the words tumbling off her sour lips. "You can barely get it up anymore, you leak your nasty blood all over everything. Even your men are pulling away," she lied.

"What's that you say? My men? I'll show you who can't get it up anymore." He transferred Lorna to his ramshackle bed, stripping off her blanket to leave her fully exposed. He fumbled with his pants, dropping them to his ankles and leered over the infant, stroking his flaccid penis as he made ready to inflict horror on the newborn.

Without warning, his head split open like a ripe melon as Suzy bashed it in with a thick piece of metal, frantically rescued from her bedroom.

His grunt of surprise was soft and feeble, just like his treasured penis which he had planned to use to rape Lorna. His body did a slow motion fold as it made its way to the dirty floor.

Crying hysterically, she sidestepped the remains of Doc to rescue her daughter. She wiped at the snot that ran free from her nose with the back of her hand, careful not to touch the baby with it.

"Oh shit."

Suzy whirled around to see Kimmey and Liselle at the door. Kimmey's face drained of color as she tiptoed to a chair, her voice a mere whisper. "I just wanted to see the babies . . ." Suzy ignored her as the stronger Liselle pushed her into her bedroom. She removed Lorna from her hands to wipe off Doc's blood which had splattered onto the infant.

Making sure baby Lorna was safe, she glanced at Seth, who remained sleeping in his makeshift bed. Grabbing Suzy's elbow, she pushed her toward the door. Suzy yanked her arm back.

"You're not getting me to go back in there." They listened as the sounds of Kimmey retching carried into the room.

"I don't know what happened here, Suzy, but if you care anything about the women of this tribe and your babies, you'd better just suck it up and figure a way out of this mess before anyone else finds out what you did." Liselle paced, wringing her hands. "Why now? He was getting ready to die anyway. Couldn't you wait?"

Kimmey and Liselle's faces drooped, flaccid and green as Suzy described her grisly discovery from yesterday.

"We were fighting again over the announcement at the council. He wouldn't commit. I thought he might be planning a fast one. I thought I could hold it over his head. Things got out of control." Suzy held her head in her hands, her voice faltering between sobs.

"But his pants are down. What . . ." Suzy looked up, sickness oozing from her eyes.

"He was going to hurt the baby . . . to get even with me for insulting him. I . . . I've never seen him like that before. I just . . . lost it." Liselle took her into her arms.

"It's okay. We just need to come up with a story, fast." They froze as they heard a man's voice from the other room.

Seconds passed as if hours before Suzy recognized the voice of her lover, Tom. Pulling away from Liselle, she rushed back into the room and threw herself into Tom's arms.

"Thank God you're here," she sobbed. Quickly calming down enough to talk, she filled him in on the discovery in the small cavern, the monster and Doc's subsequent death.

"Good God, Lorna. I don't know if I'm up to getting sucked into something like this." Tom's face screamed fear.

Stiffening her spine and relegating her emotions to the back recesses of her breaking-down mind, she took a deep breath, faced Doc's corpse and turned back to Tom. "It's all right, Tom. We have it all under control." Liselle clearly tried to swallow her surprise as Suzy rushed over to Doc's sixty-pound medicine safe.

"Come on, give me a hand." They hurried over to the safe. Directed by Suzy, they lifted it over Doc's mangled skull and dropped it on him. Liselle gulped and knelt to pull up his pants.

"That should work. No one will think much about it when I claim he was moving things to make room for the baby's stuff. I'll claim Liselle was here to see it happen. Besides, they'll be distracted when I tell them Doc finally made his decision about his successor."

Tom looked at her with amazement, guileless and clueless. "Did he tell you?"

Suzy sneaked a look at Liselle, tossing her a covert wink. "Yes. It's me of course, Tom."

"Well you sure have had a lot of luck come your way lately, Suzy." His brows knit together as if he was having trouble passing a difficult bowel movement. "Quite a bit of unexpected luck . . ."

Suzy anxiously herded him to the door. Trying to get his mind off recent events and her role in them, she kissed him softly, nipping passionately at his lower lip until she felt his manly swelling.

"I think we might have a few things to talk about later, don't you, Tom?" His eyes glazed with foreseen passion, glittery in their eagerness to forsake everything but the pursuit of sex.

"You better go now. I'll see you later." She smiled until her muscles hurt, pushing him out the door as he dreamed of their next tryst and the possibilities now that Doc was out of the way.

Suzy leaned against the door to catch her breath, while Liselle looked on with doubt in the slope of her shoulders.

"I don't know, Suzy. Are you sure you can trust him?" Suzy wordlessly nodded her head, rubbing her hands on her face, then raked back her loose, stringy hair.

"Yeah, he's a little temperamental, but he has a sweet simple side. As long as he's satisfied, he's happy and easy to control. It's stress free for me. He just doesn't want to get dragged into something that would draw the attention of Doc's men. I think he's just as afraid of them as we are."

A sudden pounding sounded on the door, vibrations tunneling straight to Suzy's hammer-tripping heart.

"Shit." The raucous pounding sounded again, the women paralyzed with fright.

"Open the damn door, Suzy."

Suzy whispered to Liselle as they clutched each other, relaxing as she identified the voice. "It's Lafe. What's he doing here? He's got a hell of a nerve."

She pounded right back on the door. "What the hell do you want, Lafe? You're not wanted here anymore."

"Shut up, bitch. I want Doc. He makes the decisions around here, not you."

Suzy bit deep on her lip, the pain clearing her thoughts. "It's Doc's decision, not mine," she shouted back. "He's had enough of your shenanigans. Your boys killed one of the Janice twins. He can't ignore that. We can't have the likes of you around now that we have the babies."

"Sounds like more of your bullshit to me."

She felt a body slam to the door but it held. "Your things will be left for you at the Council Center. Now get lost before Doc loses his patience with you," she added.

The women were met with quiet. They held their breath as they weighed the silence. It wasn't long before the odors of Doc's body reclaimed their attention. Praying that Lafe had departed, they discarded plan after plan until the simple actions of frightened women took over.

Peeking out the door to see if it was clear, they stepped outside and screamed their heads off.

Suzy munched on her peach, which she had retrieved from her pouch. The thick aromatic juices ran down her jutting chin unnoticed as she studied her two infants. Her heart swelled with vulnerable love and hope for a better life for Lorna and Seth. Grabbing a cloth, she swiped at her chin, removing most of the juices in preparation for bed.

She dipped the cloth into a cold pail of water, shucking her shirt to scrub at her grimy neck. It had been a long day and she was exhausted.

The council meeting to award the Janice twins to their man had been postponed due to the twin's death as well as the unexpected death of Doc. It would be held in three weeks after tomorrow's official mourning of the tribe's first leader.

Suzy smiled to herself. *Out with the old, in with the new.*

Doc's men had come to pay their respects this morning. None had commented on the passing of leadership to her, but she knew from the silent nods and bobbing heads that the official announcement would brook little challenge at the council meeting in three weeks.

Most of the tribe was so saddened and shocked that the women's version of Doc's death was readily accepted.

As Suzy slipped her raggedy gray nightgown down over her head, she ran to the next room to make sure the door was bolted. She kissed the babies gently, breathing in their newness and the clean milky smells that come with new infants. After giving Lorna a last loving caress, she climbed into her cot with its heap of frayed blankets. Her last thought before she drifted off to sleep was about how good her life with her babies would be without Doc around.

Morning came quickly, the babies having slept straight through the night, with not a peep from her two angels. She heard a squeak that ended in a jerky squall—Seth demanding his breakfast. As she pulled down her nighty to feed him, she glanced over fondly to say good morning to her quiet princess.

The crib was empty. Her mind blanked in panic, her thoughts unfocused and useless. She grabbed the now screaming Seth from his crib and ran to the door, which stood wide open. Lafe. It had to have been him. She groped for the sleeve of her nightgown, balancing Seth as she tried to get it up her quavering arm, distracted by the taint of sulfur in the air.

For the second time in three days, she ran outside to scream her head off.

Three weeks passed in a daze for Suzy. Liselle and the women of her inner council cared for Seth while Suzy fell apart. She wouldn't eat, wouldn't bathe, and wouldn't feed her remaining child. Other women, heavy with nourishment from their own newborns, took turns with the neglected infant.

Today, she lay in her cot, wasted from the lack of food, depressed and useless. Her only thoughts were of her kidnapped hope and dreams; her baby Lorna. She couldn't help compare it to her own kidnapping so long ago. The same defiant spark that had carried her so far for so long buried itself deep, hiding from her consciousness as it had decades ago.

"Get up." Suzy opened her eyes at the harsh words. Liselle stood at the foot of her cot, hands on her hips and steel in her voice, but softness in her eyes.

"It's time, Suze. The council meeting is in three hours. You have to pull yourself together. I can't just watch all our plans go up in smoke. So many women here have lost infants. They go on. Our plans were to make things better for everyone's babies. Think of them." Liselle perched on the end of Suzy's cot.

"Are you going to get up?"

Suzy remained silent, her eyes closing heavily.

"There'll be time to mourn. You have the rest of your life. Carry on in Lorna's name." Liselle stood up with a sigh as it became clear Suzy was unreachable. "You might as well know. Lafe has been sighted. No sign of the baby. It's rumored he'll attend the council meeting."

Suzy's eyelids flew open. She cleared her throat as steel seeped back into her eyes, recharging her. Liselle held her tongue, watching Suzy swing her legs over the cot and try to stand. Her voice croaked out the words Liselle hoped to hear.

"Over my cold dead body, he will. Get me some water and fruit, please, Liselle. And ask one of the others to bring me a bucket." She swept her hands over her oily face, cheekbones straining at the translucent skin that strived to hold her together. "I guess I'd better clean up."

With visible relief, Liselle hurried to fetch the items Suzy would need to bolster her strength. She returned with two women to help Suzy wash and dress.

"Here Suze. Drink this." She handed over a large mug of tea, filled with bits of strange leafy plants that grew in the growing field.

Downing the hot liquid gratefully, Suzy pushed herself with the blinding hatred she felt for Lafe. The son of a bitch would be made to tell where her baby is. He would pay. Turning to Liselle, she gave the woman a silent hug. Liselle uttered no words as Suzy drew further strength from her wisdom and the force of the tribal women's dependence on her. Parting, they stared somberly at one another. Liselle's intense face split with a wan smile. "Welcome back, Suze."

Chapter 9

The noise from the attendees at the Council Center filtered back to the women in rises and dips. As they approached the crowd, Suzy could see flickers of the bonfire in the center. The stench of infrequently-washed humanity brought tears to Suzy's eyes as they fought their way to the front of the noisy crowd. Men cursed and women made way as they reached the front line.

A new four-foot-high stage had been built to the side of the bonfire. Doc's most trusted men stood with mugs of their homebrew raised high, heat from the fire producing acrid sweat that streamed down brows as the merriment raged on.

Suzy stepped into the circle and stood tall as the men noticed her presence. One of the men stepped forward, raising his hands for silence. The crowd settled down as they looked forward to the night's business.

Liselle gave her a quick shove, and she found herself walking up onto the stage to a round of quiet applause, the subdued reception not what she had expected.

Looking into the slothful faces of Doc's remaining men, she glimpsed old age, disease, hostility and resentment. Her nerves strummed, wired and ready for confrontation.

"We didn't expect to see you tonight, my dear." One of Doc's most trusted men stepped forward to receive her, his courtly manner not deceiving her as she watched his eyes look over her head, searching the crowd.

"Why don't you go back home, Suzy? We have things under control here." She wrinkled her brow in confusion.

"I'm here for the announcement that will introduce me as leader of the tribe."

The old man coughed into his hand. "Well, about that matter, my dear. It seems a challenger has stepped up and claimed Doc had already named him as successor."

Blindsided by surprise, Suzy stood tongue-tied. The old man leaned in, his evil practicality dismissing her.

"What is your claim measured against the claim of a man, after all?" He turned his back to her and joined the rest of the men, who now stood clapping Lafe on the back. All distorted grins and awkward dancing, Lafe celebrated his elevation to tribal leader with his new men, a tankard of brew lifted high to rejoice with.

"No." Her shout rang like a bullet, straight and swift. The din lowered and died as all eyes turned to her. The men on the stage sneered.

"He will not lead this tribe. I was appointed by Doc himself before he died."

All eyes followed Lafe as he lowered his tankard and limped over toward Suzy, insolence twisting his deformed features more than usual. "Funny . . . Doc promised it to me." He swept his hand toward a few of Doc's oldest men, now feeble, senile and sick. "And I too have witnesses."

He stared at Suzy, his hatred washing across the stage, searing her with its power.

"You are a murderer and a baby thief." Her venom struck back as his confidence refused to slip.

"I am a man . . . checkmate, bitch."

Suzy saw red. She flew at Lafe, fist pummeling ineffectively as he backhanded her, sending her spinning to the ground away from the fire. Shaking the stars and black waves that threatened to undo her, she tried to sit up. Lafe limped toward her, his fist pulled back to give her more. The crowd remained quiet and fixated, swept up in the drama.

A low rumble sounded under their feet, unnoticed by most. A murmur snaked through the crowd as it became more pronounced. Screams were heard as the ground began to shake.

With a loud wrenching and splintering, Suzy's gelatinous monster tore up through the ground, bursting through the wood on the stage, showering them all with rubble and the stench of sulfur.

The crowd scrambled back, clawing over the old and infirm to get away. Doc's men jumped off the ruined stage to leave Lafe and Suzy to confront the beast alone.

The creature reared high in the air, looming over the terror-stricken crowd that cowered in the dark fringes of the Council Center. From the throat of the beast, a protrusion appeared. The beast formed appendages that gripped the protrusion, lowering it toward Suzy. She remained transfixed, unable to move, and determined to show no fright to the crowd. Lafe slowly inched his way off the ruined stage, kicking a fallen man aside and tripping as he reached the ground.

The beast lowered its faceless head to sway gently over Suzy as its appendages presented baby Lorna to her, safe and secure in a fluffy yellow blanket.

"Oh . . . my baby." She unwrapped Lorna to a stunning surprise. As she stared at her baby's two perfectly-formed hands, she steeled herself to look up at the beast. She awkwardly regained her footing, unbalanced by the weight of her missing infant. Swallowing hard, she forcibly controlled her tremors. "Th . . . thank you." She raised her hand as if to tentatively wave. With that, the beast retreated as if sucked back down the hole by which it arrived.

No one moved. Suzy watched her healthy baby coo up at her. Her heart swelled with fierce motherly determination. She shook off the final dredges of drained emotions and stood tall. Her voice carried to all, cutting like a buzz saw through the dark and unruly crowd.

"If I'm given any more trouble as the new leader of this tribe, I'll call it back." She eased herself down to the ground, her words greeted by a hush. Pressing her advantage, she ordered two men to seal the hole.

"Does everyone understand?"

Heads bobbed in quick agreement, Doc's men's eager voices fawning with acquiescence.

Suzy swelled with confidence. She called to Liselle and the other women of her inner circle. "These are my advisors. They will be shown the same respect you showed Doc Benjamin." A low threatening undertone could be heard coming from Doc's men. In a stunning show of leadership, Suzy turned to them.

"I need three representatives from your old council to join mine."

Surprise and respect bloomed in the eyes of the men eager to hold on to the trappings of their power.

"I would ask you, Gus." The oldest in the crowd hobbled his way to Suzy. "And you, Tom." Mutters reached her ears as she chose the youngest of the group, her secret lover.

But the biggest surprise was yet to come, shocking all.

"And you, Lafe."

All eyes turned to Lafe as he still lay on the ground. Embarrassed, he scrambled up to face Suzy, his expression as pleasant as if she had just ordered him to drink his own urine. The sparks of hate Suzy observed in his eyes subsided to be replaced with animal cunning. He straightened his shoulders, bowed to the crowd and moved toward the chosen ones near Suzy. He glanced at her as he passed, and nodded, acknowledging her win in the battle. They both knew the war had only just begun.

A groundswell of cheering and applause erupted from the tribe. Suzy held up her hand for silence. She screamed with all the pent-up passion of her thirty four years. "I want you all to look on the miracle my creature did for me. He found my baby. Look . . . look at the perfect hands of your future leader."

As the crowd roared its amazement, she held up baby Lorna for all to see.

"Your future leader . . . Lorna Calloway Benjamin!"

Chapter 10

2147 AD

Ginger Mae and Daisy sat face to face in the complicated lab where the ninety-six-year-old intellectual savant spent most of her waking hours. It had taken Ginger Mae decades to get over the fact that she was no longer her six-year-old little girl.

She gazed fondly at the sweet face she had given birth to, recognizing signs of maturity in the way Daisy had taken to cutting her hair in a tightly-layered chic crop. She wore tailored pants and cardigan sweater, found long ago in the huge supply cavern where the Kreyven had dumped the contents of a department store in preparation of their arrival.

"Mother."

Ginger Mae snapped her attention back to her daughter. "I know, I know," she said worriedly.

Daisy reached out to take her mother's hand. "Mother, you know I love you dearly, but it's time to let this go. The operation is my destiny. Netty assures me there is no danger of any kind. I will just come back . . . different. Altered, if you will."

Ginger Mae patted Daisy's hand. "I know you'll be safe with Netty. It's just that Oolaha is so far away. It's not even our solar system. I'm just . . ." She put her head down.

"You are what, Mother?"

"I'm afraid you might not come back."

Daisy shook her head, turning to call to Hud who poked around the exhibits in the lab whenever he got the chance to visit. He pulled himself away and hurried over to his wife and stepchild.

"What's up with my two best ladies?" He bent down to give them both a hug.

"My mother is ready to freak out. I'm not postponing the trip again. I want to be ready to help build our settlement when we leave here, so I need to get it done now. Once the settlement is complete, I will be going for good. Mother has had plenty of time to get used to the idea. Can you speak to her, Hud? We're leaving in the morning. I hope you'll be there to see me off."

Hud opened his mouth to speak, but Ginger Mae cut him off. "We'll be there. In the wedding cavern . . . first thing. I know this is what you want, Daisy Chain."

Daisy cringed at the sound of the old nickname. "*Mother.*"

Hud stood up. "Well, it's settled then. That didn't take long. Maybe we should head over to the kitchen now. It's almost dinner time. I heard Dezi might have a special treat for a certain little lady tonight." Ginger Mae stood up with her daughter, brushing away a few tears. She gave her daughter a hug.

"I will always love you, Mother."

Ginger Mae smiled down on the diminutive woman before her. "I know you will, baby. Me, too." Wrapping her arm around Daisy, they headed for the door, pausing as Daisy locked her lab up tight, then headed for Netty's noisy kitchen.

The sounds from the kitchen greeted them in the hallway; Maya's screams of delight the loudest. She suddenly appeared outside the kitchen in all her toddler Elder glory, throwing herself against the regal and tolerant Caesar, who grunted as the child slapped him on the head.

"My kitty."

Caesar turned his face to the wall as if she didn't warrant his time. Ginger Mae bent down to pick her up, giving the beleaguered big cat some peace. Caesar turned his big head back to watch and blinked his golden eyes, all the thanks she would receive.

The chaos in the kitchen stayed mostly in the addition that had been carved by the Kreyven, decades ago. It was where the infants stayed, supervised by Father Garcia and Maddy who had personal chambers off the main room.

Because of the size of the infants, it had been decided not to have them sleep with their parents until the settlement was built. The duties and responsibilities within the Hive did not allow for much time to care for an infant. So Father Garcia and Maddy continued to run the nursery, and the moms and dads took over at meal times and after dinner.

Ginger Mae watched from her seat at the table as the moms and dads filtered into the nursery. She felt Daisy's arm snake around her waist.

"Are you ever sorry you sent the baby back with the Kreyven?"

Ginger Mae rubbed the thin arm that circled her waist.

"No, sweetie. I'll never know where the baby came from, but I knew it wasn't right to keep her. She was such a newborn that she had to belong to someone else. I can't imagine who or where, but the Kreyven wouldn't have taken her away if there wasn't a mother somewhere feeling a hole in her heart. Maybe someday we'll have an answer." Ginger Mae brightened. "Just another mystery in this strange life we're living."

"Babe, I'm headed over to talk to Wil and Cobby. We're making plans to do some testing up above. Cobby thinks we might be able to step up our plans to resurface."

Kissing the top of her head, he headed over to the table where Wil and Cobby sat talking with Johno and Peter. They looked up as he approached, Peter sliding over to give him some space. "You're just in time. Wil has some news for us."

Hud nodded to the other men and sat. "So . . . what's up guys? We going to do the test like we planned?"

Wil's muscles tightened as he leaned in, his wings clinging tight to his body with his tail strapped around his waist. "I don't think it will be necessary, Hud. I've been informed that if we can get our materials moved to the wedding cavern, closest to the entrance, we should be good to go in about two weeks."

"You're shittin' me." Jaws dropped. "Two weeks?" The men were flabbergasted at the unexpected news. Pale faces with mixtures of joy and trepidation sat silent.

"I thought you would all be ready to celebrate?"

"It's just that it's so sudden, Wil," said Cobby, who glanced over to see Johno nodding his head slowly, pensive and calm.

"I must get my elephants ready. Tobi will be excited, but so many have never seen the outside."

"Don't worry, Johno. We'll do this in stages. First, we'll move all the building materials to the cavern. Anything that's removable will be moved there. We'll move the kitchen last. When we're ready, we'll go outside. We'll let the animals come and go as they want. Many will go back and forth until we ourselves begin to live above ground. It'll take a long time until our settlement is constructed. We'll need to build many houses, clear fields, plant . . ." Heads were nodding, hands being clenched.

"Yeah . . . we have a lot of hard work ahead of us, but it's all good." Peter grinned, his excitement infectious.

"What about the others?" Cobby asked. "Should we let them know?"

Hud held up a hand. "If you don't mind, this is Daisy's last night. Dezi has planned a special dinner and a cake for her. Can we leave it until after she leaves tomorrow morning? We can make the announcement at breakfast."

All the men agreed. They had much to think about anyway. It wouldn't hurt to have some more time to prepare for the questions that were bound to come. Containing their excitement, they scattered back to their own tables to enjoy Daisy's last night.

Scotty and Chloe, Kenya and Kane, along with Echo, Barney and Teddy, lay scattered around the fireplace, eating their cake after the knockout dinner Dezi had created for Daisy's celebration.

"But I still do not understand, Brother. Why did we not sing to the happy birthday girl?" Echo's mind aura circled in Scotty's head. He could feel it flounder blindly.

"I thought I explained that, Echo. It's not her birthday."

"But this is her cake. It must be her birthday and we must sing."

"Listen, you little rascal. Just enjoy smelling the cake."

"Is she not the guest of honor? And is she not getting her wish to go away for her operation? The empirical evidence shows, it must be her birthday. Does she not want her birthday song?"

"We only sing *Happy Birthday* on the day you were born, you know that, Echo."

"But we have cake."

Scotty hung his head. If he didn't give in to Echo, this could go on all night.

"Why fight it?" Chloe laughed. She stood, clapping her hands. "Attention. Attention everyone. Echo has requested we sing her favorite song. Tonight it will be for Daisy."

Echo scrambled to her feet as the laughter and groans came from the crowd. Standing at attention, she fluttered her wings in approval as the survivors gave a rousing rendition of *Happy Birthday*. Echo's fondness for the song was a curse they had all learned to laugh off.

"See, Brother Scotty, I told you. Sister Chloe understands. I am so happy to see that she is so tuned in. I must keep my eye on her. I have a great feeling about her, did I tell you that?" The friends erupted in laughter as Echo's aura danced in their minds.

"Yes, my sweet friend. You tell us at least once a week. Thanks for the reminder." Chloe leaned over to deposit Echo in her lap. Within two minutes, Barney had maneuvered Echo off her lap and back to his spot, reclaiming Echo as his.

Kane turned to Scotty as Baby trundled over to climb onto Kenya's chair with her; her nightly abdominal massage set to begin.

"So what do you think about the rumor I heard? You must know the scoop, Scotty."

Chloe perked up, wrinkling her nose. "Rumor?"

"Shhh, we aren't supposed to talk about it yet. Wait until after Daisy leaves."

"Oh, come on, Scotty. It's us. We don't keep secrets," Chloe reacted with indignation. When Scotty refused to be goaded, she turned to Echo. "What's Scotty talking about, E?"

"We'll be leaving the Hive soon." The auras swirled. "Change is coming. There will be much work. Much change."

Chloe's hand flew up in surprise. "That's sooner than expected."

All eyes bored into Echo as she twirled her head around in pride. "We have new life. You will mostly be pleased. Many surprises."

"Mostly pleased?" Kane picked up on the one thing everyone else failed to question.

"Every eco system has its inherent dangers for one species or another. I think the Womb has done well with the balance. As of now, your species will not last forever, so many of the dangers to you will become insignificant. One never knows with the Womb's thought process."

"Well. That doesn't sound so peachy, Echo," Kane complained.

"We must wait and see, Brother. Wait and see."

"Nothing can be any more difficult than what we've been through already. Kenya, that means the baby will come soon," Chloe remarked.

"Ummm, I sure will miss these massages from my little buddy here." Kenya's eyes glazed over, Baby's magic doing the trick. "I just can't think about the baby right now. I can't imagine not lugging this monstrosity around anymore." Her eyes snapped open, sparkling with delight and anticipation.

"Kane, you know what that means though. No more three in the bed, chickey."

Kane blushed quick and deep. "Come on, Kenya . . . not here."

The foursome erupted with gales of laughter, Chloe threading her arm through Scotty's as fond glances from the other tables reminded Scotty how great it was to have a big family.

Deep in the back of his mind, a percolating thought crept forward. Maybe once they no longer lived in the Hive, maybe . . . just maybe, a little Chloe or Scotty might be just around the corner.

With the thought warming his heart, he gave Chloe a big affectionate hug, getting a dazzling confident smile for his efforts. As he focused his attention back on Daisy's celebration, he marveled at the perfection of his relationships with his best friends. What more could a man want in life? Pushing the thought of his immortality and their eventual deaths away, Scotty partied on.

*

By morning, everyone had gathered in the wedding cavern, which would soon be converted to a staging area for materials and departure.

Daisy stood, slender and calm between Netty, Abby, and Baby. This was to be Abby's first trip to Oolaha and everyone could see she was overjoyed and excited. Wil and Jose would remain behind to begin the process of preparing the survivors for emerging from the Hive.

Ginger Mae and Hud stood to the side, trying to keep up a pretense of happiness so as not to spoil the sendoff.

"I have a few words I would like to say before I go." Daisy stepped forward, her pale face serene.

"I love you all so much." She turned gravely to her mother and Hud, then to her companion of decades, Kimir; the one other person to take her leaving very hard. Everyone knew her childhood friend and later lab partner loved her deeply. But they also knew Kimir's love would always remain unrequited. Daisy was already married to her destiny.

"I know many of you worry for me, but fear not. This step will enable me to enter the service of the Womb in a fashion that most are unable to understand. The Womb is my God and I am its servant. It is my destiny to bring its message to the cosmos; the message of harmonious life and mutual respect for all creatures. Perhaps if this planet had received such a message from one such as me so very long ago, we could have avoided so much pain." Smiling, the tiny women that so resembled Ginger Mae's six-year-old child of ninety years ago, slipped one hand into Abby's and waved to the crowd.

They watched in fascination as the threesome and Baby approached the membrane-shrouded wall that had taken the bodies of those long departed. Memories dwelled briefly on their arrival in the Hive so long ago, as Barney's stiff body was the first to disappear into the membrane.

The subsequent funerals from the Time of Seth were erased by the memories of so many happy weddings held here. And now a new memory was to be forged as they watched the travelers step up to the membrane and pass into it, before it closed around them as if they had never been there at all.

A quiet descended over the remaining survivors, the only sound the sniffles of a bereaved mother and a heart-broken Kimir.

"If no one minds, I would like to make an announcement. One that I'm sure will brighten your spirits." Wil stepped forward, nodding to Jose to take a seat on one of the chairs that had been salvaged for wedding festivities decades ago.

When he had everyone's attention, Wil began to speak. As he made the announcement, he surveyed the muddle of emotions. Just as he had expected, fright and terror shared the moment, along with trepidation and stubbornness. He knew they would adjust. They had to. It wouldn't be long before all the Elders except Scotty would leave this planet along with the Hive membranes and the Kreyven. For good.

Chapter 11

It had been a full backbreaking two weeks since the survivors had learned the Earth was now habitable.

Scotty appraised the organized chaos in the cavern. Every spot was filled with building material, tools, and caskets of precious seed and books. Books everywhere. Even Caesar looked squeezed into a small space between a workbench and a stack of used lumber. Faithfully watching him as always.

He shook his head as he wondered how they would find the time to dismantle the entire collection of the Library of Congress.

"I know what you're thinking." Chloe stood near a stack of books. "You'll thank me when our child has the books to learn from. What's better than books?" She gave him the eyeball as he strode toward her slowly. "What?"

He kept coming, a small smile tugging at his lips.

"What did I say?"

He reached her side, lifting her high to hear her cackle with laughter. Setting her back down, he studied the face he knew better than his own. "I love you."

She caught her breath, eyebrows quirked. "Well, I love you too, silly."

A disturbance in the air announced Echo; auras cast. "I love you too, Sister and Brother." Echo landed as Barney caught up, tongue hanging and dripping. She wrapped her tiny leather arms around their legs.

"Woo, watch out there, E," Chloe warned.

"I want to be silly with you."

Scotty and Chloe exchanged smiles. Echo was nothing if not predictable. No matter the time or the mood, the scamp wanted to be the third musketeer so badly.

The moment lost, Scotty picked up the golden furry creature. "We have work to do, Echo. We need to meet Kane and Cobby. You coming?"

"Of course, Brother. I have everything under control. We need to plan the growing field. Chloe and I are in charge of the planting. I must be in attendance." Echo squirmed out of Scotty's grasp. Gripping Chloe's hand, she officiously pulled her away.

"Come, Sister Chloe. We must keep our eyes on these men so they get the plans correct."

"Eh . . . Echo?" Scotty stood still, amusement in the curl of his lips.

Echo turned to cast her aura. "Yes, Brother Scotty?"

Scotty tried hard not to laugh, keeping a serious expression intact. Chloe followed suit. "They're meeting us here."

"Oh."

If a golden furry alien with a lion tail, deadly crystal antlers, and reflective radiating gold eyes could look embarrassed, it would look like Echo. Chloe turned to the golden creature, patting her hip. In one hop, Echo sat firmly in his favorite spot, a leather arm around her neck.

"I think I need you more, Echo. I need to have you sort the seeds with me. That's our duty, you know. The seeds are our responsibility." Echo cast an aura, leaning back and swiveling her neck to Scotty.

"I am so sorry, Brother Scotty. But other responsibilities call. Can you go on without me?"

"I'll do my best, Echo. I will be the first to bow to your other duties." Scotty kept a straight face as Chloe walked away. Caesar extricated his resplendent self from the puzzle he had twisted himself in and shook himself, ready to go. *He must be tired or maybe hungry today,* Scotty thought, miffed.

"Hey, you guys. Ready for us?" Cobby shouted a greeting as he entered the cavern with Kane. Scanning the piles of material, he remarked, "What a mess. How the heck are we going to carry all of these big timbers out of here?

Kane flopped down on the ground, shirtsleeves rolled up and grime around his neck. "I'm beat. Being a laborer is not for me. Give me the real dirt of the Womb's green meadows. I think I'm a farmer at heart now. Whoops, sorry, Dad. I know you had your heart set on me being a boat captain like you, but when was that? A hundred years ago?"

Cobby grabbed him in a choke hold, setting him off yelling. Unexpectedly, they stopped, turning to Echo who remained motionless. "Uh oh."

Non-threatening auras hit them all. "Do not worry, Brothers. I know they have no horse, but that they are horsing around. Correct?"

Scotty and Kane relaxed. "Well, it took you long enough to get it, Echo. What's it been, fifty years?"

"Okay, boys, let's stop with the fooling around and get down to business." Chloe clapped her hands for attention. "Don't be late for dinner, please?" She turned with a wave and walked away with Echo still on her hip, Caesar padding softly behind her.

That's my family, Scotty thought with pride. "I don't think we need to worry about moving this stuff. Johno has a plan."

Cobby spoke up. "Yeah, he said the elephants will help. Let's hope Tobi's in the mood." Making himself comfortable, he took out a role of paper. "This is the map I had Wil draw for us. Hey, speak of the Devil."

Wil's voice came from the entrance. "Hello, everyone. I thought I'd join you if that's all right? We can't afford to make any mistakes when we leave here and we need you all to get the seeds in the ground as soon as possible."

They happily greeted Wil and made room for his wings as he joined them, examining the map Cobby laid out on the ground.

Curling his long legs and tail under him, he leaned over the map. "Here's the entrance to the Hive. We're on a hill that overlooks what was formerly Scott's family home." He turned to his fellow Elder. "You know all this land was part of Netty's inheritance that her bastard first husband tried to steal, don't you?"

Scotty could see him shake off the acrimonious memory, so long in the past but still able to draw sourness.

"Here's your old house. I should say *was* your old house."

Scotty leaned in. "That's the old watering hole we used to play in."

Wil circled the area with his finger. "That's exactly where we want to start the fields. It's close to the water and the only flat land in the areas. The rest is all hills. We can build our shelters on the level foundations of what used to be your neighbors. As we build up around the hill it will give us a good defensive position."

"Defensive position?" Cobby and Kane asked at the same time.

Cobby scratched his trim beard, crinkled eyes questioning. "What would we need to defend ourselves from if we're all that's left?"

"Whoa, you men must understand. We have no knowledge of what new creatures we may encounter out there, but I can guarantee that there will be some. The Womb does not confide in us. We serve the Womb."

Scotty cleared his voice. "I gather from Echo and Baby that there'll be some pretty big changes."

Wil shrugged. "I guess we'll have to wait another day and see." Everyone did a double take.

"Do you mean what I think you mean?" asked Cobby.

Wil broke out in an eager grin, lighting them all on fire. "Yes. It's time. Daisy's due back with Netty and Abby in a few hours. We'll let everyone make a fuss at dinner, then we'll spring the surprise."

"All right." The men clapped each other on the back, excitement wild in the air.

"Listen, babe. Has the Dez ever let you down before?"

Ginger Mae shook her fingers out with nervousness, rocking from foot to foot. "I know, Dez. I just want everything to be perfect. It feels like she's been gone forever."

Dezi put down his paring knife to wipe his hands on his apron. The handmade pin that Daisy had made him sixty years ago, proclaiming him 'Kitchen Boss' sat prominently on the upper strap of the apron.

The Hive, along with his confidence and position of authority, had turned the scrawny, sad letch into a robust man with a way around the kitchen like no other. Ginger Mae gazed into the now pleasant and masculine calm face. What a wonder the Hive had done for Dezi's health and self-esteem. After all this time, Dezi still remained her most treasured confidant.

"Ya gotta let her go, Ginger Mae. She may look like she's six years old, but she's a grown woman; a woman that I can't even understand half the time." He reached out to stroke the side of her head. "I know it's hard for ya ta take, but it looks ta me like Netty and Abby have plans for her—plans that Daisy looks forward to."

Ginger Mae rested her head on his shoulder, an uncomfortable feat as she was a full head taller than him. "I know, but I don't want to know. You know what I mean, Dez." She sighed.

"Yeah, I know, babe." They both turned as survivors began to trickle in, first Clyde and Salina with the quiet Jennifer who, after all this time, remained a withdrawn and damaged woman; the effects from the Time of Seth leaving a lasting legacy.

Chloe and some dogs entered next, Echo fluttering above the ubiquitous Barney. Caesar stuck his mammoth head in to be shooed away by Chloe. That meant Scotty and Kane must be in the hallway.

"You better help Kenya to her chair. It's gunna get crowded in here soon. See if you can scare up Karen and Gloria. It's their turn tonight."

He jerked his head toward the kitchen nursery where laughter and infant voices accompanied Father Garcia's daily report to the moms on the eating and elimination habits of their babies. After all, they didn't do much more than eat and poop. Everyone else was happy to leave that area to the mothers and fathers.

"Okay, I'll go get them. I'd help, but I'm just too nervous." Waving to Hud and taking her leave of Dezi, she crossed the room to collect the evening's kitchen slaves.

After she finished admiring the infants and directing Karen and Gloria to Dezi, she heard a commotion at the doorway. Glancing up, she saw a huddle around a newly arrived Cobby, Wil, Scotty and Kane. Wil had his arm wrapped around a beaming Netty. Abby and Daisy were nowhere to be seen.

Eagerly, she made her way from the nursery, skirting tables and chairs to see her daughter. Netty reached out to embrace her. "Where's Daisy?"

"Don't worry, Ginger Mae. She's just in her sleeping quarters. She's changing into a gift Abby made her. From fabric she made out of a fibrous plant she found on Oolaha. You'll be so surprised."

"But is she okay? The operation . . ." Ginger Mae felt like she would burst from holding her breath. Netty smiled her most gentle expression.

"My dear, you will be so proud." Moving Ginger Mae along toward the tables, she shouted out.

"Come, everyone. Let's sit and get settled for dinner. Daisy will be along in a minute. Let me tell you, she's starved. The food on Oolaha leaves a lot to be desired for a normal human." Netty craned her neck to Dezi. "I'm sure our intrepid Chef Dezi will not disappoint tonight. Best of all, we have another surprise."

Buzzing and demands for hints filled the room as everyone found their seats. Shirley and Johno filed in with the keepers to add to the din.

A hush blanketed the room. Abby stood at the door. "It everyone ready?"

Ginger Mae stood up at her table, craning her neck to see Daisy. Abby hurried to sit next to Jose, leaving Daisy to make her entrance.

The atmosphere was charged with expectation mixed with arresting fragrances and mouthwatering smells as Gloria and Karen set platters of culinary wonders on the tables, then took their seats. The crowd grew restless, Ginger Mae inching toward the door.

She blinked rapidly, a gold luminance appearing at the doorway as Daisy appeared. "Hello everyone," she said in a voice no one recognized.

The child woman stood motionless, aware all were trying to digest her changes. She stood taller, wrapped in a loose sarong of the most remarkable fabric ever seen by a human eye. It reflected a golden luminosity, casting glints of ever-moving sparkles on Daisy's skin. The sparkles roamed her face, even appearing in her eyes. They gave her the look of a creature not of this Earth.

The sarong thickened at her neck to fall like a pyramid to the top of her shoulders.

A hush fell over the kitchen as Daisy reached up to part the fabric at her neck to allow it to tumble to the top of her breasts. She shook out her short hair, which roamed with sparkles, giving it a life of its own; vibrant and lush.

Ginger Mae gasped at the changes around her daughter's throat. A five-inch band of sheer, translucent material grew as if attached from her throat, forming a complete circle around her. She could actually see the throbbing of her daughter's heartbeats through the ring. Another, thicker, band of—*what . . . bone? Is it some kind of bone?*—fell in ripples down to the top of her breasts.

None of the sparkles touched the transformations. They appeared stark and barren in contrast.

"Daisy . . . what have they done to you?" Ginger Mae reached out to her daughter, hesitant and shocked, afraid to touch.

"Mother. Dear, dear, Mother. They have transformed me. You will understand. Allow me to demonstrate."

Within seconds, light radiated from the band made of cartilage around Daisy's throat and neck. The light danced, colors blinking and strobing, a light show of pattern and dimension never seen before.

From below the bands of light, the witnesses heard a humming that vibrated softly in the room, getting louder as the vibrations too began to dance, the patterns somehow more familiar.

Abruptly, the vibrations and colors vanished. Daisy replaced her sarong, now draped to cover the transformation.

An uneasy silence met her performance. Abby and Netty rose from their seats to usher her into the room, walking right past Ginger Mae, who stood stunned.

Hud rushed to her trembling side. "Easy, babe. Let them explain."

Shaking Hud's arm off her shoulder, she ran to face the Elders. "Daisy . . . baby? What . . . what just happened?" Ginger Mae's voce was hushed and choking. Abby stepped up, raising her hand. She slapped it away.

"No. I'm speaking to my daughter if you don't mind, Abby."

"Please, Mother. This is not necessary. I'm fine. Abby and Netty are just trying to help. This is my choice."

Ginger Mae's face caved in, suffused with blood and anger. "You're still my daughter, young lady, and you still answer to me."

Hud appeared alongside Ginger Mae. His face filled with hurt for his wife, he tried again. "Hon, let's just sit down and talk about this. Daisy doesn't answer to anyone. She's a grown woman, honey."

Ginger Mae stared into the face of her daughter. She still saw a six-year-old stare back, looking like she was playing dress up. As she hesitated, Hud snaked an arm around her waist, ready to catch her as she collapsed into tears. "Shhh, it's okay. I'm here, babe. I'm here." Hud stroked her back in rhythmic circles until she reduced her sobs to sniffles. Abby handed her a hanky. Everyone watched the tableau, remaining silent.

Daisy approached her mother. She held out her thin sparkling arms. "I love you, Mother, and always will. Please. Can you just remember that and let me go?"

Ginger Mae knelt down to embrace Daisy, the strange lumps of cartilage under her sarong pressing into her breast to frighten her. They pulled back, Ginger Mae wiping her tears and taking a breath. She furrowed her brow and shook her head at Daisy. "I'm sorry, Daisy Chain. I just can't help it." Daisy winced at the nickname.

She patted her mother softly. "I understand. Truly I do, Mother."

Ginger Mae brightened. "Well then. Do you think you can tell me what that demonstration was all about?"

Daisy's smile ran from ear to ear, the sparkles dancing quicker. "I was talking, Mother." Daisy turned to include everyone.

Clyde slapped his hand down on his table top. "What do you mean, you were talking, girl? I didn't hear a gosh darn thing. Well, except some vibrating. You got one of those ole cell phones on you?" Clyde's ever belligerent voice slapped everyone in the face. They all accepted he was a changed and damaged men since the horrors of the Time of Seth, but many thought he was often tiresome, the lone challenging personality in the happy Hive.

"No, Clyde. As many of you know, I've been studying the languages of other life for many decades. It's one thing to be able to now read in the thousands upon thousands of dialects my mathematical brain allows me to decipher, but to truly communicate, one needs to be able to speak.

"My operation has enabled me to do just that." She pulled on her sarong, revealing the effect of her operation.

"Not all species have a voice box or tongue like we do. Many species speak in sound, like our animals do. Many speak with light frequencies—some of which you cannot even see." She placed her hand to her face.

"What appear to be decorative sparkles are really a combination of hormones and enzymes, produced by my skin from the graft of a gland during my operation. It reflects and interacts with light when I wear this gown. That's why you can see it. It enables me to interpret frequencies of light you can't see, many not even found on this planet.

"My new growths around my neck are actually made of cartilage that grows from inside my new . . . voice box, if you will. It's an organic organ grown just for me and transplanted inside me to allow me to talk in the language of frequencies. The bottom of my new growth is reserved for allowing me to talk in the frequency of sound. Again, some so silent a human ear can't hear them. Just like the way Tobi and her herd communicate subsonically through the pads on their feet over long distances. I hear through the receptors on my bib, as I call it. I also send out my own subsonic signals through the bib. That's what you heard, Clyde."

Ginger Mae, stood nervously. "That's all so . . . interesting, Daisy." She swallowed hard. "And if that's what you need to be happy right now, then I'm all for it." She gave her head a resounding shake for emphasis. Plastering on a phony smile, she grinned at Abby and Netty. "Well, if this is all over now, why don't we sit down and eat?"

Cheers and hoots rang out as the hungry survivors dug in to Dezi's mouthwatering grub, Daisy's and Hud's eyes lingering silently on Ginger Mae.

Everyone sat as the subject appeared to be closed, laughter, gossip and drinking distracting them all, and the evening returned to normal.

Every once in a while, Ginger Mae would catch Daisy glancing at her pensively.

She just kept that big ole smile plastered in place like any good mother dying of heartbreak would. For she knew exactly what this operation would mean. It meant she would lose her daughter for good. She would lose her to the stars. It was just a matter of time.

As dinner wore on, Chloe, Scotty, Kane, and Kenya looked forward to the announcement they knew was sure to come. Unable to keep a secret from the girls, they had shared the anticipation of a surprise.

After squashing her massive abdomen up to the table, Kenya spoke up. "Chickeys, you darn well know the only surprise that will interest me is when I get surprised by the birth of this watermelon."

"I wish you wouldn't call the baby a watermelon," Kane said.

Kenya rolled her eyes. "Oh, reallllly? Care to carry it around for the next two weeks? This babe is ninety years old. That's how long I've been lugging it around. I want to be normal again. I don't even remember what normal feels like." Kenya's voice rose a couple of octaves.

Scotty and Chloe shot Kane a dirty look. Cringing, Kane swiveled his head wildly, Baby not in sight.

"Where is that little dude when we need him?" An aura stuck them all as Baby crawled out from under the table.

He scrambled free, expanding his wings and flexing his tail. He snapped his wings back in place, taut against his body.

"I am here, Brother Kane. I knew you would need me." Baby's solemn furry face turned toward Kenya.

"Do not fear, Sister Kenya. If a watermelon is taking up space for the baby, I am here to rectify it." Baby held out his elongated, leather fingers, the cup-like suctions at the end now crinkled and flexing.

Kenya pushed herself away from the table, all eyes on her bursting belly. She held out her hands. "Come here, my little man. You're the only one that gets me." She gave Kane the evil eye. "If you were just a little taller, I'd marry you." She gave Baby a juicy kiss.

Baby just stared, silent and transfixed. An aura finally hit them. "If you were more cerebral, Sister Kenya, I would take you to Oolaha when I leave this planet."

The friends were stunned. Scotty sat straight up, his jaw hanging.

"I don't know if I should be flattered or pissed," Kenya complained.

"Echo, what's this about leaving?" Scotty words reflected everyone's surprise. Echo gave a quick bow, moving back to Barney, who waited anxiously at the fireplace.

"I don't like the sound of that," Scotty stated.

"Neither do I." Chloe raised her eyebrows. "Should we try to drag it out of her?"

"No. If she wanted to tell us, she would. Look . . . Netty and Wil are speaking." They all turned their attention to the front of the room where Netty and Wil stood laughing.

"And now that we're finished with this wonderful dinner, I would like to thank Dezi," Wil said.

Dezi waved from his seat next to Hud and Ginger Mae.

"I would also like to take this chance to say welcome back to Daisy, Abby and my lovely wife." Wil turned to Netty, who stood at his side, snaked his lion-like tail around her waist and leaned in for a very public kiss. She laughed at his antics.

Wil faced the members of the Hive again, his eyes flashing and twinkling more golden than usual. He waited a moment, dragging out the suspense. "And . . . I would like to announce that tomorrow after breakfast, we will take our first journey topside."

Screaming and cheers erupted. Tears were shed and embraces were shared all around. When all eyes were wiped, they settled down to hear more.

"The next day, we will begin to move material to a staging area. Johno, I am putting you in charge of the heavy stuff. There's very little that we can't manage, but Tobi and her herd will be a great help. By the end of the day, I would like you to turn them free. They may try to follow you back inside. That's okay. When they're ready to roam, they'll just go.

"Please, take your keepers and begin to release the rest of the animals. Big cats first. They'll quickly disperse, looking for their own territory.

"I suspect many of the primates will stick to the trees around our settlement. The birds, turtles and goats will stay with us too.

"Don't worry about safety. Their implants will not be removed for several months, maybe longer. We will assess as we go.

"Kimir, I want you and Jennifer to take charge of providing supplemental feeding for the animals outside. Pick two of the keepers to work with you. We'll need several staging areas for different groups. Most likely, all the animals will continue to be dependent on us to some extent.

"We'll continue to sleep and eat in the Hive, except for lunch. Salina, can you take charge of running lunch to everyone? All able-bodied men will be on the construction crew. Our first day will be spent exploring the best sites to build.

"I think the first building will be our headquarters. We can use it for all of to sleep in until we build individual homes. We'll relocate Netty's kitchen there. It will make things easier if we can wean ourselves away from the Hive as soon as possible.

"The only problem is the growing field." Wil turned to Scotty and Kane. "Guys, how many saplings do you have that will transplant easily?"

Scotty and Kane looked at each other in confusion.

"About fifty, maybe less," chimed in Chloe. "But they're two years away from producing fruit. We have bushes and vegetables that we could transplant. That is if the growing conditions are good."

"I'm sure things will be different, but the Womb has made sources of food available for the current creatures out there. I'm sure there will be things we can eat while our crops mature. One of the other jobs I need volunteers for will be to dig a root cellar."

Across the room, Kimir fastened his damp brown eyes on Daisy. Feeling the heaviness of his gaze, she turned to meet his eyes. He watched as she excused herself from her table and made her way back to his secluded corner of the kitchen. He couldn't fail to read the sadness in Ginger Mae's face as she watched Daisy move toward him. *I guess I can forget about any privacy here.* His face flushed through his warm russet complexion.

"Kimir, would you mind if we walked back to the sleeping caves?" asked Daisy, holding out her hand.

Relieved, he slipped her tender tiny hand into his equally youthful one, the hope fading from his eyes as he began to finally accept the futility of his love for her. Eyeing her changes and admitting her commitment to their implementation, he shivered.

Quietly, the youngest survivors and long-time companions left the kitchen to talk. One simply to say hello, the other to say goodbye as the decades of unrequited love came to an end.

Back in the kitchen, the excited survivors planned well past their normal bedtimes, finally being chased out of the kitchen by Father Garcia and Maddy, who wanted to put the babies to bed.

"See you all in the morning." Cobby set off to bed with Karen at his side. Excited goodbyes were exchanged as Father Garcia and Maddy settled the babies, crawling into their private rooms to sleep as the membrane lights dimmed and the wondrous tendrils of the night crept out of the walls to begin the last few months of their unending cellular repairs.

Chapter 12

Morning found every single survivor gathered at the cave entrance. A progression of dogs, Caesar, Chance, and even Tobi and her herd waited impatiently in the larger cavern of the survivors' inaugural night.

Bonnie stood with Tobi, the elephant's trunk resting lightly on her shoulder. Echo wobbled on the ground at her side. "Please, Echo. Make sure she understands. We need to make sure it's safe for them first. There's no telling what might be out there. And that goes for Barney and Chance too. If something happens and we need to make a run for it, Chance won't fare well with those tiny feet of his. And keep all the dogs here with you."

"I will make sure they understand, Sister Bonnie."

They glanced up as Scotty shouted from across the cavern. "Come on, Bonnie, we're leaving now." Bonnie bent down to kiss Echo then ran off to join the excited survivors.

Cobby, Clyde and Johno were the first to step through the opening as the membranes parted. Scotty stood behind with the rest of the crowd as they all were assaulted with the heavy, steamy smells of green growth in a humid atmosphere.

Sounds of knives hacking through undergrowth filtered into the corridors, and the crowd grew impatient as they waited to emerge into the open air.

"Kenya, if you want to go back and wait . . ." Kane expressed his concern, holding Kenya around her waist.

"Not on your life, chickey. I want to see what we're getting into as much as the next person. You're not leaving me outa this."

Kane gave her a big kiss. "That's my girl."

Johno poked his head into the corridor. "Okay, sorry for the delay. We had to clear a pathway. Foliage has grown right up to the entrance."

Following Johno out, the survivors made their way around and past the huge granite rock. The weather was oppressively humid, vines and low growth saplings lay hacked and thrown to the side as they made their way through the new woods to stand at what was once the edge of the forest that had looked down on Netty's farm and Scotty's small neighborhood of modest homes.

Hearts tripped madly as all remained silent, assessing the vista before them. Tears slipped down faces held up to see the sun . . . the glorious sun. Wil, Netty and Baby stood quietly, reliving bittersweet memories.

"It sure is quiet." Cobby squinted at the sun, familiar and welcome.

Scotty looked down the hill where his neighborhood street used to be. He remembered the first time he ran up this hill into the woods to nurse his pain over his violent, abusive father to later discover Echo. His thoughts resonated with tenderness. An aura pierced his brain.

"I remember too, my Brother." Sending Echo a warm thought, he scanned the topography as the rest of the survivors pointed and exclaimed to each other in hushed tones.

The silence was eerie. Small mounds of greenery sat where each house had rested, hiding the skeletons of the building material and treasures worshiped by families long gone. The small mounds resembled graves. The final resting place of the crumbled and rotted traces of a civilization time and the elements had failed to completely eradicate.

"Look." Johno kicked his foot in the soil, his toes covered in red. He dropped to the ground, scooping up a handful of claylike dirt to let it crumble through his fingers. He brought it to his nose and sniffed. "Praise the Womb. This looks like the same red soil of my great country in Africa. I can feel it, can't you?"

He looked from the uncertain faces of his fellow survivors, the keepers falling to their knees to scrape up the soil. "This is a sign; an omen from the Womb. My eles will be happy. Tobi will know the difference." He swept his arm wide to encompass the strange but verdant landscape before them with its unfamiliar trees and vines.

"It feels like home." Johno grinned wide with infectious happiness. "I know we can do this, my friends. Are you with me?"

The survivors hesitated then broke out with claps and hugs. Tears flowed all around as they realized their lives of exile would end. Even Kenya began to wail with happiness. The wailing got louder.

"Please, please, Mr. Womb, not now," she moaned.

As all eyes trained on Kenya, Kane stepped back. "Babe?"

She continued to wail, her hands shaking high in the air. "Help me down, chickey." She suddenly bent at the waist. "Ohhhhhh, noooooo." Kane helped her ease to the ground as Crystal, Salina and Netty ran to her side.

She looked up pitifully, her brown eyes wide as saucers. "My water just broke."

"Oh my heavens!" Crystal broke out in tears, bending down to hug Kenya. "Finally, your day has come, baby girl." The men began to clap Kane on the back, laughing and hooting it up.

It didn't take long before everyone noticed Wil and Netty's drawn faces, the golden light from their eyes dim and muted.

As the silence surrounded Kenya, she looked up, her stomach contracting visibly. "What? What's wrong now? Netty? Wil?" Her head rotated from one to the other. "Someone better tell me what the heck is going on. Ahhhhhhh." Her stomach contracted again.

Kane stepped to her side, shouting to Scotty and his father.

"Come on. Help me get her back to the Hive."

"No," Netty shouted. "You must not!"

They turned to her in shock. She stepped over to Kane. "Go into the Hive. Take Scotty with you. Bring back as many blankets from the supply closet as you can handle." She turned to Bonnie. "I want you to bring me a pail of water and a box of whatever Dezi can throw together for four or five people. And tea. Get tea. Have Dezi give you some of the special tea for Kenya. She will just have to drink it cold." Salina stood, her face furrowed with indignation.

"For the love of the Womb, Netty. Let's get this girl inside where we can attend her."

Netty ignored Salina, strolling over to link her arm with Kane's, moving them both closer to Kenya. "I'm so sorry, my dear. But you cannot go back into the Hive. It could mean your death and that of the baby."

"Are you crazy, Netty? Ahhhhhh. Get me back into the Hive. Right! Now!"

"Baby, can you help?" Netty called to Baby, who quickly clumped his way to the circle around Kenya. Placing his hands on her abdomen, Kenya immediately relaxed, the next pain lessened significantly.

"Ahhh. Oh yes . . . yes, that's better, Baby. Thank you, chickey. You're my man." Kenya took a deep breath.

"Can you just cut to the chase, Netty?"

"I told you. If you go back into the Hive before the baby's born, the process will stop. Your contractions will stop and any damage done to the placenta and your womb will hurt the baby." Disbelief glazed every expression. "Depending on where the baby is, it could kill you. The only answer is to have the baby out here."

Crystal crouched down next to Baby. "You poor kid."

"I'm not a kid, Crystal. I am a grown old lady. Ohhh."

Kane, Scotty and Cobby sidled up to Wil.

"Have you noticed how quiet it is, Wil?" asked Kane.

"Will the kids be safe out here? Who knows how long the baby might take. It might get dark," Cobby commented.

"I'll have two of the keepers stay with you if it gets dark," Johno volunteered.

They all turned back to Kenya; who appeared in less pain and much calmer. Wil took charge. "Okay now. Peter, Clyde, Johno and one of the keepers. Let's lift her up and get her back to the Hive entrance. Go Scotty . . . you too, Kane. Bring back the supplies we need. Bonnie, why don't you bring back lunch for all of us? Use Netty's cart. If Dezi wants to come back with you, let him. This is a chance for him to check things out. Go . . ."

As everyone scrambled to get back to the Hive, all backs were turned away from the panorama of the site chosen for their new settlement.

No eyes witnessed the dark gliding shadow that flitted over the precious land as its maker patrolled its territory from dizzying heights, backlit by the oppressive sun.

Her five-inch razor claws hugged her improbable body, translucent feathers concealing the ruby scales that protected its massive two-hundred-and-fifty-pound frame, making her feathers appear to flame in the blue sky. Her twenty-two-foot wingspan banked on placid wind currents, forcing an occasional wing flutter as she scanned the land with her torpedo-shaped head that concealed her snake-like fangs, looking for prey. She preferred the carcasses of the dead, but enjoyed the occasional live prey when unable to locate the maggot-filled decaying flesh she preferred.

As the vacuum cleaner of the land, she did a marvelous job. But, during one certain time of the year, it became necessary to prepare to feed other mouths. Live prey was always an option. In this humidity, it decayed quickly once a lightning and skillful boring through the prey's skull rendered it harmless. Eyeing the retreating figures on the hill, she made note of the prey's location and wheeled back to the nest that contained her eggs.

"Kenya, I want to stay out here with you and watch the baby come." Kane's stubborn pronouncement did nothing to alleviate the pain of Kenya's contractions.

Cobby pulled him away as she glared and began to moan again. "I don't think she wants you here, kiddo."

"Kiddo? Dad . . . really?"

"Sorry, but you're still my kid. I can't help it." Cobby gave Kane a playful punch in the arm.

They stood up against the granite rock that played such an important part of their lives. Offering shelter from the unexplored Earth, it was close enough to the Hive opening to feel safe.

Kenya lay atop a bed of blankets. Towels and water sat handy for the big arrival, the granite rock waiting to be the first to welcome her baby to the new world.

It was decided that two of the keepers would station themselves down the path, a lookout for possible danger. Netty and Abby would attend the birth, with Cobby standing by to offer assistance and be their go-between back and forth from the Hive.

Kenya clearly didn't want Kane around for the messier parts of the process. "Chickey, there's no way in Hell that you're going to watch me shit myself when this baby comes. When the two of you meet, I'm gonna look like a princess who's here to present you with your own royal baby. Now, why don't you pleeeease go back into the Hive? Go pick out something nice and slinky for me from the supply closet. This girl is aimin' to get her sexy back on as soon as the watermelon decides to come on outtttttttttt—ahhhhhhh!"

"Breathe, Kenya," Netty said. She looked up wide eyed and flushed, sweat beading heavily down her neck.

"I am! Oosh, oosh, oosh, oosh."

Cobby lit the bonfire the men had constructed during the day. The keepers took their bedrolls down the path with them, saying a goodnight as Kane and Scotty made their way back into the Hive.

Netty dipped a cloth into the water to soothe Kenya. Six hours had passed, and everyone was tired. She looked over to Cobby. He leaned up against the rock, eyelids drooping. "I think the crown's rounding. It shouldn't be much longer. Why don't you wake up Cobby?"

Abby nodded her head, skirting over to Cobby. She shook his arm, startling him awake.

"The baby?"

"No, not yet." Abby smiled gently. Cobby stood and stretched. He threw another log on the bonfire, embers from the burning logs spitting and riding high in the air to be wafted away, a message for unknown creatures to stay away,

"Guess the heat from the fire knocked me out." He yawned. "Want to take walk?"

Abby raised her eyebrow back at Netty.

"Go ahead. Nothing's happening here for a while, but I'll need you both alert later. Don't go far. It might not be safe. Come running if I call."

"We'll be just around the corner," said Cobby. "Can't go far in this jungle of vines."

Cobby and Abby skirted the rock tightly to avoid the vines. The night air away from the fire felt refreshing and cool. The moon dimly cast their shadows over the foliage, its full strength saving itself for another night. Or was it the cloud cover? They scanned the night sky, hoping for feelings of familiarity, but instead shivered under the vastness.

"You cold?" asked Cobby.

"No, I just feel small out here. It's so different from the coziness of the Hive."

Cobby leaned up against the rock next to her. "I know what you mean. I never felt that way . . . before. We'll get used to it. Did you notice the absence of sounds during the day?"

"Yeah. It's not what I expected. Echo will know. She'll tell us if it's something the Womb has done or if it's just a natural occurrence. Our animals can't be the only species on the planet. It takes so much more to sustain an ecosystem." Abby fell silent, oddly aware of Cobby's warmth next to her.

"I don't get to see much of you in the Hive. Usually just at meals and then Karen is so busy with our baby."

Abby nodded. "Yeah . . . Karen." Surprising herself, Abby detected a note of something unidentifiable in her comment.

Cobby turned toward her, his arm touching hers, even as her wings felt crushed against the rock. "What do you mean by that, Abby?"

She looked deep into his eyes, his handsome face so dear and familiar. Something inside hitched, waves overcoming her. She saw something in Cobby's eyes. Was it confusion? His lips parted as she leaned toward him, unable to make herself stop.

Cobby's hands went to her face, kissing her hungrily. She heard him groan. "Oh God, Abby."

She felt her breast heave and her breath came in short gasps. "Cobby."

"Yes, Abby. I've dreamed of this . . . for such a long time."

She felt herself tremble. Cobby snaked his arm around her waist, mashing her to his hard body.

Abruptly, she pulled herself free. They stared at each other, ragged breaths loud and unexpected. Cobby's eyes filled with passion and longing. He swept his hand over his face, taking another deep breath. "I'm so sorry, Abby; it's just that for so long . . . ."

"I know, Cobby. I know exactly—"

From down the pathway a sudden shriek, then a heart-rendering scream, abruptly silenced. They looked toward the pathway and saw a dark shape move across the sky, briefly obscuring the moon.

"Oh my God, Cobby. The keepers?"

Cobby's lips set in a grim line. "I better go investigate."

She clutched at him in horror. "No. Let me go. I can protect myself. I won't have you put yourself at risk. Stay with Netty and look after Kenya." She gently touched the side of his face, then stepped away from the rock to flex her wings. Then she was gone.

All her confusing thoughts about Cobby were pushed to the back of her mind to savor in privacy as she flew over the path to the hill where the keepers kept watch.

Touching down on the ground, she saw one of the keepers prone and unmoving, half his skull missing, blood pooling under his neck. Hurriedly looking around, she was unable to locate the other keeper, even as his bedroll remained heaped in disarray. They had no bonfire, even though a pile of kindling and larger logs lay piled in the clearing.

She sniffed the air, redolent with the faint stench of carrion. This was not good. Stillness greeted her ears, haunting in its overwhelming eeriness.

Taking wing, she wondered how she would have the courage to break the news to Johno.

A rustle in the bushes announced her return. Stepping into the clearing, she beheld Kenya's tired smile and the jubilant grins of Netty and Cobby. In Kenya's trembling arms lay her newborn baby girl. The first and the last child to be born to humans in the new world.

*

The joy over the birth of Kenya's baby was overshadowed by the death of the keepers. Losing two members of their tightly-knit community was a loss felt by all. Worse yet was the prospect of danger it presented for their fledgling settlement.

Understandably, the mothers were the most vocal.

"Cobby, you can't expect us to put the babies in danger. Our lives are fine here. We have everything we need." Karen's voice strained with her arguments against moving to the settlement.

"Are you out of your mind? If you think any human will choose to live underground when we have the chance to reclaim our world, you're crazy. And the baby would never grow up. Is that what you want?" Cobby's words unexpectedly stung.

Her voice low, she responded, "I'm just thinking of our safety."

Cobby took her in his arms, surprised at his shortness. "I know you are, Karen. I know. Try not to worry. We have plenty of time to investigate. It's going to take us a good year or more just to get the settlement in enough of a rough shape to move into. We're down two men now. That's going to cost us. It might take us longer than we expect. We have so much to do. And you need to help. I'm sure we'll have a complete picture of the dangers before we give up the Hive." He gazed into her trusting eyes.

"Promise?"

He held her again as he tried to fight his century-long and futile desire for it to be Abby in his arms. "Yes, I promise."

Chapter 13

2148 AD

Lorna surveyed the construction site. If only her mother, Suzy, had lived to see this. Her dream of freedom was what had driven the women of the tribe to overthrow the diabolical control of the barbaric men who had ruled them during the first twenty eight years of life in the mines.

She had no memory of her father, Doc Benjamin. The memory of his rule glowed bright and embellished in the minds of the men of the tribe. Quietly, that is. The female leaders of Lorna's inner circle allowed the worship without comment, instead preferring to encourage a healthier discourse of kindness and sharing. The women knew the memory of Doc Benjamin's reign would die out after the next generation.

Lorna and her twin brother Seth were now sixty one and relatively fit. They attributed their health to the miracle produce from the growing field which no one seemed to remember planting.

Under Lorna's leadership, the men had gradually been convinced to participate in the work around camp, reducing their caloric intake and losing some of the puffy chubbiness that came from ingesting prodigious amounts of fruit.

Lorna's habit of banning a man from his home and his females had curbed much of the formerly rampant crime. Unfortunately, not all abuses had stopped, but just went unreported or underground. Lorna and her inner circle knew the men had an unknown ringleader who thwarted their every move, but they had made progress all the same. Mostly with the women. It was amazing how manipulative a woman could be with sex when it was applied for the greater good. It was a weapon the subversive men did not have in their arsenal.

And of course, her mother had been the chosen leader; chosen by Doc Benjamin himself.

Her own leadership had been preordained. She herself had seen sparks of resentment and jealousy from her brother Seth as they were children and well into their teens. But Seth had come around. Just as their brother Lafe had.

Lafe had become her mother's most reliant member of her inner circle. When the older members of her father's old entourage had balked at a new directive, Lafe had been the first to take her mother's side. He had been an elder adviser when she had taken over after her mother's death sixteen years ago in a drowning accident at the falls when she was visiting Tom, an old family friend who operated their power grid.

She had continued to consult with Lafe up until his death ten years ago. Surprisingly, Seth had been beside himself at his funeral, throwing himself at the foot of Lafe's funeral pyre even as it burned. She had no knowledge of their relationship and shrugged it off, the control of the burning funeral pyre more of a concern.

Fire had become her friend. Fire kept them healthy. Whenever an outbreak of disease struck, she ordered everything they had touched to be burned and the sick quarantined in another cave with no contact from the others. Their meals and water were left at the mouth of the cave. When the healthy were healed, they rejoined the tribe. The bodies of the dead and all their belongings in the cave were burned.

They had been lucky to find a cave that evinced an upward draft, allowing the smoke to escape. The disposal of the dead for any reason became another event for fire. It cleansed. That was all that mattered.

The tribe had lived in the mines for eighty seven years. Three years ago, the council had voted to send out scouts for the first time. A great ceremony had been held to honor the two men chosen for the dubious distinction. There had been no guarantee they would come back alive.

It had taken the scouts three whole nail-biting days before they appeared with garlands of green vines on their heads and strange mushroom-shaped red growths that had hung from branches of a tree they had failed to recognize.

"It's okay. We saw squirrels . . . yes, squirrels and odd little glass boxes with wings eating them. The corner of the boxes had beaks so we guessed they were birds. The sun was out . . . everything's green. We can go outside now. It's safe."

The scouts babbled about the abundance of life. Deer the color of plums, huge rabbits with legs that enabled them to walk and run like a man. So much food to trap.

"No. There will be no trapping and eating of the animals. We live long and healthy lives with the produce we grow. We have more than we'll ever need. Our bodies were not made to eat the flesh of another. There will be no more death. Life is for the living."

And so Lorna had made a decree that had saved them from the wrath of the Womb. Unknowing to them, they would be granted the same last chance granted to the survivors of the Hive; the same chance that came with the same unfortunate downside. For strangely enough, not one child had been born to the tribe in the three years they had begun to build their village and live under the watchful eye of the bright and humid sun.

Lorna stood on a hillock which gave her a good view of the village with its ramshackle lumber holding together their attempt at permanent homes. A large building that served as the Council Center was ringed by dwellings in the same pecking order as in the mine. Lorna smiled as she admitted to herself that they were unimaginative creatures of habit. But it gave everyone a sense of comfort. A feeling sorely needed in their sometimes-dangerous new world.

She turned to greet Seth as he joined her on the hillock. "Everyone battened down?" she asked.

"Yes, Lorna. The flamer'll go without a member of our tribe this year. Do you think it's a new one or the same one each year?" Seth scanned the sky, cupping his eyes from the beating sun. His bland good looks and slight build created a stark contrast to Lorna's large and Amazonian dark stature.

"It's the same one. They seem to be territorial. That's why we've never seen more than one at a time. She should show up any day now. All the other creatures are in hiding. Did you notice the sudden silence yesterday? We'll never get a better warning than that."

Lorna turned and left the hillock, Seth trailing behind. "Did you put together the team for my excursion to Lily Pond Road?" she asked.

Seth frowned. "No, not yet. I'm working on another project that needs my strongest men."

Lorna raised an eyebrow in surprise. "Your men?"

Seth winced. "No, of course . . . I meant our men."

Lorna stopped and reached her hand out. "Show me the map."

Reluctantly, Seth removed a newly-discovered map from under his layers of rags. The map had been found during the last cleanout of the mine. It had remained hidden under discarded debris for decades.

Opening the map of Sussex County, New Jersey, Lorna studied the word Franklin, then traced her fingers northwest to the town of Andover where she stopped at the words, Lily Pond Road; a simple left turn off the Newton-Sparta Road which was a twenty-five-minute drive from where they stood. She estimated it would take them less than two days to get there if they stopped to sleep under some cover. The hardest thing to do would be to cut through all the overgrowth and evade the sharp eyes of the flamer.

"I want to leave now. The flamer might not return for a while yet. We might have one more day of safety if we get started right away. Prepare the men to leave after lunch. Are you coming with us?"

Seth blinked, his face neutral. "Of course, dear sister. I can't have you going off on your own. It's too dangerous. God forbid any danger affect you. I just don't want you to set yourself up for disappointment. They might be long gone. And Grandfather will have died long ago. Mother said she thought he was an old man when the bombs fell."

Lorna shook her head. "Mother said he drove a truck to make a living. He was still working when the bombs hit or Grandmother wouldn't have been alone in the resort town in Florida. Mother remembered the beach," Lorna reminisced dreamily. "She always said she wanted to see it again before she died."

Shaking her head of foolishness, she added, "Grandfather couldn't have been too old if he was still working. He must have been carrying supplies for the bomb shelter. He might have been working for the old government. I have to know for sure. They might have resources we can use. Or maybe we can share our seeds with them to some advantage."

She turned back to Seth. "Make sure you bring seed with us. Just in case." Without waiting for an answer, she handed him the map and walked toward the Council Center.

Seth trudged back to the mine where his men waited. This was not good. He would look weak in their eyes. He steamed with frustration and bitterness over the influence his sister exerted in the tribe. It was his birthright. It should be him. Just as Lafe had drummed into him since he was a child old enough to talk. And old enough to see the pleasure he had given Lafe in their stolen moments of passion.

His heart shuddered with pain as he thought of his deceased love. No man could come close to the pleasure they had found in each other's arms. The forbidden moments, Lafe's hot, fervent whispers and cajoling demands. Demands made of a child, but lusted for as an adult. Demands Lafe insisted they keep a vital secret from all. In public, they appeared to be disinterested brothers, albeit Lafe was adopted. In private, Lafe took him to heights of pleasure no man was meant to experience outside of a woman's arms.

While they had reveled in their stolen moments, Lafe had taught him the truth of Lorna's rise to power. A fabled eyeless beast she controlled and the false claim of Doc Benjamin's appointment testified to by his mother's second-in-command, a woman named Liselle. Too bad Liselle had met an accidental death by drowning at the waterfall a few years later. Seth smirked.

But by then it had been too late. Lorna and her inner circle had wormed their way into the hearts of most of the tribe with improvements in health, rights for the women and education for the urchins.

So Lafe had encouraged him to seek out like-minded men of the tribe; those that nursed grievances or dark passions against women. Many a night deep in the mine, they'd bring an unsuspecting young girl, lured away with sweet promises. She would meet her end in their protected cave, safe from discovery as the men raped and tortured the girl. Lafe and Seth always enjoyed the scene from afar, after a raucous spate of passion for themselves first.

It had been Lafe that had taught him to keep his shriveled gimp hand hidden among the layers of rags he wore until most forgot he even had a defect. But *he* never did, he never forgot. How could he when he confronted the perfection of his sister's miraculously-healed hand on a daily basis?

All the while, they both functioned in public as loyal confidants of first Suzy, then Lorna.

Making his way in the dimness with only a tallow candle, the electricity lines long taken down and restrung in the village, he ran his hands along the tunnel wall he knew so well.

"It's about time. Where ya been? Did she take the map?" His current lover, Andrew, paced in their cavern; the other dozen men quiet and anxious.

"Plans have changed. Our excursion to the arsenal will need ta wait."

Seth opened the map and pressed it flat to the floor. His grimy fingers followed Route 15 until it converged with Route 80. It put them closer to New York City, but still far enough from what they suspected might contain enough radiation to still bring on the sickness.

It was an acceptable risk. Less than a quarter of a mile before the merger with Route 80, the map showed hundreds of acres marked Picatinny Arsenal U.S. Army. An Army base for munitions and civil engineers, it had been an important employer for the county for eighty years until the economy had busted after the last war. They hoped it would be a gold mine of weapons waiting to be unearthed. They would salvage them to bring back to the tribe for the coming insurrection that would imprison the current inner circle, including his sister, and install him and his men as the new leaders of the tribe, as he so richly deserved. Lafe would have been so proud.

"Let's make some notes. Lorna might just decide ta take the map away from me, the self-righteous bitch. We need ta be prepared."

Amid his men's indignant voices, Seth dreamed of the moment of success and the shocked look he would find on his despised sister's face. He laughed to himself. He knew he had failed to distinguish himself in the eyes of the inner circle. He often thought himself an unnecessary pet Lorna kept on her leash.

Lafe had been right . . . keep your enemies close, the better to blindside them and grind them under your feet.

Lorna and Seth trudged along the red dirt road, cement and asphalt long broken down and vanquished by the elements. Vines and overgrowth made staying on what they guessed to be the road difficult.

The third day of the journey was half over, the sun directly overhead. It was time to stop for lunch. They were accompanied by a mixture of inner circle members and Seth's men to pull the wagon that carried their supplies, weapons, bedding, and seed.

Their journey was non-eventful, most creatures taking refuge until the flamer had laid her eggs, and hatched and raised her newborn, forcing them to migrate to other lands until the next breeding season. It was almost like the winters of old when creatures hibernated. They stored up resources for the winter months and emerged in the spring. Only now, they emerged when the flamer was gone. An occasional stray deer or oddly-colored bird was seen hunting for food. All bound to fall victim to the flamer eventually.

"I think we should go this way. Have the men cut through that overgrowth. It should put us on Lily Pond Road if we aren't already," Lorna directed as she studied the map.

As the men cut away at the overgrowth, the scouting party turned a bend. Everyone froze as voices wafted down a hill rising above an open plain, clearly an old subdivision location.

They slowly crouched down to observe the figures standing at the crest of the hill, all with their faces turned up to the sun.

"Holy shit. Do you see what I see?" Seth's face was alive with awe, his voice full of unmitigated fright.

"Yes . . . I see. Several of them have wings. Do you see the small golden one?" Sunlight hit the horns on the winged figures' heads, refracting bright rays back to the scouts hidden in the bush.

It was clear they had just arrived. If it truly was the people from their grandfather's bomb shelter, they had better rethink their plans. The disclosure of men and women with wings had them reeling.

"What should we do, Lorna?" asked Seth.

Lorna watched them all turn away, carrying one of their members who appeared to have been struck with a sudden sickness. From above, the deadly shadow of the flamer floated over the hillside, the strangers oblivious. The scouts froze.

"I think we need to return home, Seth. I need some time to think about this turn of events. We'll return during the flamer's migration when the danger has passed. We need to take care of our own tribe right now. This will keep. At least I'm satisfied." Lorna's face sagged as her mother's story was verified. Her heart ached for what could have been.

"They were here all this time. So close . . ."

Keeping low and clinging to bushes, they made their way back to the tribe, Lorna excited about the opportunity this could mean for her people.

"This must be it." Seth studied the map Lorna had left in his safe keeping. He and six of his men stood in front of a swath of low bushes and young trees. The younger growth usually masked a road that had taken time to degenerate enough to allow trees to take a foothold.

The men were hot and tired. They had lost their enchantment for Seth's hair-brained idea about a week ago when they had balked at investigating any more of his false leads. All they wanted to do was get back to the tribe.

It was insane to be risking their lives with the flamer on the loose. She had most likely laid her eggs by now and was collecting live prey to rot in the sun for her hatchlings. And, as they well knew, every once in a while the flamer chose to eat something herself. Usually alive. This time of the year, with most creatures in hiding, the number of carcasses remained low. Nature adapts to what is available and they had no intention of being on the menu.

"Okay, this will be the last spot we check. Let's just take a look around. If it's not the arsenal, we'll head back."

After much bitching from the men, they finally cut through the bushes and passed through what once had been the proud gates of Picatinny Arsenal.

The men walked the vast acreage which sported low growth and young trees, evidence of a huge network of roads with rotted and collapsed buildings.

They soon stumbled upon a derelict railroad, the iron rusted and eaten away, leaving channels to mark its ghostly track.

"Hey, Pedro. Didn't your old man work for the railroads?"

"Yeah, boss. But this must have been private. The track channels seem awfully small to me. They probably used it to transport heavy munitions to a loading dock. Or underground storage."

Seth eyes lit up. "Underground storage? That's just what we need to find. Let's go, boys."

The track went on for two miles before it ended precisely where Seth had hoped.

The warped and useless iron door to the underground bunker lay flat on the ground—on the inside. Seth suspected the force from one of the New York City bombs had blown it off its mammoth hinges. They were only a mere seventy five minutes from what used to be the George Washington Bridge; the fabled bridge that had once spanned New York Harbor to connect New York and New Jersey.

It didn't take them long to realize that the leather-clad armaments stored in the bunker were too unstable and dangerous to move. No one wanted to risk blowing themselves up for one of Seth's megalomaniac plans to take over the tribe.

As the men headed back outside, Seth noticed a small door near the entrance. Pitted and covered with vines, it had been easy to overlook. Taking a crowbar to the door, they managed to wedge it open. Daylight made its way in to expose a network of intact metal, protected from the elements by the sealed door.

"We have something here. Don't know what the Hell it is, but why go home empty handed? Let's see if we can get it out of here and loaded into the wagon."

Ripping away the unyielding door took some doing as it no longer sat trim in the door frame. The wider the door moved with the crowbar, the more sunlight pierced the gloom to expose a medium-sized skinny cannon on an iron frame. Hooked to the side of the cannon hung a half dozen finely-crafted long metal spears with a nasty, elongated arrow on the end.

"What the . . ." Seth's heart sank. The men wanted to get home. His time was up.

"All right. Let's pull it out. We'll take it with us. We can scrap it and use the metal. We might get something out of this trip after all." Seth walked out of the bunker's mouth, disappointment heavy on his brow. He tried to show confidence to his men, but Andrew knew him better.

Approaching his lover, compassion in the sag of his face, Seth shoved him roughly away. "Not now, faggot."

Andrew skittered away without comment, a loyal dog licking his wounds after a vicious kick from his master.

Seth did a slow simmer, all thoughts of his victorious, tribal coup up in smoke. What could he hope to achieve without a significant weapon? How would he depose Lorna now? He clenched his fists. *Lafe . . . if only I still had Lafe. He would understand. He would tell me what to do.* Seth stifled a sob.

A noisy clatter forced his thoughts back to his current failure. Turning, he forced himself to re-examine the hunk of metal they had found.

Andrew sidled over to him tentatively. "Do you know what it is, Seth?"

He honored Andrew with a raised eyebrow. "Well, spit it out, Andrew. You obviously think you know something."

Andrew danced on his toes, mincing with excitement. "It's a harpoon gun. I saw pictures in one of our books. They used to kill whales with them."

"Kill, you say?" Seth took a closer look.

"Do you think we could make it work again?"

Everyone crowded around the old seafaring weapon. One of his men ran his hands over the metal.

"It's sturdy enough. Not too much rust. We can clean that off. Maybe take a few potshots at something with it. Check it out, it might be effective."

Seth walked around the metal heap, dismantling a harpoon to examine the tip. He frowned. "Hmmm. I need to think about this. We might have just found the answer to our plans. If we can bring down the flamer with this, we'd be heroes."

His men shrank back. "You won't get me anywhere near that flamer." The rest of the men grumbled their assent.

Andrew whispered in his ear, one hand tenderly on his arm. "How will that make us the new leaders, Seth?"

Shrugging away Andrew's arm, he replied, "Don't question me, faggot. I know we're on to something. Let's get this baby home." He turned to his men. "Load 'er up boys."

As they began the long walk back to their village near the Franklin Mine, Seth's mental wheels turned, a bright gleam in his eye. He knew he didn't have a plan yet, but he also knew that someone . . . somewhere, was going to suffer a whole lot of hurt.

His shriveled heart expanded and sang.

Chapter 14

The months flew by swiftly for the survivors at the Hive. The shock of losing two of the keepers had been felt for weeks with everyone frightened for their own safety, slowing down their plans to build by months. Then a miracle happened.

One morning, Cobby, Johno and Clyde returned early from their daily surreptitious explorations above ground.

The survivors were sitting around Netty's kitchen gossiping after a light lunch of green rolled apple and walnut fritters when the men burst into the room.

"Quick, everyone. Come outside. You have to see this."

Netty and Wil stood together. "What's the matter, gentlemen? Is everything okay?" Netty moved toward the gathering crowd, concern wrinkling her brow. The men wore grins that split from ear to ear.

"Come on, see for yourself."

The survivors raced through the Hive; Caesar, Echo, Baby, Barney and doggy posse in tow.

As soon as they hit the fresh air, sounds met their ears; musical, wonderful, alive sounds. They ran down the pathway to the edge of the woods. Looking down the hill they saw magic in the making.

A small herd of plum-colored deer were grazing near a stand of young trees covered with dangling red ornaments that had attracted the attentions of bird-like creatures, graceful in their improbable box-like figures, their bodies glinting in the sunlight like square diamond rings.

Giant butterflies flitted from one spot to another, angling to show their electric colors to their best advantage.

An odd gingerbread figure, all spongy and featureless, jumped from a high branch to float to the ground surprising a blue, mouselike creature, popping it into a mouth that flashed with needle-like teeth.

"Oh my." The survivors stared and listened, the sounds joyful and overwhelming. Life had come back and life was good.

Wil breathed a sigh of relief. "I think we can move forward with our plans." He turned and held up a hand for slaps from the other men.

"I don't know what's just happened, but I'm sure we'll figure it out in time."

And so the survivors moved on. They lugged wood, cleared land, set boundaries, planted crops, and nurtured saplings. And at night they returned to the Hive to care for the animals, eat, laugh and make love.

It was a heady time. They felt safe.

From time to time, Father Garcia and Maddy even brought the babies to visit. Little Maya liked dancing alongside as if she were the supervisor in charge, her tiny wings uncontrolled and her tail wrapped tightly to her waist so it couldn't be pulled; a favorite pastime of the jokesters in the group.

As the first dwellings began to go up, some of the men transported the bones of Netty's kitchen to the first completed building. It was a painstaking job to remake the fireplace, having dismantled it stone by stone.

Johno turned out to be a master at knowing something about all the phases of construction, having built his mother and father's house in Africa. It had been a home to rival the neighbors with his first earnings as a keeper when he was a young man.

Luckily, the new red dirt under their feet made superb bricks, just as it did in Africa. Mixed with chopped weeds for binding, and loose gravel where they found it, the fresh bricks piled up, drying quickly in the hot sun. It was a simple matter to preserve their limited lumber for bracing and roof joists.

The roofs presented another problem. They had no shingles. Clyde suggested they tear all of the doors and paneling out of the library. Most of the paneling was buckled and split from the rough conditions during the underground journey to the Hive. But no one saw that as a problem. They decided to fit doors and pieces of walnut paneling over the roof joists as underlayment. On top, they laid mats of woven reeds held together with saplings. The reed mats were then plastered with elephant dung.

When dried in the sun, the dung became a weatherproof barrier, keeping out rain and hot sun. Altogether, a very satisfactory solution.

Kenya and Chloe rested under an acacia tree near a rock outcrop to get a respite from the heat of the noon time sun. Caesar, Echo and Barney lay panting under a deciduous tree that trickled leaves from its branches, signs the weather might soon start to cool. Scotty and Kane hauled lunch and containers of water from Netty's new kitchen.

Only now it was called Dezi's. He cooked, cleaned and lived there along with Father Garcia and Maddy, who had eased up on their responsibilities for the infants as the parents had taken over, bringing them in at breakfast for nursery care only.

Chloe reached into the box. "I see something good. You want some, Kenya?" She pulled out a huge wedge of berry tasset, a rich mixture of greens from Oolaha that Dezi ground into a paste before adding all kinds of berries and roasts. The paste puffed up, encasing the fruits inside a hard, crusty, spicy shell.

"Chickey, if you think I'm gunna apply any of that rich temptation to my new beautiful thighs, you have got to have your brain examined." Kenya preened on her back, posing with her lovely, svelte legs high in the sky.

"Okay, we get it. You have the best legs on the planet." Chloe laughed.

"Oh, chickey, thank you. Them words are music to my ears after decades of lugging—"

Kane crashed down near her, grabbing her by the waist to sling her over his lap. "Lugging what . . . your watermelon?"

Kenya pealed with laughter. "No, you gorgeous hunk of old man. My darling baby girl. Our baby girl."

Kane turned to Chloe. "Did I tell you how beautiful she looked this morning? Those big eyes of hers, just like her smart-ass beautiful momma." Kane turned back to crush his lips down on Kenya's.

Chloe looked out over the field. She was happy for her friends, although she had trouble admitting to the twinges of jealousy. It was long past the time she had first hungered for a child for her and Scotty. It wasn't easy accepting it would never happen. She fought off the tears that threatened to spill over.

"Hey, hon. Got some more of that in there for me?"

Chloe reached in to get a hunk of tasset for Scotty, who reached out with his foot to give Kane a kick. "Get a room, you two."

Kane snorted and sheepishly reached into the food box.

"Sorry, gang. It's just like we're on a honeymoon after being cooped up for so long in the Hive. And now that Kenya's not pregnant . . ."

Chloe rolled her eyes. "Yeah, yeah. We get it Kane. You don't need to spell it out." She ripped off a piece of tasset.

"Here, Barney. Want a piece?" Barney scrambled up and stepped toward the tidbit. He stopped and looked longingly back at Echo. Eyeing the goody, he licked his lips, but, with another look back at Echo, returned to her side to curl up. He nestled in closer to the creature without taking his eye off the treat. Echo slipped her arm around the little white dog's neck then sat up to wobble over to retrieve the goody and offer it to a grateful Barney.

"They really love one another, don't they?" Kenya asked.

Scotty watched his two favorite buddies as he chewed his lunch, nodding his head. "Never seen anything like it before. It's an odd pairing, but I'm happy for them both."

Kane changed the subject. "Looks like the weather might give us a turn. The leaves are falling from some of the trees."

"Don't worry, Johno said these acacia trees only grow in dry, warm climates. I don't imagine it gets too cold around here at any time of the year. I sure hope he's right. I don't relish what six inches of snow would do to our crops."

Kane leaned back, scanning their hard work that now covered five acres. Five acres of shimmering fruit trees and long rows of healthy vegetables and mystery plants supplied from Oolaha. They estimated they would lose 15 percent of all crops to hungry wildlife. That number would rise sharply when they released the Hive wildlife.

Their biggest concern was keeping the elephant herd out of the field. They hoped to rely on Echo to communicate the need for them to find their own food sources. Hardly a chore in their new environment, which supported such a wild variety of conifers and deciduous trees.

Most of the edible fruit, vegetables, and nuts had been harvested from the Hive. The survivors had banded together three months ago to help Netty can everything and move it to a root cellar behind Dezi's kitchen. It had only taken four men a week to dig the vital storage and install a door. Most of the survivors marveled at Netty's forethought to keep the canned supplies hidden until just this moment.

"Do you guys have any idea why the wildlife was missing when we first surfaced? When we lost the keepers?" Chloe asked.

Scotty wrapped up the covering of his tasset, tossing it toward the box. "I don't know, babe. But I guess it had something to do with whatever took the keepers." No one mentioned the fact that the body of the second keeper had vanished while Abby had gone for help.

"I think the native wildlife is just as afraid of the thing as we are."

A golden aura stabbed at Scotty's mind. "You will learn to cope with danger just as other life has learned, Brother. We are watched."

That got Scotty's attention. He grinned at Echo. "I know, the Womb watches us all."

"Yes, but the Womb is not the only watcher."

"Exactly what do you mean, Echo?"

But Echo would say no more, tucking herself and Barney closer to Caesar.

Kane yawned and wrinkled his nose. "Now that Echo says it, I've had that weird feeling now and then. The last few days, I think. Just a prickle on my neck as if someone's standing behind me and watching."

Kenya fluffed her hair. "Are you sure it wasn't me, babe? You know I love to watch you. Even with your clothes on." Kane's face turned color as Chloe and Scotty burst out laughing.

"Come on. I'm not telling you guys anything anymore." Kane stood up. "Let's get back to work. Isn't the Kreyven going to make our irrigation trench today?"

"Yeah, Wil said it'll come from the Hive's water supply. The Kreyven will tunnel through the hill, giving a natural path to the well we dug. Thank heavens we won't need to lug water anymore. I think we're close to being self-sufficient."

Scotty stood, flexed his tail, and stretched his wings to their full, glorious span. "Ahh, it's so good to be out in the open. I feel like I can breathe. And the stars. I forgot how awesome they look at night."

Chloe linked her arm through his as he folded his wings tight to his body. "Tonight will be our first night under the stars. Dezi has a cookout planned."

"I can't wait to get our housing assignments tonight," Kenya said.

"This will be the last night we sleep in the Hive. Tomorrow begins the release of our animals." Scotty shook his head. "I don't know how we're going to make this work. Wil better have some good ideas to share."

"Come on, Scotty. We need to get back to the fields. Why don't you and Kane go check to see if the Kreyven has shown up? Kenya and I will clean up here and catch up with you."

Scotty and Kane hurried off to leave the girls to return the remains of their lunch to Dezi's kitchen. Echo and Barney strolled after them, leaving Caesar behind with the girls. Gathering the remains, Kenya chatted merrily about her plans to decorate the baby's room. "Do you think it matters what colors I use? I just can't find much pink cloth in the store room."

Kenya turned to Chloe and watched her sit under the acacia tree. "What's wrong, chickey?"

Chloe rested her head on her knees then raised her head, wiping at a tear. "Don't mind me, Kenya. It just gets the best of me sometimes. We're very happy for you and Kane. It just that . . ."

Kenya's face fell. "Oh, chickey, I'm so sorry. Sometimes I'm just plain thoughtless." She moved toward the acacia tree and immediately froze.

"Chloe?"

Her head rested back on her knees.

"Chloe. I'm going to ask you to not move a muscle."

Caesar padded closer, a wicked growl announcing his presence.

Chloe took that moment to raise her head and change her position, frightening the timber rattlesnake that had surfaced from its den while they ate. It struck hard and lightning fast.

"Oh my God." Kenya screamed as Caesar lunged to Chloe. In one breath, the rattlesnake went back to its den, leaving Caesar hissing and sputtering at Chloe's side.

Kenya ran to her and dragged her away.

"Chloe, doll. Are you okay?" She frantically tore at Chloe's shirt, exposing the spot on her chest where the snake had bitten her.

"Kenya, Kenya . . . stop. I'm fine . . . I think." Chloe felt around, breathing heavily.

"Easy . . . breathe slower." The girls hung tight to one another, Caesar pacing in agitation.

When Chloe had her breathing under control, she held up Scotty's gold coin that still hung around her neck. She examined it closely.

"I think this is what saved me. I don't have a scratch on me." She glanced up at Kenya. "Let's keep this to ourselves. I don't want to upset Scotty. He hates to let me out of his sight as it is. I forgot Scotty told me this area used to be called Snake Hill."

She picked up the box from lunch. "Let's get out of here. We'd better tell the others that we spotted a rattlesnake. But promise me you won't say any more. I'm just starting to feel comfortable with this new confidence. I can come and go as I please, yet Scotty is always afraid something might get me. We still don't have a full handle on the new wildlife here." She turned to point to Caesar.

"What actual harm will come to us, anyway, with that huge beauty around?" She wrinkled her brow; her short, dark hair swinging with her words as she admired Caesar's vibrant colors, the sun making his coat gleam. "Hmm, shouldn't he be with Scotty?"

Kenya rubbed her arms. "Let's just get out of here, chickey. That snake gave me the creeps. It figures that the creepy crawlers would survive the bombings." Throwing one last look back to the rocks near the acacia tree, they headed to Dezi's kitchen, Caesar following, silent and calm.

As they made their way through the new settlement, Caesar stopped, the girls unaware. He padded to the edge of the settlement to stare unblinkingly at a distant band of trees and wild hedges. From deep in his throat came a mashed growling. A sapling moved and all was silent. Caesar slowly turned away, the hair along his marvelous withers still raised and bristling.

"Pass me the tapod." Clyde held out his hand to accept the survivors' favorite spice that Dezi had managed to improve with the addition of a new fuzzy nub he had found growing on the east side of a strange tree near the newly-dug well.

Whenever anything needed to be tested for safety before consuming, Dezi presented it to Baby. The survivors would often see Dezi and Baby roaming through the woods and the fields picking all manner of edible surprises.

"Clyde, aren't you full yet? I need to clear the tables and get ready for Cobby and Wil's announcements." Salina nudged Jennifer, prompting the quiet woman to help.

"Bring me back some tea, Salina," directed Clyde, his tired bones resting heavily from a difficult job on the last roof. "I hope this is a short talk tonight. I'm beat."

Salina bent down to give him a hug. "I'll hurry everyone along and we can sneak away early. I'll just let Bonnie and Peter know. I want to give my grandbaby a hug."

As Salina cleared the tables with help from Jennifer and Karen, Crystal poured tea for all. It wasn't long before Cobby rose, handing their baby over to Karen.

Salina watched as Cobby approached Wil and leaned down for a discussion. Wil stretched, taking his place at the head of the first table. All eyes rested on his golden glow, undimmed by the setting sun.

When the conversations and joking had finally stopped, Wil began.

"Before I turn this meeting over to Cobby, I need to inform you all that Netty, Baby, Jose, and Abby and I will be leaving."

There was no reaction from the survivors.

"Where you planning to go, Wil?" Clyde's natural curiosity carried to the front of the room. "You headed to the city?"

Wil scanned the faces around the tables. "I'm sure you all realize that you've become self-sufficient." He turned to Cobby and nodded. "I was going to leave it to Cobby to announce, but the dwellings are now finished. You've only to decide who wants to live where."

Clapping broke out among the survivors.

"So it's time that I need to let you know—within one week we'll be leaving for Oolaha."

"When you coming back?" shouted Johno.

Wil looked down, his radiant eyes closed. "We won't be coming back," he whispered softly.

Salina looked over to Netty, who had her arms around a frightened Abby. She walked up to Wil as if a trance. "Is this what you want?"

Startled by Salina's challenge, Wil countered. "It's not about what we want, Salina. It's about our duty. We're needed elsewhere. You no longer need us."

Salina faced Cobby. His face drooped, drained of color. "Did you know about this, Cobby?"

His eyes watering, he looked back at Netty and Abby. She heard him whisper, "No."

Johno stumbled from his table, overcome with surprise. "You can't leave us, man. We need you."

Slowly, the survivors turned their attention to where Hud and Ginger Mae sat with Daisy. It took a few minutes before they realized they were the center of attention. Ginger Mae flew to her feet, pulling her daughter with her. "No! I will not allow it. My daughter is not going with you."

Daisy squirmed in her mother's grip.

"Hud. Tell them. They can't have her."

Hud stood, his sympathetic face telling all he had been waiting for this to happen. Wrapping his arms around his wife, he held her close as Daisy slipped away to join Netty and Abby at their table, her new physical changes looking normal in their presence.

"I'm a grown woman, mother. We've been over this before. This is my destiny. You and Hud need to lead your lives without me."

"Now calm down, everyone." Wil tried to silence the crowd. "You'll have time to get used to the idea. Now let me turn this over to Cobby."

The crowd erupted with questions. Cobby swiped at his own eyes as he shook off the deluge of demands. "Hold on. Hold on. One at a time. First let me say, everyone needs to bring anything they want to salvage from the Hive down here in the next few days. We'll draw numbers to assign shelters to each family unit. I assume you men want to stay together?"

The remaining keepers all nodded in agreement.

"The animals will start leaving the Hive tomorrow. Wil, Netty and Abby will handle that. They should all be free by tomorrow night. The cats first. I've been told they'll quickly disperse into the wild to look for their own territories, except for the moms with young cubs. They'll look for cover close by until the cubs can travel. We'll continue to offer supplemental feedings on the outskirts of our compound, as far out as practical.

"Many of the animals will choose to stay nearby. The primates, our birds, most of the dogs, Tulip and her many litters. Dezi, you keeping Chance nearby?"

"In the kitchen with me at night," he answered.

"Then we have the goats and camels. We'll get this all worked out. The only possible problem will be Caesar and Tobi. I doubt Caesar has any plans to leave Scotty. Tobi is another matter, right Johno?"

Johno shrugged. "Tobi will do what she wants to do."

Unexpectedly, Jennifer spoke up. "Why is Scotty staying here? He's an Elder."

"Eh, Jennifer? I'm right here. If you have a question about my choices, why don't you ask me?" Scotty stood mystified, looming large over Jennifer, his wings spread wide in the falling darkness that was lit only by lanterns.

"Well, I don't see why you need to stay. We don't need you here. You should leave with your own kind."

He turned on her, aghast at her dismissive words. "My own kind? You are my own kind. You are *all* my own kind. I refused to leave my home, Chloe, or my friends. Where's this coming from, Jennifer? What's your problem?" Scotty's voice grew louder and louder.

Clyde rushed to her side. "She doesn't mean nothing by it, Scotty. She doesn't understand." He lowered his voice. "She's just not the same since the Time of Seth."

"And take your little creature with you." Jennifer's voice slithered out another attack.

"You better get a handle on her, Clyde. Echo doesn't deserve this."

From the spot on the ground that the dogs, Caesar, Chance, Baby and Echo had chosen to claim, Echo stood. Her aura hit them all. "Danger, my Brother, we are watched."

Wil and Cobby beckoned for Abby and Netty, who joined them to scan the sky. Echo's aura quickly clarified.

"Danger comes not from the sky. Danger comes from the ground."

Peering into the gloom, they heard a twig snap. Netty and Abby stepped forward, their horns swirling with steaks of gold red and black, and prepared to open. They stepped away from each other to open their wings; long, golden hair streaming and lion tails switching high overhead.

A voice pierced the darkness. A woman's voice. "Hello? Please don't shoot. We come in peace." And into the light stepped the first glimpse of humans the survivors had seen in over ninety years.

They counted half a dozen. Three women in the lead, a solitary man, then two more men in the back. They were dressed from head to toe in rags, but looked to be healthy, the men on the portly side. And, except for the two men in the rear, they were old, very old. The tallest of the women carried a rifle. She stepped forward, her eyes blazing at the sight of the Elders.

"I want to speak to your leader." She looked around, spotting Cobby, Johno, and Clyde, who stepped forward.

"We have no leader here. All are equal," Johno announced. The man behind the three women stepped forward.

"Can we please have a word with someone other than your token black dude?"

The strange woman recoiled, and one of the others yanked him behind them.

The tall woman spoke again. "Please forgive my brother's rudeness. I'm looking for anyone that can tell me about a relative of ours."

Wil stepped forward, the strangers shrinking back as his wings rippled and his tail flexed.

"Madam, I am quite sure we know nothing of your relative. Can we inquire as to how you managed to survive the bombs? Where do you hail from?"

The tall woman stood speechless, staring at Wil as her face began to crumble. She swayed on her feet, clearly overcome.

Cobby swiftly ran to support her with a chair. "Water. Karen . . . get me some water," he shouted.

Carefully holding a cup of water to her mouth, she drank even as she tried to wave him off. "Thank you. That's fine . . . I'm fine. It's just . . . the disappointment."

The members of her party gathered around on the ground. Netty approached. "May we offer you something to eat?" She turned to Dezi. "Any more of your pie out of the oven, yet?"

Dezi jumped up and ran to the kitchen shouting to Jennifer to give him a hand.

The newcomers eagerly chewed pieces of Dezi's fruit pies. As Salina passed out mugs of tea, the tall woman remarked, "I see you have no problem growing fruit. Neither do we."

"I know," Netty answered. The woman glanced up at Netty in surprise.

"You know? What do you mean, you know?" Netty remained silent. The rest of the survivors, sensing tension, began to stir.

The tall woman handed her plate to Wil and stood to face Netty. "Just exactly who are you?"

More silence from Netty.

A shout came from one of the survivors. "What the hell is going on here? Do you know these people, Netty? Do you mind clueing us in here?" Clyde's loud and demanding voice carried to all in the clearing.

"They are just survivors like us. Nothing more," explained Netty. "We learned decades ago that some in their starving group had developed unsavory . . . habits . . . that preyed on the vulnerable infants in their group."

The tall woman brought her hand to her chest. "How did you know of that? It was never proven. My mother told me in confidence. I demand you tell me what is going on here. What kind of creatures do you harbor here? Are you the spawn of the Devil?" The tall woman signaled her people and all fell to their knees as she led them in a prayer.

"Dear Lord, Father our God, please deliver us from danger. I have led us blindly in my search for answers to my mother's delusions. I pray you spare us and guide us back home through your heavenly embrace."

"Stop."

Those praying looked up in shock.

"You pray to a false God." Wil towered over the newcomers, his tail snapping angrily. "We are the ones that provided you with the means to grow food."

At a sound from the survivors at the tables, Wil turned around, guilt in the slump of his shoulders. Clyde stepped forward. "More secrets, Wil? You knew there was other people alive and didn't think to tell us?"

"Clyde, please don't start now. We'll explain all of this later."

The tall woman stood slowly, shock draining her face of color. "Clyde? Your name is Clyde? No . . . it couldn't be. You're too young."

Wil and Clyde threw each other a look. Clyde stepped closer to the tall woman, emotions rippling across his bulky face, confusion and doubt reigning. "Madam, what is your name?"

The woman paused at the unexpected question. "Lorna. My name is Lorna, and this is my brother, Seth."

A strangled gasp from the survivors pierced the air, then an eerie wail emanated from one of the tables. Everyone watched as Jennifer stood, shaking. Her eyes glazed with saliva dribbling from the corners of her mouth. "Aaaaaaaa," she shrieked. "Noooooooooo."

Clyde scooted behind her as she slowly made her way to the newcomers as if sleepwalking. Her hands flexed spasmodically.

"Baby, what's the matter? It's okay, Jennifer. It's okay, I'm here, Grandpa's here. Salina . . . help me."

Jennifer approached the newcomers, her hands held in front of her as her head jerked from face to face, seeing no one. "Grandma . . . help me. Seeeeth."

Salina ran forward, wrapping her arms around Jennifer as the tall woman backed away, eyes wild and frightened.

Clyde grabbed the woman by the shoulders.

"Who are you? Where did you get those names? What are you trying to pull on us?" Clyde was restrained as the woman began to cry, Cobby and Johno pulling him off the terrified woman. Netty pushed her way through the throng around her, guiding her back to her chair.

"Mama was right all along," the woman sobbed. "My poor momma." The cries were filled with deep anguish and pain.

Netty stood still as the woman's tears fell, slowing with exhaustion and gulps of air as she brought herself under control. Quietly, the woman began to talk, her face down, her voice flat.

"My mother was the leader of our tribe. She managed to take control from the first brutal leaders who enslaved our women. Women they kidnapped from their families during the chaos of the bombing about a century ago.

"My mother is a legend. She prayed for freedom and equality. She said if her grandpa couldn't find her, she would go to him. On Lily Pond Road. He had a sanctuary where crops were grown and afflictions were cured." The tall woman's face rose slowly, her brother moving forward, a look of astonishment directed at his sister.

Bitterly, the woman continued, "She died before we moved out of our shelter at the Franklin Mines. But I never forgot." She stared at

Clyde. "You ask who I am. My name is Lorna Calloway Benjamin. My mother was Suzy Calloway Benjamin."

It was Clyde's turn to cry as the woman's story unfolded and Jennifer let out a scream. "Suuuuzzzy. We need to save Suuuuzzzy." With that, she fell into a dead faint.

Chapter 15

It had only been three days since the return from what Lorna referred to as her Aunt Jennifer's home on Lily Pond Road, and Seth felt kicked in the stomach with betrayal. By his mother—that really hurt. And by his sister—to be expected.

Now he understood the real reasons for his lack of success in the tribe. They were all plotting against him. His whole life. Lafe had been right. You had to grab while the grabbing was good. Before your own blood kicked you in the teeth with their selfish plots and plans to demean and use you. That sadistic bitch, Lorna. She was probably laughing right now.

Seth rolled over on his dingy bed, pounding the filthy covers impotently.

Why couldn't he have been born in the Hive instead of the Franklin Mines where his mother had been exposed to the virulent winds that had given him his gimp hand? He softly stroked the fused fingers of his desiccated claw, bitter tears falling to soak his bed as he thought about the tales of his mother's beast which had helped hand her the leadership of the tribe. It should have been Lafe. Seth's bitterness threatened to explode, his head shouting with the pain as he tried to massage it away.

What a bunch of chumps. The beast had turned out to be some kind of servant of something they called the Womb. What the fuck? He was now supposed to believe that?

His head reeled with the lies they expected him to swallow. The tribe's crops had been secretly planted by the beast and the funky golden creatures that had wings like the humans. They called them the Elders. *They must take me for a fool.*

The only revelation that stymied him was the man named Clyde's claim to be his great-grandfather. He looked like he was a few years younger than himself and Lorna.

Yeah, Lorna. His stomach contracted with pent up anger and hatred, bile looking for a place to overflow.

The stupid bitch had swallowed it all. He had been forced to watch them all hover over her as she hugged Clyde and the young girl named Jennifer, who had slowly recovered. *If the girl would just stop her sniveling. How in the world could she be their aunt? The only thing she looked good enough for was as a toy for the boys.*

He grinned at the thought of the small pleasure, making his dick ache in his pants. Releasing it, he distractedly stroked, wondering if he should wait for Andrew. He felt like punishing someone and Andrew was such a willing victim. Trying to think about Andrew's soft lips on him was hopeless. The harder he tried, the more his hostility toward the new people returned.

How in the world would his plans to take over the tribe work out now? As the evening had come to its conclusion, Seth had found himself alone in the dark catching suspicious eyes glancing his way. What the fuck? The rest of his people had either gone back to their temporary camp or joined in conversations with the new people. But no one had bothered with him.

He had overheard Clyde and one of the winged Elders propose that they join forces on Lily Pond Road. Seth had to admit their dwellings looked a hell of a lot more substantial than those back at the mines. It should all be his, anyway.

He was Doc Benjamin's son! *Lafe, where are you when I need you so?*

Pulling his hand from his pants, he had a thought. As he had sat ignored in the darkness, he had felt eyes studying him. Squinting into the gloom. he had caught glows from the orbs of the two winged nightmare creatures that sat with the dogs. One in particular had been curled up with a white dog's head on its lap. He had noticed the dog stuck to the creature like glue. It was clear they held a favored place in the hierarchy, as several times the Elders showed deference to the creatures.

A germ of an idea began to form in his brain; a passing wish that drew power from the demonic force of his hatred. If he couldn't win the tribe just yet, why should Lorna be handed this opportunity to make hay out of the probable Lily Pond merger? She would only gain more power, defeating his plans for ever.

What if he were to kill one of the winged golden nightmares? The image of his newfound harpoon danced in his head. If it worked in the water, why not on land or in the sky? He wondered how fast the golden bugger could fly.

If he was successful, and he made it appear that Lorna was the culprit, the merger would be postponed, maybe even cancelled. The thought of the chaos and distrust that would be directed toward the tribe by the new people warmed his heart.

Would there be retribution? A battle perhaps? Seth preened. He had always fancied himself a general that could lead troops into battle. He sat up abruptly, pounding his claw into his fist. *By God, I think I'm back in business.*

Chapter 16

Lorna sat with Clyde and Salina, her arm around Jennifer as they watched the last of the animal release. It was near dinnertime, and Dezi and Crystal were carting food to the tables to feed the hungry wranglers.

Bonnie sat astride Tobi as they encouraged the huge skittish herd to move along toward the old swimming hole at the rear of the field.

The cats had long departed, breaking for freedom and slinking off into the bushes. Scotty and Kane lugged the last of the feed for various animals to pre-arranged staging areas far from the settlement with Nettie's well-used cart.

Dezi crawled on the ground with Maya on his back. The little Elder screamed with delight as she rode her new horsey around the tables.

Lorna and Jennifer laughed as Kimir regaled them with the antics and obstacles of the now thousands of beloved creatures as they first tasted freedom.

It had been a long day of tears and happy smiles as Clyde's fragmented family took the entire day to get to know one another. There was so much to tell . . . so much pain and loss . . . so much horror.

The difficulties of the truth about Seth and Suzy's kidnapping had taken their toll on all of them. But the joyous healing was well under way. They were all alive . . . safe . . . and optimistic about the future.

Lorna filled the blanks in with what little she could and explained the dangers of their new territory, including that of the flamer.

"Clyde, I have a special favor to ask, if I may." Lorna shyly turned to her great-grandfather. "I'm sure you noticed how Seth hangs back and fails to join in."

Clyde visibly tensed at the mention of Seth's name.

"He has a debilitating complex over the deformity he was born with. He hides his hand, but it's difficult for others not to stare and be put off by it. Most of us in the tribe are used to deformities by now, but Seth can't seem to get over it. It caused many . . . difficulties . . . in our relationship as children, and I fear he's still nursing a grievance." She held out her two perfectly-formed hands.

"Since I now understand the principals of your healing tendrils, I was hoping . . . praying really, that if I spoke to Miss Netty, she might allow Seth to sleep in the Hive and have his hand healed. Just as mine was as a baby." Her voice pleaded as she added, "Miss Ginger Mae filled me in. I am honored by her sacrifice . . . giving me up and hurting for my mother. I'm grateful for the sake of my tribe, but . . ." Lorna's sad and wistful voice trailed hints of the preference she might have enjoyed had she grown up in the Hive with her family instead of the mines.

Clyde looked at Salina blankly, searching for an answer. Turning back to Lorna he said, "I don't see why not. It's no big deal. You'd better get him back here soon. The Elders are fixin to leave soon, and the Kreyven and Hive membranes will go with them and return to the Womb."

Clyde leaned in and lowered his voice as other survivors began to gather for dinner. "Why don't I go with you to talk to Wil and Netty after dinner?"

Lorna's eyes lit up with excitement. She stood and threw her arms around Clyde in a hug. "Thank you so much. You have no idea how much this will mean to Seth."

Salina reached out to rest her arm on the older woman. "We're happy to help, Lorna. It's the least we can do for one of Suzy's children. We're family."

Three hours later, the survivors and their guests sat around a huge bonfire in the middle of the settlement. Scotty and Kane had planned the surprise. As they carted food to the outer reaches of the settlement, they had scavenged wood and kindling for the celebratory fire which would mark the passage of their treasured wildlife into the real world that would become their home.

Many of the animals failed to go far. Lorna could discern the dark shapes of members of the elephant herd in the gloom. She watched a huge amount of dogs scatter themselves in and around the group, and a creature called a monkey skirted around looking for mischief.

Lorna had never even seen a dog in her lifetime as they had all been eaten long ago. She was understandably frightened when two large pit bulls named King and Queenie strolled by to give her a sniff.

Running to her rescue, an Elder named Jose gathered the pair. "They can't hurt you. They may look fierce, but they're as gentle as babes and as trustworthy as anything you could hope for." He leaned down to hug them to his chest, receiving a tongue washing for his efforts. He looked back over to Lorna, pure love for the big dogs in his reflective eyes as he cleaned his cheeks of the zealous traces of canine affection.

"They're part of our family." At the sound of a broken lawnmower, they stared across the fire. A tiny brown dog was leaping like a hot potato from group to group, finally settling down on a large brown and white dog named Penny. He made a bed in her deep, flowing feathers and promptly fell asleep. Next to the content dogs sat Scotty, Chloe, Kane and Kenya with their entourage of more dogs and the creatures called Echo and Baby. Of course, Echo lay possessively wrapped around the body of the curly-haired dog, Barney.

"What's the story of the golden creatures, Jose? Why are Echo and the white dog so inseparable?"

Jose eased down next to Lorna, folding his wings tight into his body. "No one's filled you in yet? That's such a long story. I don't how much Clyde and my mother told you, but let me fill in some of the holes."

Lorna started with surprise. "Your mother? Is Netty your mother?" Jose chuckled lightly.

"No, no, Salina. She's my mother. My stepmother really, but she raised me since I was very young . . . another long story." Jose broke off, his forehead knotted.

"Do you hear that?" Lorna looked around, seeing nothing out of the ordinary, just groups of survivors laughing and horsing around. She watched as Wil, Netty, Abby, and Scotty turned their faces to the sky. Jose stood up, concern puckering his face as he glanced toward Baby and Echo. The two golden creatures tottered to their feet, alert and expectant.

Listening deeply, Lorna began to panic as she picked up the sound of wings in the sky. The flamer! She jumped to her feet screaming. "We must hide. Run."

As she and her inner circle women leaned to run, Jose grabbed her around the waist. The sounds got louder and louder, Baby and Echo taking wing low over their heads, the dogs barking.

Everyone looked up to the sky to witness dozens of white four-legged creatures with tight curly hair flutter overhead, Baby and Echo in the middle, their wings beating in synchronization with the strange creatures.

"Relax. Echo says to relax." Jose sat her back down and took a seat next to her. They watched as the golden creatures dipped and swayed in the air as the oddly familiar-looking creatures greeted them. As if tired of play, the swarm took to the ground, everyone relaxing and waiting for an explanation.

Echo's dog, Barney, stood near the fire, every fiber of his small body taut with emotion, his tail wagging, tongue flickering and back legs doing their own harried assessment.

"Oh my heavens," exclaimed Jose.

Lorna scanned the circle, observing similar looks of amused astonishment. As she beheld Baby and Echo making such a fuss over the new creatures, it hit her.

With the exception of their more rounded bodies and vaguely reptilian heads, eyes that sat on each side of their skull and extended snouts that gave five or six inches to a steel-trap mouth, they looked just like dogs. Plump dogs with curly white hair, that looked just like the eager Barney, who vainly continued his eager prancing, anxious to be noticed.

And wings, of course. They wore well-muscled white wings, tight with short feathers curling back toward their tails, which wagged just like Barney's.

High-pitched whining could be heard from deep in Barney's throat as Baby and Echo pranced and fondled the new creatures, who preened and bowed to their attentions.

Netty joined the throng, letting the creatures jump on her and dance back as she lounged toward them. Her musical laughter rang loud in the darkness, the flames from the fire setting her long golden hair afire.

"Don't worry, anyone. These are nooglets. From Oolaha. The Womb sent them here to see if they would be an asset to the environment. Back on Oolaha, they are the most habituated creature on the planet. They learned long ago they could derive benefits for their species by intertwining themselves into the fabric of the Oolahans' lives." She lurched forward as Echo fell against her after an enthusiastic pounce from one of the nooglets.

Without warning, the nooglets took to the air, followed by Echo. An aura hit all the survivors, including Lorna and her inner circle.

"Don't worry, Brothers and Sisters. I will return. I have been called."

And they were gone, leaving Lorna shaken and astonished, her hands to her head with wonderment, questioning her own senses.

Baby tottered over to Wil, hands out begging to be lifted into his arms.

Lorna gazed at Barney as he stood silent and stunned, his tail curled tight and his head downcast. She followed him with her eyes as he crept away from the warmth of the fire to find solitude on the fringes of the gloom, his friend, the ever-present moon, vanished behind nocturnal clouds.

Quickly dismissing him from her thoughts, she turned back to Jose to urge him to begin his stories, the din of the happy survivors returning to its normal clamor.

It wasn't long before the survivors decided to retire to bed. The comfort of their new dwellings may not be as relaxing and luxurious as the Hive, but they belonged to each of them, fashioned from their own labors, their own hopes and their own plans for the futures of their families.

The various primate tribes bedded down on their respective trees, chosen by the troop as the most beneficial for nocturnal safety. A distant chuff echoed from afar, alerting Tobi as her herd rested for the next day. Heaps of dogs bedded down in and out of shelters, alphas ever alert for the slightest sounds.

A hurt little dog named Barney trudged alone in the woods. Forlornly hoping to pick up the smell of his beloved Echo, who had not returned, the confused canine instead followed the human trail left by Lorna and her inner circle women as they began their overdue trek back to the Franklin Mines.

Seth stood before the gathering of the tribe. In Lorna and most of her inner circle's absence, he had called an emergency meeting of the tribe to announce his plans over the objections of the rest of the inner circle.

Scanning the faces of the worked-up crowd, he glowed with satisfaction.

Only a born leader like him would be able to pump them up like this. Keeping his deformed hand inside his layers of rags, he raised his good fist high over his head.

"We too can have finery to adorn our backs like the Others do. We too can have magic that will heal us as they did my misguided sister as an infant. We too can rule the power of their beast as my mother claimed to so long ago." He stalked the stage like a political orator of bygone days, promising riches and the easy living of the Others. Unfortunately, human nature had failed to evolve far in the last century as his promised goodies had them eating out of his hands.

"Are . . . you . . . with . . . me?" Seth shouted with maniacal rage. He could feel himself get hard as the crowd shouted back his name. Now all he needed to do was capture one of the golden creatures. That was the surest way to demonstrate his powers. With the creature as his captive, he would be successful in his negotiations to secure access to the loot that remained in the Hive. If Lorna refused to go along, his harpoon would speak for him.

Searching the screaming tribe, his eyes lit on Andrew who stood wetting his greedy lips at the edge of the stage. Seth felt his erection strain, begging for release. His glittery eyes signaled to Andrew, then he left the stage amid chants of his name, the voices mostly those of the men. Ignoring the significance, Seth hurried passed Andrew to hasten their beckoning moment of hot primal sex.

The next morning, Seth and his men set out for Lily Pond Road. His men dragged the harpoon behind them, slowing their progress to a crawl. Seth trudged along, wondering what his next step would be, distracted by the long night with the subservient Andrew.

And where was Lorna? She'd been due back days ago. His blood boiled at the royal treatment that had no doubt seduced her into delaying her departure from Lily Pond Road. He pulled his claw from behind its protective rags.

I bet they wouldn't treat her so royally if she had one of these. His claw twitched as if it could hear his thoughts. Shoving it back under his clothes, he continued on, puffs of dry red dust layering his worn boots. He took a swig of water from his bag, his parched throat adding to his discomfort and misery.

Through a stand of trees, his scout stealthily emerged. His entourage stopped, the harpoon gun catching up slowly and nosily. Seth turned, his face hostile with annoyance as the clatter of the heavy wagon reached his ears.

"You might want to take a breather. Lorna and her inner circle are up around the bend, headed this way," announced the scout.

Seth clenched his jaw. *Great.* Signaling his men, he motioned for them to join him. He took stock of their weapons. A few old rifles, some chains and Andrew's machete. His claw tingled as he enjoyed the sight of Andrew stroking it absentmindedly in the sun.

It didn't take Lorna long to arrive. Confusion and the hot sun prevented her from seeing clearly as she rounded the bend and was confronted by the sight of her brother.

"Seth. What are you doing here?"

He approached his sister carefully, not wanting to alarm her. His men circled around her back to the rest of the women.

"Here, Lorna, you must be thirsty." He held out his bag of water. As she reached out to the bag, Seth's men seized the other women before knocking them to the ground and relieving them of any weapons.

Seth reached over to grab Lorna's gun at her belt. She slowly lowered Seth's bag of water from her wet mouth.

"What do you think you're going to do with my gun, Seth?" She pierced his eyes with her own, her glacial reflection goading him with its dismissiveness.

Cocking the pin on her revolver, he moved swiftly to the women who lay on the ground and pulled the trigger on each one before his shocked men could blink.

Lorna stood frozen in shock as the red dirt displayed the spattered brain matter of her most trusted confidantes.

Seth signaled his men, who quickly surrounded a defiant and uncomprehending Lorna.

"What's gotten in to you, Seth? There was no need for this!"

Seth slowly circled Lorna, his nerves on fire, his claw twitching a dance inside his rags.

"Get on your knees, Lorna."

Her eyes filled with confusion. "So you're going to kill me, too?"

Seth laughed briefly; short and crisp. "Get on your knees, now."

Lorna slowly lowered herself to the dirt, never taking her eyes off Seth.

"You didn't need to do this, Seth. I had a surprise for you. Something special. I just wanted you to be happy."

Seth eyes flared his mouth in a grimace. "You just want to belittle me, just as you always have. You with your perfect hands."

Lorna sat back on her heels, comprehension dawning. "Is that what this is about? Your hand?"

Seth removed his deformed claw from its hiding place. He reached out to his sister, slowly drawing his claw down the side of her face. "Is this what you call a hand, dear, favored sister?" Seth's eyes glittered with fever as Lorna flinched when the claw caressed her face. Inflamed, he reached for Andrew's machete. "Hold her down."

Lorna struggled and screamed as Seth's men stretched her out on the dirt path. Seth loomed high over her, blocking the sun and, with one strong stoke of the machete, he removed her right arm, four inches down from the elbow.

"Whoops, I guess I got more than I planned." He giggled manically. Lorna lay in shock, her heartbeats spilling her life's blood out on the hot red dirt, staining it black.

Before anyone could do anything further, a rustle was heard in the bushes near the bend in the road. The men drew their guns. Seth squinted, shading his eyes with his claw.

"Come out of there," he shouted. The bushes rustled again and then parted, revealing a small curly, white-haired dog, his face eager, his tail wagging.

Seth's mouth split into an expansive, vulpine grin as he recognized the lonely Barney, who had been following the human scent of Lorna and her now deceased inner circle.

Chapter 17

Back on Lily Pond Road, Echo had still not returned. The Elders were in the midst of preparing for their departure, and Jose stood with Scotty and his gang.

"I can't leave until I know Barney's safe. There's no reason we can't delay for a few more days." His words were laced with anxiety.

"I agree," chimed in Abby. They all looked up as Baby came wobbling toward them. His aura included them all.

"I will find My Barney for Sister Echo."

Chloe spoke up. "How will you know where to start, Baby? He could be anywhere by now. And it could be dangerous out there. I think we need to split up and start a search." Her worried face said what everyone else was thinking.

"Okay. How about Baby takes to the air and goes south while Chloe and I set out with Caesar toward the hills in the other direction? If he hears us, he'll come. He's probably hungry by now. We just better hope none of the cats have found his trail. There's no telling—"

Abby threw her arms around her brother. "Don't worry about that, kiddo. Barney won't wind up as a meal for any of our animals. I haven't removed their implants yet. I needed them to become more familiar with their new environment and scatter further before I called the implants back."

Kane spoke up. "I think you need me to go with you, bro. We can't have you getting lost on us." Kane good-naturedly ribbed his best friend.

Scotty refused to rise to the bait, his concern over Barney overriding everything. "No, you stay here in case Echo comes back. Make sure you tell her I have plans to have a few words with her. It's just not like her to be so insensitive. Especially to Barney." Scotty

172

shook his head with dismay. "Promise you won't leave until we come back with Barney, Ab."

Abby rubbed his arm for reassurance. "We promise, hon. If Netty and Wil can't wait, they can go on without us. Although I doubt they'll leave without Baby." She gave Chloe a quick hug. "Maybe you should take Jose with you, Chloe. Your brother can look after you." Abby quirked a questioning eyebrow at Jose.

"They don't need me, Abby. Scotty and Chloe can handle it on their own. Besides, I need to stay here to look after things."

Abby laughed. "Look after things? What's to look after?"

Jose shifted his eyes to the ground after a long scan of her face. "Never mind. Let's just get the search party off."

Abby stared at Jose, confusion and reluctance lurking in her expression. Closing her mouth, she urged everyone to come back safe.

With that, Baby's aura faded as he fluttered up in the air and flew south.

"I'm going to grab a knife from Dezi's kitchen," Chloe announced.

Chloe slammed into the kitchen to find Dezi sitting at a table with a book open, his shoulders hunched in concentration. "I need to borrow one of your longest and sharpest knives, Dezi."

He looked up from his reading, casually slipping the book in his apron. "Bring it back in one piece, please." He handed her a long wicked carving knife, tapered to a razor edge.

"I don't think I've ever seen you read before, Dezi. What caught your fancy?"

"Nothing you'd be interested in, my dear. Now be careful with this. It's very sharp." He handed her a cloth bag to slip it into. "Just to keep the blade from cuttin' you.

"I hear you're going lookin' for Barney. Remember to be home for lunch. And keep your eyes peeled, we don't know what's in those woods yet."

Chloe threw him a kiss and hurried out the door.

*

Chloe, Scotty and Caesar reached the edge of the settlement. The morning sun beat lightly on their eyes as they searched for an easy way through the brush to head for the hills.

"I think if we make it to the base, we can climb up and see around the valley. We might even spot Echo and her friends. We could sure use their help to find Barney. I'm very surprised at her. I thought she'd be back last night." Scotty's disappointment showed in the tone of his voice.

"I know what you mean, babe. I'm just as surprised Barney took off. It's not like the rest of the dogs rejected him. I guess he has one true love and that's that. I sure wish he'd come to us first."

Chloe stepped aside as Caesar plowed through the bush, leaving a massive hole for them to slip through.

"Barr . . . ney," Scotty shouted.

"Barr . . . ney," Chloe echoed.

They chomped through the underbrush for the next hour, finally breaking through with Caesar's help. The sun began to heat up, forcing them to stop and catch their breath. They stood at the base of the first hill, now appearing craggier than it had from their settlement.

Scotty pulled detritus from Chloe's short hair as he examined the bramble cuts on her arms and legs. Caesar was covered in brambles and pieces of brown leaf litter which had caught in his magnificent fur. But Scotty was the worse for wear, his wings covered with burrs, feathers missing, and no longer sleek against his body.

He shook out his tail and tucked it back around his torso, his voice suddenly concerned. "I don't see any sign of Barney. I wonder why we haven't seen any wildlife? You'd think we'd have spotted some of our own." He scanned the trees, Chloe following his line of sight, their backs to the hill.

"Not even a bird. And I didn't see a single primate when we left the settlement. We must have at least a hundred. Where can they be?"

She puckered her forehead in wonder. "Do you notice how quiet it is, Scotty?"

A whoosh from behind forced them to turn, just as a giant streak of gleaming flame sunk its talons into both of Caesar's thick ribs, piercing him deeply and lifting him off the ground.

He roared with pain and struggled, Chloe screaming like a banshee.

As the flamer flew higher into the air with the six-hundred-and-fifty-pound tiger, Caesar panicked, flailing wildly and gouging the creature's leg. It instinctively released Caesar to send him plunging to his death.

With no thought for their own safety, Scotty and Chloe plunged back into the thick brush to Caesar's side. The poor cat was still breathing, steam rising off his bloody coat.

"Oh my God, Caesar," Chloe cried, throwing herself on top of him, Scotty kneeling at her side.

"Hey, big guy. Don't worry." He placed his hands on Caesar's steaming pelt to hopelessly stem the blood that still poured from his broken body. Caesar tried to lift his head, a broken groan escaping from his throat.

"Please don't leave us." Chloe's shoulders shook with tears, her eyes frantic. "Scotty, get your tail out. You can save him."

Before the words had left her mouth, Scotty's tail stood high, extruding the membrane which emitted the healing pressure that would save the iconic cat. Chloe clapped with delight as Caesar tried to right himself, faltering and crashing back to the ground.

He finally stood, chuffing softly and licking the blood from the side of his chest. All that was left from his nightmare was the smell of sulfur and Chloe's relieved tears.

Astonishingly, Caesar's hair bristled. He turned and snarled, then let loose with a deafening roar, his hot breath bathing Chloe in terror as she slowly turned to see the flamer seize an unsuspecting Scotty in its talons.

Time stood still as Chloe watched the only man she had ever loved rise high into the sky. She squinted her eyes, her hand blocking the searing sun as he flailed madly, disturbing the monstrous creature so much it reared its head back, screamed and brought its huge scaled bill down on Scotty's golden head, cleaving it in half. It then calmly flew away as Scotty struggled no more.

"Nooooooo." Chloe watched the bird disappear behind the crest of the hill. In shock, slowly sinking to the ground to silently curl up, she lay dazed.

Chloe lost track of time as she lay numb in the red dirt; grasses and weeds cocooning her small body. Her mind emptied of all thought as she willed herself to die, the blistering sun witness to her hopeless surrender.

Her ears vaguely registered the rustle of grasses through her miasma of pain and despair, unconcerned for her own safety. She fought the sensation of hot breath on her face which lay pressed sideways in the grass, unwilling to be drawn to reality.

The heavy weight of Caesar's paw slapped the side of her chest. She opened her eyes to stare into the face of the tiger, three inches from her own.

Silently and slowly, she closed her eyes again. Caesar crept another inch toward her, his hot breath demanding, his throat chuffing and still she lay unmoving. She felt the big cat rise, feeling pressure as he grasped her in his terrifying mouth and pulled her along the ground.

The dirt and weeds ground into her face, rocks riding under her inert form to leave bruises as Caesar pulled her up the hill. Unable to stand the pain any longer, her reaching hand stayed the relentless cat. He dropped his grip and sat quietly as she rose up, her face slack, her eyes unfocused.

Breathing shallow breaths, the sweet gamy odor of Caesar's pelt forced her stomach to rebel as she vomited in the grass. Tears slipped down her face as she slicked back her hair, which lay plastered with sweat against her feverish neck.

Caesar opened wide and let loose with an ear-splitting roar.

"Geesh . . . Okay, Caesar, I hear you."

The great cat watched as Chloe pulled herself together, comprehension flooding back into her face. She wiped her mouth with the back of her hand and stood looking up the hill, a glint developing in her eyes. Her hands searched for the cloth hooked to her belt, the carving knife still nestled inside and infusing her with strength.

Her eyes found those of the huge tiger. Caesar stared unblinking and stoic as she lost herself in the strength of his piercing gaze.

Together, they turned and began to ascend the hill, renewed purpose launching bitter anger through her veins. She knew just one thing. She must kill the flamer. She must avenge Scotty's death if she was to go on living herself.

She slipped her right hand under the cowl of her neckline to retrieve the chain that held the gold coin which had hung around her neck since she was sixteen. Scotty's gold coin . . . Netty's gold coin. She squeezed it tight, feeling a grateful tear course down her cheek.

It had been the fateful coin that had brought them this far. If Netty hadn't stolen it for revenge from her disgusting husband, Robert, it would never have been found by her Scotty. He would never have discovered Echo. He would never have met her on the beach in Sarasota. They would have all become victims of the bombs like the rest of the world.

She took the coin and raised it to her lips, her heart now inflamed with emotion. It would see her through her task; one more assistance with revenge. The coin would witness the death of the flamer and give her the strength she needed to complete the slaughter. Her heart beat stronger. It was almost as if she held a piece of Scotty in her hands. A piece that would stand witness to her retribution.

The hill became steeper as they neared the crest. The stench of carrion emanated down the hillside, evidence they neared its nest. Chloe unsheathed Dezi's evil carving knife, the blade glinting in the searing sun. Adjusting her grip, she crept slowly to the edge of the crest, Caesar's heaving breath assuring her of his assistance.

As their heads cleared the last of the crest, they feasted their eyes on the nest of the flamer. The flamer itself, nowhere in sight.

The nest sat protected by a copse of large rocks giving the interior a circumference the size of an automobile not seen since the bombs a century ago. Assorted bones stuck in the rocks cupping the nest, evidence of mama's housecleaning. She studied the bones and remains of previous meals, a half-eaten lion roasting in the sun and thick pools of drying blood sending waves of stench to abuse her stomach. Her heart beat faster as she wondered if the long bone near the lion carcass was human or animal. Her eager eyes slowed as she realized the thatch of golden feathers that littered the nest floor belonged to her beloved Scotty. She clutched at the few that clung nearest to her, tucking them into the cloth bag at her belt.

Bloodlust filled her breast as she gazed further into the nest. Two flamer hatchlings lay quiet amid the carnage, eyes shut and vulnerable, their red-scaled bodies not yet sporting the translucent feathers of their mother. They squatted exposed, their bodies no bigger than that of a full-grown chicken.

Chloe signaled Caesar to move forward. He didn't budge, his attention fully on her.

"Well, if you aren't going to help, can you at least watch for their mama?" she whispered.

The big cat stayed silent, detached and observant. Shrugging her shoulders and miffed, her rage at the loss of her lover overtook her hesitation. Lifting her legs over the thick edge of the nest, she lowered herself to the floor. Creeping along, she summoned all her strength to ignore the soft golden feathers she stepped on. Her targets beckoned.

When she reached the hatchlings, she stood up and her rage boiled over as she prepared to strike, the carving knife high over her head.

One of the hatchlings opened its eyes.

"Werrrk." The other hatchling opened its eyes to join in the call of its hungry sibling. "Werrrk."

Chloe stood suspended and ready to strike as the baby creatures watched her. They tried to jump toward her, but their strength had not yet matured enough to maneuver. Instead, one fell over in its awkwardness, encouraging the other to take a swipe at its nest mate, leaving a tiny drop of drawn blood.

"Hey. Don't do that." She lowered her arms as the creatures watched her, naïve in their fascination. Their huge eyes covered most of their faces as their still-growing beaks made them look as if drawn by a child with his first set of crayons.

She raised her arms once more, the carving knife suddenly heavy and vengeful in her hands.

"Werrrk."

Gritting her teeth, she cursed the fate that had brought the three of them within range of the deadly flamer family. Her arm slashed down to rest alongside her aching legs, covered in blood from the abattoir the flamer called its nursery

Dispirited, she turned to go. Caesar sat watching her from the edge of the nest, frozen and immobile, eyes only for her. He chuffed softly.

Sheathing her knife, she moved to climb out of the nest and hurry back to the settlement. How in the world would she be able to report the devastating news? How could she tell Abby?

Chloe and Caesar moved stealthily, retracing their steps through the foliage from their earlier trek. She examined broken branches. Had Scotty touched that one? Is that the one he stopped from snapping back at her? Her feet moved forward, one leaden foot at a time as her cracked lips ached for moisture, her saliva thin and pasty.

She remembered to look for Barney, but her efforts were halfhearted. She existed in a stupor; a zombie, the walking dead. Only the efforts of Caesar kept her moving. If she stumbled or halted, threatening to sink to her knees, Caesar growled threateningly, nudging her forward.

Before long, they reached the edge of the settlement. No one was in sight as she made her way to the center where most of the survivors gathered for dinner, their voices and laughter sounds from another lifetime.

Kenya was the first to spot them. Her scream alerted them all as Chloe and Caesar approached. She appeared as a sunburned wraith, sweat stained, filthy and smelling of death. Caesar appeared no better, his fur matted with burrs and dried blood.

"Oh my God. Chloe, what happened?" Kenya sat her down as Bonnie ran for water. Crystal offered her a cup of tea.

"You poor girl, where did you leave that man of yours?" Shirley glanced back toward the edge of the settlement as Caesar sat heavily at Chloe's feet.

"Hey, now." Crystal pushed him with her foot. "Johno, can you get this brute out of the way?" Johno rushed to feed the tired cat some water.

"Miss Chloe, why is Caesar not with Scotty?" His question was met with silence, her chin resting on her chest. The gathering crowd parted as Abby approached, Cobby rising as he glimpsed the fright on her face.

"Chloe, where's Scotty?" Abby's low voice, whispered out like a frightened fawn, wobbly and unsecure.

Chloe lifted her dirty face, her eyes full of the pain which spoke for the broken woman. She began to leak tears, her head moving from side to side in denial as the words refused to materialize.

Abby grabbed Chloe's shoulders, her fear transforming her into a hysterical Elder. Cobby, coming from behind, wrapped his arms around the escalating Abby.

"Shhh, Abby, give her a chance. She's traumatized." Cobby led Abby away, signaling for a pensive and anxious Jose to hold on to her.

"Dad, can we help?" Kane's worried face broke out in sweat. "I need to know where he is. What if he needs help? I can get it out of her."

Cobby searched his handsome son's face. "Okay, give it a try. Go easy." He slapped Kane on the back as he turned to approach Chloe, who had begun to sway in her chair. He knelt down in front of her.

"Hey, Chloe. It's me, Kane." He smoothed her dirty face with his hand, observing a flicker in her eyes.

"Kane." Her voice was little more than a whisper.

"What happened, honey?"

Chloe's eyes began to twitch and blink frantically. "The flamer . . ."

"The what?"

"The flamer, the flamer, flamer, flamer . . ."

Kane reached out and slapped her face. She stared at him in surprise and began to cry. He reached out his arms and she fell into them sobbing.

"Scotty's gone. The flamer attacked Caesar, lifting him into the air. He was too heavy . . . the monster dropped him. He was dying, so Scotty healed him. We . . . we weren't paying attention. The flamer came back . . . grabbed Scotty. He didn't have a chance." Chloe's heart-rendering story came out between her sobs. She reached into her cloth bag and removed the golden feathers, crushing them to her heart, as she recounted the rest of the tragedy to the survivors.

"I couldn't kill them. They were innocent. Their mother was just trying to live the life the Womb gave them." She looked up at the survivors for condemnation. None came.

"I'm sorry," she whispered.

More tears were shed as they turned to Abby, who stood crying in Jose's arms, Netty and Wil hovering in the background. Chloe stood and held her arms out to Abby. The two women slowly embraced, sharing the pain of the death of the man they both loved so deeply.

"Where's Echo? I need to talk to her very badly." Chloe's voice was tight, repressed anger focusing on the missing minion.

"She hasn't returned," said Abby.

Chloe opened her mouth to speak as the ground began to shake.

Abruptly, the earth burst open to announce the Kreyven, menacingly silent with streaks of light flashing through its gelatinous mass and emanating its identifiable odor of sulfur and raw organicness.

Swiftly, the Kreyven rose up in the air to hover over Netty and Chloe, dipping down to wind around one then the other. Before anyone could shout out, the Kreyven rose back in the air, Netty calm and Chloe straining, her fists pounding on the unfeeling mass. Then they were gone; sucked back down the hole in the ground as if they had never been there to begin with.

Chapter 18

Baby fluttered to the ground, tired and discouraged. Not finding Barney had displeased him. It had been a full day and night since he had set out to help Brother Scotty and Sister Chloe locate Sister Echo's treasure.

Deciding to walk for a while, Baby shuffled along a slight, beaten path; the stamped weeds revealing the rich red color of the soil. As Baby traversed the pathway, he reflected on the surprise that a mere dog could feel the power of rejection. It had been surprising enough to discover that Tobi and her elephant herd contained as many emotions in their brains as humans. Perhaps he should study the canines further.

He made a metal note to forward recommendations to the Womb. Echo was another matter. Perhaps it was the difference in their ages. Echo was still a mere babe, but should have known better by now. Baby nodded to himself. Well, maybe not. This was her first new world, after all. She could not be expected to realize a minion never leaves their charges or their partners on a new world. Too dangerous.

Perhaps the recommendation to the Womb had been a mistake. But he had thought the noogies would be a fitting choice for this new world. He had forgotten to factor in their shared memories. Of course Echo would have had an instantaneous attraction and fondness for the creatures. They were the favorite of minions everywhere.

But where did that leave Echo's poor rejected love, Barney?

Baby stopped to send his aura out to Brother Scotty to check on their progress. At this distance, only an Elder could hear his aura. An Elder with a close bond. Like the one he had with Sister Netty.

For some reason, he could find neither one. Baby rubbed his temples and tapped on the bridge of his nose. Trying again, he cast his aura. Maybe his relationship with Brother Scotty needed some work. Nothing. Reaching out to Sister Netty would produce results, but he feared she was nowhere on the planet. He had felt sure she would not leave without him.

Baby shivered as he suddenly felt small and lost without Sister. He wanted to go back and be with her.

Rounding a bend in the pathway, Baby came up with a start. Lying in the dirt were the bodies of three human women. The dirt surrounding them contained pools of their lifeblood.

The sight was so unexpected, Baby's mind spun. *Could it be?* He moved forward to examine the women, searching for signs that their deaths were not caused by man. Praying it was the work of a natural, hungry creature.

No luck. It was clear to Baby the damage had been wrought by another human. Only Homo sapiens killed for pleasure without eating the kill. His heart sank. This was very bad news. The Womb was sure to know of this by now. If humans wanted to kill themselves, so be it. But Baby's nerves turned to ice with the knowledge that a killer did not stop with one species.

He must hurry and find Barney. There would be a grave need for preparations. He must get back to the Hive as soon as possible.

Shuffling around the Sisters he saw footprints that had stepped in the life blood. Large footprints, and many of them.

No. Oh dear, no. Three smaller prints revealed themselves, clear as could be seen. A small dog . . . *Barney.*

He must have followed the new Sisters' trail after they had left the settlement. It would be natural for the rejected canine to seek out another source for attention, thought Baby.

Plowing forward, Baby skirted the body of the tall Sister, who sat apart in a pool of drying blood, her arm hacked off and missing.

Trying again, Baby sent his aura out to Brother Scotty and Sister Netty only to be met with a blank. Taking to the sky, Baby followed the pathway, hoping it would lead him to Barney and a quick trip back to the Hive.

Baby sat atop a flat roof near the square where most of the humans surrounded a small stage. A Brother was waving part of an arm in the air, screaming at the people who watched, Brothers cheering and Sisters adorned with fearful expressions.

As the Brother turned, Baby saw him wave his own arms. One arm ended in a fused and withered claw. Brother Seth; the quiet brooding sibling of the tall Sister. Could it be possible? Could he have killed the tall Sister?

Scanning the crowd, Baby's eyes latched on to a group of men off to the side. At their feet sat Barney, tied tightly to a large metal contraption the men leaned on. The contraption exhibited a projectile with a sharp, evil-looking, hooked end pointed toward his hiding place. Clearly a weapon of some sort.

Baby's antlers began to swirl, red and black streaks moving in rhythm as he devised a way to rescue Barney without involving the humans. They were no concern of his. But he knew full well if the need to protect himself arose, the humans wouldn't stand a chance.

Tentatively, his aura reached out to Barney. He watched as the dog startled then jumped, giving a ferocious show of enthusiastic barking. He sent another aura to calm the aroused dog as one of the Brothers kicked him viciously in the ribs.

As Baby witnessed the Brother laugh at Barney lying unmoving in the dirt, his anger escalated, his antlers flashing.

Stay calm, my little friend, I am here to take you back to Sister Echo.

Barney whined, his tail thumping as he looked toward Baby's rooftop.

"Hey. What's that? Up there on the roof. That light?" The humans turned to look as someone spotted Baby's swirling antlers, backlit by the sun and casting refractions down to the crowd.

Brothers ran toward the building even as Baby squatted down, his heart pumping madly. *No time, I must act now.*

Taking to the air, Baby flew toward Barney; his tail held high, extruding his healing membrane to send its pressure to the dog's injured ribs. He split an antler, sending a projectile to devour the restraints that bound the dog.

"Get ready to run Bar—" Baby felt something slam into him. It plowed through his chest and shoulder, pulling him from the sky to crash soundly to the ground, landing a few feet in front of the now healed and free Barney.

The last thing Baby saw was Barney being tossed into a makeshift cage as the evil Brother called to Brother Seth, who stood frozen on the stage. Darkness slowly descended on the ancient, brave Oolahan.

Seth jumped from the stage, his astonishment galvanizing him into action.

"Are you kidding me?" The tribe crowded in to see the strange creature which had fallen from the sky. Shouts of 'be careful', 'is it dead?', 'stomp on it', rang from the clan.

Seth fell to his knees in front of the golden creature. He turned with annoyance to the crowd. "Boys, can you give me some room?" His arms waved them back as he barked instructions.

"Andrew, get me a sack. Cut the harpoon off from the gun. No. From the gun. I want to leave the harpoon in the creature."

Within a few minutes, a sack appeared. They slid it carefully under Baby, wiping iridescent green fluid from their fingers with distaste.

"Is it dead?" Andrew peered over Seth's shoulder.

"I don't think so. It's still warm. It must have missed his heart. We need this sucker alive. It's our new ticket to power. We can negotiate our way into some goodies with this thing." Seth scanned his men's eager faces.

"And we still have the dog. The other creature will be interested in him if this one dies. I'm going to force them to fix it so our babies can be born again. They must know the secret. They all have babies. Get them loaded on the wagon."

Seth's men dumped the harpoon gun to the ground with a crash. Lifting Barney's cage, they placed it in the center of the wagon, dumping the awkward sack containing Baby and the deadly harpoon next to the frightened dog.

Andrew slithered over to Seth. "I don't think your relatives will be too happy with what we did to their creature. I don't think this was a good idea, sweetie."

Seth fixed him with a glacial stare. "I didn't ask for your opinion, now did I, Andrew? For your information, I don't intend to tell them we did it. I'll tell em we found the dog and graciously returned him home. The winged creature was on the verge of being eaten by the flamer. When Lorna ordered the flamer shot, she missed and hit the creature, allowing the flamer to carry it off. There was nothing we could do."

Seth hung his head mournfully while shooting a vulpine smirk to Andrew. Clapping his hands together and giving a quick hop, Andrew leaned in for a kiss.

"Not here you fool." Seth stepped back with displeasure, glancing around. "If you can't contain yourself, you can stay here. I don't need you to dispel my conquering hero persona when the tribe awards me the position of leader for discovering the Others' secret to childbirth. That, dear Andrew, is why we need to go back there. I now have a bigger justification to demand the tribe follow me. Furthermore, it's my birthright. Announcing that Lorna planned to steal the women and take them to her relatives took care of that obstacle neatly. You saw how worked up the men were."

"Yes, Seth. But the tribal women . . . they didn't appear convinced."

Seth waved him off. "Piff . . . Just watch them fall to their knees when I tell em they can have children again. The stupid bitches won't be a problem. Now go pack, I want to be gone."

Seth returned to the hustle and bustle of departure, glancing at the wagon to see Barney huddled and shivering on the floor of his cage. His deformed hand, hidden deep in his pocket, tingled.

They had been on the road no more than half a day when they began to spot wildlife, first deer and then birds. As they noticed the phenomena, they paid more attention, spotting a few turtles, rabbits and other vermin.

One of the men speared the biggest turtle ever imagined. It must have weighed fifty pounds with its shell.

"Good meat tonight," he bragged, his yellow teeth showing empty holes.

"I don't believe I've ever tasted meat before," another commented. "Are you sure it's okay to eat?"

Seth's man pulled out the limp head, stretching the long neck. In one chop, he sliced it off and tossed it to the other man who jumped back in surprise.

The noble turtle's head lay in the dust and the weeds as the men cackled and mashed it into the grass with their shabby boots, before moving on.

As evening approached, they set up camp and built a fire to cook the turtle meat. In the last hour alone they had been forced to take cover as lions, bears, camels and wild horses joined them on the path. They could hear all manner of beasts tromping and snorting their way through the underbrush out of sight.

Seth dismissed his first sensations of alarm. A growing impression had overtaken him within hours of the first sightings.

The animals were all traveling in the same general direction. The same direction they were going. He glanced back at the bundle on the wagon. *Could the creature be calling them in hopes of escape? Naaa, that weird dude could barely breathe.* At least he hoped the thing was breathing. It was hard to tell.

Seth spotted one of his men tending the fire.

"Build it up high, Booney. We need some protection tonight. And don't forget it's flamer season."

Booney kicked at the fire with his boot, sending sparks wafting high in the dusk.

"Sompin's not right with them animals, boss. Not a one seems to be in a hurry. And they don't even seem to notice us. Aren't lions supposed to hunt in the dark? You can bet I'm keeping one eye open tonight and Momma here tucked in with me." He patted his rifle.

Seth felt another twinge of unease. He had noticed the same thing, but had kept it to himself while he pondered on the why.

"When you get around to it, Booney, gather up another man and bring that sack over to me. I want to see if it's still alive."

"Why, we gunna cook it too?" He glanced over to the other men busy with their bedrolls.

"Tell Whop he's got another hunk a meat to skin."

The men crowded in. "We gonna have more meat, boss?"

"Can someone just bring me the sack? If it's dead, you can have it. Not much point luggin' a dead hunk a meat around. And I must say, fruit and dried vegetables are tasty, but I would sure love to try some meat. Who even knew we could kill these big boys so easy?"

With agreement from his men, he continued, "I think we'll do some killing on the way back. I'd like to get me one a those deer, and a big cat. I have dibs on the head, is that clear? We need something to celebrate with when we tell the tribe our good news."

"Here ya go, Seth. There's not enough left on this carcass to make it worth skinning." Whop dropped the cumbersome sack on the ground, peeling back the cover and pulling Baby out by a shriveled leg.

The harpoon remained embedded halfway between Baby's chest and his shoulder. There wasn't much left of him. His chest was caved in, sunken and emaciated, his limbs puckered and desiccated. Even his fur lay flat and matted, dried fluid coagulating around the harpoon's entry point, strangely iridescent in the approaching darkness.

Seth placed his hand on the creature's chest, feeling nothing. No warmth, no heartbeat. *Does it even have a heart like we do?* Seth wondered.

He leaned in, placing his ear to the creature's chest, his hands still in place as he listened. Nothing, it must be dead.

Pulling back he eyed the creature again.

"What the—?" Pushing himself back, he scrambled with his feet, giving a swift kick to the creature.

"What is it, boss?"

Seth's mouth dropped. The creature's chest now looked rounded and firm, its legs supple and healthy. Its eyes snapped open, golden luminance lighting up the camp.

From above, the men heard a soft fluttering. Seth felt his stomach turn over as he slowly turned and glanced overhead. His face drained of all color as his bowels released.

"Holy shit!"

Chapter 19

Ginger Mae sat with Dezi in the kitchen feeling every bone in her body ache. *Welcome to the real world,* she thought ironically.

"How you feeling, Dez?"

He dropped the bowl in his hand and turned to face her at the table with a mournful sigh. "Oh, babe. I don't know how we can go on. Everyone's exhausted from the stress, no one eats, no one sleeps." He nodded over to Father Garcia and Maddy tending the infants, Netty's three-year-old, Maya, petulant and cranky. She missed her mother. "They're the only ones that get any sleep. The sleep of babes . . ."

His face had aged. Ginger Mae had noticed the trait in many of the survivors, Scotty's death a difficult blow to recover from. He had been close to so many. Kane had not even spoken since Chloe had disappeared. And Abby couldn't stop crying, Jose helpless as a third thumb as usual.

It had been two days since Chloe and Netty had disappeared with no explanation. To compound things, Echo, Baby and Barney remained missing. No one knew what to make of it.

And if that wasn't enough, the morning before had started what would become an incredible sight, frightening in its ambiguity.

The animals were returning to the Hive. Not just their animals. All the animals. Ginger Mae had first laughed with Daisy when they saw the first troupe of rabbits walking on hind legs like a man, up the hill to the Hive as if on their way to the cinema.

The moment had passed quickly as the ominous overtones became apparent. Slow and steady, heads down, they all came. In groups, single, flying, plodding.

"How's Bonnie making out with Tobi?" Dezi sat next to Ginger Mae, dropping his small spice box at his side.

She shook her head disconsolately. "Not well. No matter what she does, Tobi wants to move the herd inside. Peter just wants her out of the way. But you can't stop an elephant when she wants something. It's going to break Bonnie's heart."

Dezi knitted his eyebrows. "She can go in the Hive to visit. What's the big deal?"

Ginger Mae gave a start. "You haven't heard?" She raked her short bob back with her fingers to hide her tremor. Lowering her voice, she whispered, "Wil told Hud the animals are going right into the membrane. Through the membrane."

Dezi blanched. "Eeww. That's not good. I don't like the sound of that, babe."

Ginger Mae looked around, the other survivors were out of earshot. "I don't think Wil and Hud want anyone else to know yet." She reached out for his hand and squeezed tight. "What can we do?"

He drummed his nails on the table, shaking his head. "Nutin we can do. It's not like someone's gunna drop a bomb anymore."

They laughed together, forced and strained.

"We gotta move, one foot in front of the other. You won't catch me goin outside with the flamer on the loose and our cats and bears on the prowl, though. I want to talk to Hud and Cobby about rigging up some kind of inside privy."

"Don't be ridiculous, Dez. It's not that bad yet."

Dezi rolled his eyes. "I'm just sayin'." He picked up his spice box. "Well, back to work. Maybe someone will eat tonight." He rattled the box as he rose to get back to work. Lifting the lid, he set the box back on the table in disgust.

"I can't cook like this." Ginger Mae looked into the box, found it empty and looked up at him quizzically.

"You need something from the field? I'll go get it for you."

"Aw, babe, you'd sure be doin' me a solid. I need some of the reddish mushrooms that hang down from those short yellowish trees. The ones with the tiny leaves?"

Ginger Mae picked up the box. "I know what you mean. The salty mushrooms."

"Yeah, I grind them up to use as a salt substitute. Can you tell how much better things taste since we found them?"

Ginger Mae looked pensive. "You know, you're right. I forgot how much I missed salt. I'll be right back."

Taking the empty box, she stepped out into the sunlight, its power weakening as it made its inexorable journey toward the horizon. Peering up towards the woods, she saw survivors in clusters, gathering strength from each other as they tried to guess the reason for the animal invasion.

She watched as one of the keepers jumped in front of a massive reticulated python that steadfastly strutted its serpentine muscles up the hill like a stealth missile locked on its target. No reaction. *Where the heck had that come from?*

Biting her lip, she slowly made her way to the edge of the settlement. She scanned the trees that stood as sentinels guarding the entrance to what Johno fondly called the lowvelt.

She could hear rustles in the bushes, invisible creatures disturbed from their precious little lives, unable to fight the magnetic pull of the Hive.

Stepping closer to the yellow trees, she was puzzled. No red mushrooms hung upside down from their long slender stems. Her eyes crawled down the trunk to the ground where the mushrooms lay, shriveled and dead. Picking one up, she turned it in her hand, dropping it quickly when she discovered the white mold that had rotted them overnight. She was sure they had looked fine yesterday.

Wiping her hand on her pants, she headed back to Dezi. Halfway there, she encountered Cobby coming toward her, his face drooping in its solemnness, eyes hot with red streaks that declared worry and sleeplessness. Scotty had been like a son to him.

"Hi, Cob. How you doing? Karen good?"

"She's fine. She's always fine. I left her with Dezi and the babies. Everyone's headed there now. Do you have a second?" He took her elbow and shepherded her toward Scotty and Chloe's empty shelter.

"I don't think I can go in there right now, Cobby." Ginger Mae hung back, bewildered by the request.

Cobby urged her forward as if he hadn't heard. "I remember when the kids insisted they have this spot." Cobby's voice broke as he looked her in the eye. "Did you know this is the spot their house used to sit? This is where they lived when their mother died, where the Gomez family lived with them after Salina's first husband took off." Cobby kicked the ground with his toe. "Well, I guess he's long dead. Salina gets the last laugh." His comment fell flat. Ginger Mae looked close, had that been a sob?

Clearing his throat, Cobby continued, "I never had roots myself. I didn't get it, I always wanted to be at sea, even as a boy. We moved to where the jobs were. The old man was a sailor." He looked at her begging for help. As if she knew. She shook her head not knowing what to say.

"It's Abby."

Cobby pulled her around the side of the dwelling to the rear. There she was. Sitting on the ground, leaning against a dead oak tree, its grand branches broken and denuded, dignified in its quiet naked death.

"What's she doing here?"

Cobby put out his hand stopping them a distance away, his anguish impossible to disguise.

"She's saying goodbye." His voice was a whisper as his eyes closed against obvious pain.

"Goodbye? Noooo." Ginger Mae gripped his hands. "It's too soon. Is it Oolaha?"

"Yes . . . they're all leaving. Tomorrow morning. She said the Hive is closing. It's leaving two pathways open. One is for the Elders to get back to Oolaha. Baby and Echo will go too, but who knows where they are? I can't stand to see her like this. Can you convince her to come to dinner? It will be our—her last memory. I can't . . . it's not right . . ."

"Sssh, I understand. You go. I'll take care of this."

Cobby took her in his arms. "Thanks, kiddo. You were always a stand-up broad." He took one more look at Abby, his breathing quickening, his hand raised, but no . . . he turned and left Ginger Mae alone to face the beautiful human Elder.

Ginger Mae moved toward the tree, a tired smile held tightly on her lips.

"Abby? Mind if I join you?"

Abby didn't even look up. A few moments passed between them before she spoke. "This is where it all began. We were just kids." She rubbed the smooth bark of the oak. "We had such hopes, full of innocence and naïveté."

She looked up to give Ginger Mae a distant smile, her eyes no longer luminescent, but dim and dull.

Ginger Mae gave a start as she realized Abby still had the same clothes on from two days ago, her hair was matted and snarled, the feathers on her wings uneven and clumped. Wrinkling her nose, she thought Abby could clearly use a bath. But her elegant and murderous horns still swirled with color, shimmering and smoldering even in the falling dusk.

"I understand from Cobby that you're planning to leave tomorrow?"

"Cobby . . . um, yeah." She looked down again, a weed in her hand, running it mindlessly through her fingers.

"I don't expect you to be happy right now, Abby, but maybe you could put on a front on for the rest of us. The others are going to be upset when word gets around. We're scared enough as it is. No one seems to know what's happening with Netty gone. How could you even think of leaving us now? We're your family. You need us now, too. We haven't even had a service for Scotty."

Abby nodded her head, the weed now sitting in her lap as she began to shred it.

"Abby, could you look at me?" Ginger Mae heard a sob as Abby raised her head, tears streaming down her face. *Oh no*, thought Ginger Mae, *I know that look.*

She placed Abby's hand between her own. "It's Cobby, isn't it?"

Abby didn't move, didn't speak. She just let the tears flow, her eyes expressing her struggle with a tide of overwhelming emotion.

"You love him?"

A tight nod, and she bowed her head, swiping her nose with the back of her hand. "But I can't. Jose . . . I can't do that to him. It's too complicated, you wouldn't understand."

Ginger Mae patted her hand. "I understand more than you know, Abby. I've known he loved you since I first saw you together aboard the *Lucky Lady* when we made our break from Sarasota."

More nodding and dripping tears. "It's just that I have this duty now. I'm an Elder."

"I also know you don't love Jose."

Her head popped back up. "That's not true. I do love him. Just . . . differently."

They stared back at one another. Two women recognizing the eternal struggle between duty and true love. Ginger Mae knew what the outcome would be. She stood and pulled on Abby's arm. "Come on, let's get you pulled together for dinner. We can't solve this tonight, can we?" She looked hard into Abby's eyes, recognizing the robust fiber of her womanhood. They both knew what Abby's decision had to be.

Arm in arm, they made their way back to Dezi's kitchen, the wildlife still moving up the hill.

Abby excused herself at Dezi's door. "I'll be right back. Five minutes. Let me just change at least."

"Okay, five minutes, no more." They parted with a quick hug and brief sincere smiles.

Walking through the door, Ginger Mae could tell the word had circulated. She didn't think the atmosphere could get any grimmer.

"It's about time, babe." Dezi closed the book he was reading with a loud snap and tucked it in his apron's wide pocket.

"Sorry, Dez. Abby needed me." She enunciated the words slowly and quietly, raising her eyebrows so he would get the message.

"Eww, she's still bad?"

Ginger's face registered agreement as she trolled the huge room with her eyes, spotting Hud in the corner with Wil.

"Can you excuse me, Dezi? I need to find Daisy. I guess you heard the Elders are leaving. I need to see what Daisy's plans are." She moved to leave.

"Hey, hey. Where's my mushrooms?"

Chagrined, Ginger Mae handed over his empty spice box. "Sorry, Dezi, it slipped my mind. There are no more mushrooms. Not a one on the trees. They're all shriveled up on the ground, covered with this slick white fungus." She shuddered. "Just throw another spice in your pot. We can live without the taste of salt. We did for almost a century."

Dezi grumbled and turned to his shelves, shuffling bowls and jars around nosily. "Well, it's just not gunna be the same. What else can happen today, for Womb's sake?"

Moving across the room, Ginger Mae felt Cobby's eyes on her as he held his baby on his lap, Karen hovering with Gloria and Billy, their baby asleep in Father Garcia's arms. She refused to meet Cobby's glance, leaving his unanswered question clouding his eyes.

She gave a salute to Hud and Wil, before finding Daisy holed up in another corner with Peter and Bonnie.

"Where's the baby?" She slid into a seat next to Bonnie.

"Asleep. Maddy's keeping an eye in him. I'm just too exhausted." Bonnie looked like hell. Her normally cheerful demeanor had vanished to be replaced by a solemn and weary grown woman in the body of a ripe teen.

Peter didn't look any better. His eyes tried to hide his concern, but Ginger Mae knew it was grave.

"You heard?"

They shook their heads.

"Yeah, we heard." They turned in unison to Daisy, waiting for her to speak.

"Mother, can we please discuss this later? You know I must go. Let's get through dinner and we will talk about it then."

Ginger Mae reached behind Bonnie to give her a hug.

"Sure, Daisy Chain. I'm a bit tired now, myself."

Abby chose that moment to enter, looking fresher but downcast. She nodded to a few survivors, ignored Cobby, and took a seat next to Jose.

Salina and Shirley began to set the tables for dinner, Dezi still grumbling about his missing mushrooms.

Dinner passed quietly, the survivors jumpy with the pace of the animal call to the Hive escalating. Noises filtered into the kitchen: chuffing, snorts, hoofs on the ground. At one point, Johno thought he heard an elephant trumpet, which caused Bonnie to run to the door.

"What? Oh, my gosh!" Her expression appeared terrified, luring the other survivors to investigate.

Wil pulled them all away from the door as they gazed up into the air to watch a massive flock of flamers, their first true glimpse of the horrifying predators. Three out of every four of the monstrous reptile birds carried a huge ball of nesting material clutched tightly in their evil-looking talons.

Ginger Mae turned away from the door as Abby sat back down, her head in her hands, Jose's arms wrapped protectively around her.

"So that's the creature that killed Scotty and my boys," Johno lamented sorrowfully. "What's the purpose of the balls of material they fly with?" He turned to Wil.

"I think their chicks are inside. They would never leave them behind."

Johno scratched at his ear, his naturally placid demeanor slipping. "How can the Womb justify calling the flamers to the Hive? That's where they're going, isn't it? Miss Lorna said this territory supports only one for the season." His eye grew large, the whites stark against his caramel skin. "There must have been at least thirty of them in the sky."

Wil answered with kindness, clear but firm, "Johno, you know the Womb respects all its children, favoring few, treasuring all their lives. There will be another home for the flamers. The Womb will guide them to a path through the Hive membrane, wherever the Womb deems appropriate. Even they deserve a chance to live their lives."

Everyone had taken their seats again. Restlessness and nerves turned the group into a frantic knot at Wil's words.

Salina rose to serve tea and two of the infants awoke, crying to be fed. Bonnie and Karen rose to tend their boy and girl before they woke the others.

"Pick me up, Daddy," came the demand from Maya as she escaped Maddy's watchful eye.

"Ahhh."

The sound of Salina dropping the teapot drew everyone's attention. She stood blank faced, staring at the doorway. All heads turned to observe Netty and a timidly-smiling Chloe standing there.

"Mama," shrieked Maya, running to the doorway.

The shocked silence from the other survivors was palpable. Finally, Clyde summed it up for them all. "Holy Mother of God."

Chloe walked into the room. Assisted by Netty with Maya wrapped around her legs, she sat in Kenya's old armchair near the fireplace, clearly eight months or more pregnant.

Chapter 20

Seth sank to his knees, terror gripping him in its choking vise. His own stench from the release of his bowels floated up, adding to his nausea.

He was surrounded by the menacing dog-like creatures that had flown into their camp unnoticed until it was too late.

Around him lay the skeletons of his men, picked clean to the bone, dressed only in their saggy rags.

Carefully, he edged away from what had once been his simpering lover, Andrew, his firm, familiar flesh eaten away by minute black and red creatures, reducing him to a screaming horror of boiling flesh that called out to him for rescue with his last breath.

Seth tried to calm down, taking deep gulps of air as he watched the other golden creature called Echo approach him. The winged-dog creatures swiveled their salivating lizard faces toward the tottering Echo as if responding to a whistle.

Four of them crept closer, snatching the live body of Seth's harpooned creature in their mouths and dragging it away from his reach.

He could hear the frantic barks of the dog in the cage. The Echo creature turned to the wagon, its luminous eyes and swirling antlers sending refractions of light into the darkness. The dog suddenly whined then ceased barking, sitting quietly in the cage.

"Okay . . . easy now. You want your buddy? You can have him. I meant no harm." Even to himself, his squeaky voice suggested guilt. He offered his hands in supplication. "I was just bringing him back to you. This is how we found him."

As Seth continued to beg, Echo flipped her long tail high in the air. The bulbous end extruded a membrane. The air filled with pressure. Seth wrinkled his nose as the smell of sulfur hit him.

To his surprise, the creature on the ground reached up and slowly pulled the harpoon from its chest, leaving a gaping wound which healed itself before his eyes.

The Echo creature approached the healed one, fingers to each furry cheek that now gleamed with health. Together, they turned to stare unblinkingly at Seth.

His heart beat so fast he couldn't catch his breath. He fought off a cramp from his bowels as the Echo creature shambled over to the wagon and hoisted itself up. The white dog went mad with excitement. Unlatching the cage door, the creature was bowled over by the dog. They lay on the wagon floor, the creature grooming the dog, its face pressed to the dog's side.

Together, they jumped from the wagon and made their way back to Seth's creature. The winged dogs gathered around. To Seth's astonishment, the two creatures gathered the dog between them and, without a backward glance, took to the air. The winged lizard dogs flew after them, a protective layer underneath the now squirming dog.

"Holy shit." He climbed feebly to his feet, wondering what to do. He could not continue to Lily Pond Road. Out of the question.

He shriveled inside knowing his leverage with the tribe was gone. They would never let him lead after this. How could he make them understand what a valiant effort he had made to save his men? If he had not had the good sense to hold his tongue, the creatures may have inflicted more horror. He began to sob, knowing his story would be a hard sell.

Why does my life always turn to shit? I deserve more than this. They don't know who I am . . . I'm Doc Benjamin's son! He shook his deformed hand to the sky.

Seth was left sobbing and alone with the skeletons of his dead men and the uncomfortable, wet smell in his pants; alone as the flying creatures vanished from sight, leaving him to listen in the darkness as the bushes rustled and growled around him.

Chapter 21

Abby rose from her seat next to Jose, shrugging his arm from her shoulders. She walked toward Netty and Chloe, her posture combative. "How could you leave us like this? And what's the meaning of this?" She pointed to Chloe's abdomen. Her face crumbled, dissolving into tears as she began to shake.

"Where have you been?" Her lost voice fell, emotions cascading as her whole body conveyed hurt, disappointment and the accusation of betrayal.

Netty rushed to her side to embrace her.

"We needed you, Netty," she continued to sob.

"My dear, it is all right. We're back now. Please . . ." She glanced around the room, spotting Johno. "Johno? Perhaps you and Dezi can brew us up some tea?" She nodded at him knowingly. "And my medicine, please. I think we could all use a dose. We need to calm down and discuss these events rationally." Her eyes searched for Wil, brightening when she located him. He stood up to go to her side as Abby continued to sob on her shoulder.

"Can you get me a chair for her, please?"

Wil retrieved a chair and placed it alongside Chloe, who reached out with a smile and a hand as soon as they settled Abby.

From outside the kitchen they heard an intense roar that resonated in everyone's bones. The door pushed open and Caesar poked his head in. The big cat gave a chuff and speared them one by one with his laser gaze. As soon as he focused on Chloe, he leaped into the room, landing inches from her side. He instantly rubbed his head on her legs, his back arching high like a house cat and tried to unsuccessfully squeeze himself between Abby and Chloe's chair, settling for curling up at her feet. He leaned his leg against her legs, yawned and closed his eyes, apparently fast asleep.

Clyde spoke up. "Well, that tiger's certainly happy to see you. We wondered what had happened to him. He hasn't been seen since the Kreyven carried you off."

Netty accepted her tea from Dezi and took a sip, sighing loudly with pleasure. She then favored Clyde with a response. "And that is exactly as it should be."

The survivors stirred uncomfortably and Wil placed a chair for her to sit down on. "I think it's time you gave us some explanations, love."

Netty's hand went to Wil's cheek, stroking it lovingly. She turned to the crowd, her radiant eyes now flashing as she tightened her wings around her body and sat. "As you can see, Chloe is pregnant. The baby is Scotty's."

A gasp from the crowd forced Netty to raise her hand.

"Hear me out. This will all make sense to you and then I will answer any questions. The Womb sent the Kreyven to fetch us and bring us back to Oolaha. It appears we have been gone for only a few days, but, in fact, we've been gone for over a year. It was quite difficult for Chloe and I, but well worth it in the end . . . as you can see." She turned to Chloe and shared a smile.

Questions peppered Netty like a downpour in late winter, miserable and unwanted.

"Okay, okay. Let me explain how. The part of the membrane where we disposed of our deceased is actually the entrance to a portal. That is where we set out on the journey to Oolaha. In fact, there are many different . . . you might call them roads . . . in the portal; and many different kinds of road.

"If one were to stumble in without the knowledge of the Womb . . . well . . . you may not care for the road you wind up on. It takes the Womb's guidance to walk the correct path.

"The pathways are collapsing now. The Womb, as you all know, is signaling us to leave. We will take Baby and Echo with us, of course. We leave in the morning.

"As to Chloe's pregnancy. It was a reward from the Womb; you all owe her your undying gratitude."

Netty and Chloe grinned from ear to ear. "I suggest, unless you lovely ladies want children, you better explore some kind of birth control, starting tonight."

The room erupted, claps and shrieks mixed with more than a few happy tears.

"But how? I thought the Womb didn't want us to have children. We're viewed as a scourge on this planet," stated a perplexed Karen.

"Yes, you were," continued Netty. "But the Womb, in all its benevolence, always planned to give Homo sapiens one last chance. A chance that would signal you understood life. That you were willing to sacrifice for life other than your own species. Some earnest act that would show hope.

"So . . . the Womb gave you The One."

The only sound in the room were those of the infants as the survivors digested this revelation.

"But Scotty died. We lost him. How could . . .?"

Netty rose, setting aside her teacup to stand behind Chloe, her face unreadable as emotions flitted over her posture. "I'm sorry to tell you this, but Scotty was not The One. It was always Chloe."

Again the room erupted with accusations.

"But Caesar was here to guard him," Kane cried. "I heard Echo tell Scotty, Caesar knew he was The One on the *Lucky Lady*."

"No, Kane. You heard Echo tell Scotty he thought Scotty was the *right* one. The one to be Chloe's consort. You might recall that Caesar marked Scotty with his urine. He was making the choice indelible.

"Chloe was recognized as The One the very first day Scotty met her on the beach on Sarasota." Netty looked down to see tears flowing down Chloe's face as her hand slowly rubbed her abdomen. Netty gave her shoulder a squeeze.

"I know it's hard to hear this again, Chloe."

"It's okay, I understand."

Netty turned back to the stunned crowd. "Chloe didn't know it, but Echo was hidden in a baby carriage with one of the dogs so she could join them in a jaunt on the beach. Echo recognized it the minute she laid eyes on Chloe.

"As you know, Chloe lived down the beach with Omar who'd had her kidnapped from Costa Rico as an infant. She had been marked then as The One. It would always be her. Events conspired, sometimes with our help, to bring us to this moment.

"We never knew when she would emerge with the deed that would change your history. We were forbidden to even acknowledge her. When everyone assumed it was Scotty . . . we said nothing. It was a simple deception. Caesar was here to guard her. It was the only interference we were allowed. You assumed it was Scotty being guarded because they were always together." Netty scanned the room full of astonished faces, recognizing the slow comprehension.

"Remember the night we discovered that Baby held you captive in the Hive, Hud? Scotty was with us, but not Caesar. Scotty had ordered Caesar to stay and guard the women on many occasions. But Caesar would have stayed behind anyway. He's incapable of leaving her side." Everyone watched as Chloe's hand dipped down to stroke the magnificent tiger's head, getting a rub and a sloppy tongue in appreciation.

Netty continued, "I'm sure you can well understand what happened when Elias died. He knocked Chloe down after striking her. Caesar naturally jumped to her defense with tragic results. But he could no more stop himself than he could stop himself eating or breathing."

Cobby spoke up. "Is he still forced to guard her?"

"I'm glad you asked. Caesar is no longer under the influence of his implant. But after this many years of conditioned response, he will stay by her side of his own volition."

Bonnie stood to ask a question. "Netty, this is wonderful news, but how can we be sure the light from the Hive didn't make our procreation enzymes die off completely? We've lived out here for months now and still no one is pregnant."

"It's no longer the lights, Bonnie." Netty reached into her robe and pulled out her hand. She leaned over to spill the contents on the table. Out rolled the reddish mushrooms from the yellow tree that Dezi used as salt.

"My salt mushrooms. No!"

"Yes, Dezi. You were using them as salt. The one thing we could count on that everyone would ingest. A property of the mushrooms alters the pH environment in a woman's uterus, preventing the union between a sperm cell and the egg."

"But the mushrooms have all died from a fungus. I tried to gather some today," said Ginger Mae.

Netty nodded. "That's true. It was necessary. The reward granted from the Womb to you all through Chloe's act extends to the entire race. That means the tribe from the Franklin Mines, too. At the time, the Womb felt a strong likelihood that communication between the two groups would cease. So the mushrooms were eliminated."

That statement was met with raised eyebrows and incongruous bluster from Clyde. Waving her hand to shush him, Salina stood up, her complexion gray and muddy with mourning. "But my Scotty, why did he have to die if you knew all this?"

"I am truly sorry to lose our Scotty, from the bottom of my heart. But the Womb works in mysterious ways, as you know. I cannot question the wisdom of the Womb. I can only be guided by it, Salina."

"Miss Netty. You've left something out. What was this worthy deed that granted such a privilege to us?"

Netty turned to Chloe, hesitation in her voice. "Do you want to tell them, hon?"

Chloe shut her eyes and nodded her head. Taking a shallow breath, she began the story of Scotty's death at the hands of the mercenary and brutal flamer. She relived the horror in a halting tale, every harsh moment felt by all in the room.

"So when I discovered the flamer had two chicks . . . I just couldn't do it. They were so innocent and vulnerable. My bloodthirst for revenge simply dissipated. The flamer is dangerous, yes. But it's a creature that has only one thing while we have so much more. It has a life. A life that feels pain when hurt, hunger when starving, and loss when its offspring are killed. I knew I did the correct thing, the only thing.

"I don't hate the flamer for what it did to Scotty. I blame myself. The Womb provided us with the intelligence to learn how to avoid the flamer when it was in our territory to nest. Just as the other wildlife takes cover. When we noticed the silence, we should have heeded the warning.

"The flamer or the chicks didn't deserve to die for our stupidity. As much as I was still in shock, I knew this to be true . . . in the deepest corner of my soul."

With those words, Netty concluded, "The Womb was very satisfied. This was but the first deed the Womb will expect from our Chloe. Her potential . . . or gift . . . as identified by Echo, has more potential. It may rest with her."

Netty looked with pride at Chloe and turned to Abby. "Or with your new niece or nephew."

A look of wonder transformed Abby.

"Chloe represents what is left of Scotty. Life. An extension of Scotty. And hope. You can leave knowing a piece of your brother lives on."

"And the pregnancy? How did that come about without cells from Scotty's . . . body . . . to clone from? I assume that's how you did it?"

Chloe reached into her pocket and withdrew a folded cloth. Unrolling it, she extracted two feathers and held them to her heart. "Without these, it would not have been possible." Her voice broke.

"It was a simple matter to clone cells from minute DNA strands found in the skin traces attached to the ends of the feather shaft."

Abby stood. "If you all can excuse me? I need to be alone for a while. I'll be here early in the morning to say my goodbyes, but for now I think I need a good soak in the bathing caves. This has been . . . . hard." Kissing Chloe, Netty and Jose goodnight, the now fragile Elder joined the relentless animal progression to the Hive.

Jose closed the door after watching Abby progress safely up the hill to the woods.

"How's it looking out there, Jose?" asked Cobby.

"No change," Jose answered curtly.

Salina and Crystal made the rounds again with tea refills. Chloe beckoned to Jose to join them.

"Hi, Sis, you look beat," he said.

Chloe smiled wanly.

"I want you to take Chloe to your shelter. She's not ready to face a night alone in her old one . . . with Scotty gone . . . Would that be okay with you, Jose?" asked Netty.

"Sure. Want to leave now?"

Netty and Jose pulled Chloe up from Kenya's old chair.

Jose grinned shyly. "This baby looks almost ready."

"Two more weeks to go, I think," said Chloe, bracing herself on Jose's arm. "Okay, I'm all set." She turned to everyone in the room. "Goodnight, everyone. It feels good to be home." She reached out to grip Netty's hand, then let Jose lead her out the door.

Netty made her way over to Johno, Cobby and Wil, now huddled in conversation at the table.

"So gentlemen . . . might I ask where Baby and Echo are?"

All three looked guilty as she hovered over them, waiting.

"Sit down, love. We need to talk about a few things," said Wil.

Quietly, Netty folded her wings, molding them securely to her body before sliding into a chair.

"Baby and Echo never came back. We've seen nothing of the nooglets either. It's been almost three days." Wil's voice resounded with trepidation.

Cobby's temper flared. "And that's not to mention the parade of wildlife through the settlement. Did you know they're going through the membrane?"

"Yes, of course. We encountered them when we came out of the portal. It was unsettling. But our only thought was to let you know we were back and safe." She turned to Wil. "You have no idea what this is about?"

"Not a clue. It started right after you left with the Kreyven and hasn't let up. Netty, even insects are on the move."

Johno bobbed his head up and down. "Yes, Miss Netty, yes. I've seen this before. It's similar to the great migration in my homeland." He stopped himself, gave a strangled cough. "In my old homeland," he corrected. "The great migration was for food. Many species would participate, even though they all encountered great danger at the Mara River with the powerful jaws of the crocodiles. This migration is very similar, but different. All species are participating."

"Netty, you must know something about this. Are we in any danger?" demanded Cobby.

Perplexed, Netty felt defensive, "I promise you, Cobby. I know nothing. We need Echo. The Womb does not communicate with me. It's done only through the minions."

Johno got up from the table to check on the migration. Smells of musk and rich feces drifted in on a warm evening breeze. "My lord."

The unexpected terror in Johno's voice drew everyone to the door. The dark sky flared with dozens of monstrous flamers, all following the migration. Not to feast, but to join; all flying toward the Hive.

"Abby's there," cried Cobby.

"Where are they all coming from?"

"Please . . . shut the door. Why take any chances? Just let them pass." Salina and Crystal shooed everyone back to their seats.

Cobby remained standing. With a look toward Karen and Maddy, who were putting the baby down, he moved back toward the door.

"I think I'm going to scout around a bit. Can someone make sure Karen gets home safely with the baby?"

Wil shook his head and waved.

The night tasted wrong. He couldn't put his finger on it, but Captain Cobby knew it wasn't just the strange wildlife migration to the Hive. His arms got goose bumps as the last of the flamers flew over his head. Instead of fleeing in panic, the rest of the wildlife continued their placid and stoic climb up the hill.

He had no real fear for Abby's safety. She was an Elder after all. Her lethal horns had the power to strip the flamers down to chicken bones.

He tried to push thoughts of her out of his mind with no success. He kicked at the dirt as he paced, frustration over their history and his unsatisfying life with Karen getting the best of him.

It was his own damn fault, anyway. If he hadn't been so timid back in Sarasota, she wouldn't be leaving now. He remembered the first time she had come to visit him on the *Lucky Lady* when Jose had taken off to find Salina and his sisters. Long before he found out about her changes. He could feel the attraction even then. His gut clenched with the memory of how he had wanted to sweep her into his arms that moonlit night she had come to see him.

But she had been his boss. He had wanted to remain professional for the sake of some stability in Kane's life. How would it have looked to Kane if Jose had come home and fired him for making a pass at his girl? He blushed to himself as he admitted he wanted to do more than just make a pass.

He realized Abby had been young and in the midst of her newfound puppy love for Jose. He knew it would wear off in time.

He sighed to himself, raking his strong fingers through his dense and dark curly hair, amazed at the outcrop of sprinkles of gray that had appeared in the time since they'd left the Hive. The difference in their ages had stopped being a factor decades ago; too many decades to count.

But by the time she had turned to him for support, it had been too late. Her changes had intimidated him. Half the time he hadn't known what was up and what was down as they had made their break from Sarasota to reach the Hive. With all the unforeseen complications from the deadly bombs, they had all had enough to cope with without adding a jilted Jose into the mix. Abby had had more than too much to cope with in her life as it was. His decision to just be there to support her was a lasting and painful one.

And then along had come Karen. A good sport, she also knew when not to bug him. She had become a distraction from the pain, a good sport to share a laugh with. Before he'd known it, they were a couple. As the picture of their lives became clearer, he had known he was stuck with her.

The burden of his feelings for Abby colored everything. He had kept it hidden well, but his marriage to Karen hadn't helped. The baby was a blessing, a hopeful chapter of his life, giving it new meaning. But how long could a guy stay engaged when all the baby could do was smile and burp at you?

The bottom line was the fact that he didn't love Karen. He never had. It just never came, even as he knew he was grateful in the lonely nights when he felt her next to him.

Cobby's heart leaped anew; hope bursting wildly after the night of his grandbaby's birth. He was nuts about Kenya and the kid, and the few stolen moments with Abby had almost made up for the many decades of torment. Unfortunately, he had never found another opportunity to talk to her candidly since. He cursed the flamer under his breath. They had lost two lives that night, and he had lost his chance to tell her how he felt.

He cringed remembering the shape he had found her in today as he spied her heading to the rear of Scotty and Chloe's shelter. He had followed her, knowing this could be his last chance. It was not to be. He had found her in the midst of an emotional breakdown, feeling the loss of her brother, her home, memories of her mother's death . . . 'a life unfulfilled', she had mumbled.

Finding Ginger Mae appeared to have snapped her out of it, and the news of Chloe's pregnancy had certainly helped.

He briefly wondered why he had never given Ginger Mae a tumble. She was a rock and good to look at. He remembered how Karen had dogged his heels the first few years in the Hive.

He stopped pacing and admitted his feelings for Abby would have intruded there, too. He took a deep breath, redolent with the exciting aromas that said life was afoot. Taking a last quick glance at the migration up the hill, he headed toward his shelter, completely missing the click of the kitchen door as it closed on the figure that had been watching him.

Abby luxuriated in the sensation of the warm water on her toes as she flipped her leg out over the pool where she sat on her favorite rock in the bathing cave. The beauty of the sultry shadows, effervescent minerals, and colorful jewels made her wonder if Oolaha offered anything comparable. She imagined it would. The Kreyven originated there and had undoubtedly learned its craft there as well.

She felt she was almost ready to say good bye to Earth with the knowledge that Chloe would be fine as soon as the baby was born.

She knew her own life would take a positive turn once she removed herself from the temptation of Cobby. After the night Kenya's baby had been born, her ache for him refused to abate. Only

Scotty's death had been able to push her constant dreams of him to the back burner. Poor, loyal Jose. He deserved better. But her deep feelings for him had worn off sometime after their first year in the Hive.

She knew her duty came first. Their destiny together was on Oolaha, and anywhere Netty and the Womb chose to send them. As she stroked her wing, she admitted nothing could ever change that. They were an Elder couple forever.

Sniffing herself in the steamy air, she grimaced. Hurriedly peeling off her clothes, she stood up on her rock, stretching her lush and strong body, shook out her magnificent wings, then pulled her long, straight hair back from her crystal horns and prepared to dive in.

"Mind if I join you?"

Abby jerked as if stung, her solitude shattered. "Sure, come on in, Karen. I was just going in myself." With that, she dove off the rock, sending ripples across the placid water ending at Karen's feet.

The tall and lean Karen stood staring as Abby surfaced, making no move to join her. The silence stretched.

"You coming in?" asked Abby.

"You're pretty good at flaunting that body of yours, aren't you?"

Abby blinked, caught off guard by the statement. "I was alone, Karen. It's no big deal. If you're uncomfortable, I'll get dressed." She swam to the water's shore, rising like a goddess, and made her way back to the rocks where she'd left her clothes.

Pulling on her pants, she arranged her hair to cover her breasts.

"Don't bother for me, your charms are wasted here."

In no mood for whatever bug Karen had up her butt, Abby ignored her and twisted her hair to wring out the water.

Karen laughed, throwing back her head.

"You look just like a whore standing up there."

Abby compressed her lips into a white line, her heart tripping faster. She sat to tie on her shoes.

"I bet you wouldn't run this fast if my husband were here, would you? You tramps are all the same. Has he fucked you yet?"

Abby froze, all thoughts of her last evening in the bathing cave gone. She searched her mind, desperate for something to say, something safe. "You're out of your mind. Cobby doesn't deserve that."

Karen turned purple. "Now you're going to tell me what my husband deserves? A tramp like you? You don't fool anyone with those looks you throw at him. I knew you were trouble the day I set eyes on the two of you. But he picked me." Spittle flew from her mouth as she shouted loud enough to wake the Kreyven wherever it rested.

Abby watched a cunning gleam appear in Karen's eyes.

"You had no idea what you were up against. I've been through the ringer with whores like you and I decided never to give you a chance to get near him. Where did you do it? I said, where did he fuck you?"

Abby knew this was a dangerous situation. Trying to slip past Karen, she felt her head jerk back.

"Where do you think you're going, bitch? I'm not finished with you."

"Let go of my hair, Karen." She kept her voice low and relaxed.

Karen dropped her hair and reached into her pants, pulling out an ugly black handgun. "Get on your knees, bitch."

"You have to be kidding me. Where did you get that?"

Karen signaled with her gun. "I won't ask again. On your knees."

Just to humor her, Abby sank to the ground.

Karen laughed gaily. "I flew planes, remember, stupid? We're always armed. Never can tell when a gun might come in handy. Hijackers, terrorists . . . whores that fuck your husband." A satisfied smile stretched across Karen's handsome face.

"You didn't think I'd notice his change in behavior? It must have been the night Kenya had her baby, right? That's the only time he got out of my sight long enough to do it. He walked around like he was mad at the world after that. Is that what you do to them, Abby, drive them mad for you?" Karen's voice shivered. "I'm going to make sure you stay away from my husband, you got it?"

"What are you talking about, Karen? I'm leaving in the morning."

"Oh really? It never crossed your mind to stay here now that Chloe's pregnant with your loving brother's baby?"

"No. I—no. Definitely not."

"Your answer fails to reassure me. So this is what I'm going to do. I'm going to stick like glue to Chloe tomorrow. I know I can't do much to physically hurt you, but Chloe's baby is another matter."

Abby blanched. "You wouldn't."

"Oh, yes I would. You threaten my family, my baby, my life." Karen began to rage again.

Out of the corner of her eye, Abby caught a glimpse of movement behind Karen's back. It was Tobi, silent and strong, swaying with agitation as Karen's rage got out of control.

Closer she crept, her trunk held high until she was close enough to swat the distressed woman to the ground, knocking her out cold.

Abby ran to Tobi, plastering herself around her front leg.

"Oh, you big beauty. Tobi to the rescue."

The matriarch wrapped her trunk around Abby, soft rumbles coming from deep in her stomach. They turned to look at Karen, the gun still in her hand and waves lapping at her feet.

"I'll get that, girl." Abby picked up the gun and held it over her head, throwing it as far into the water as she could reach. She looked down at Karen, her breathing normal.

"She'll come to in a while. Let's get out of here, girl." They turned and walked out of the bathing cave leaving Karen alone to recover on her own as the water began to lap further up her legs.

Abby and Tobi hurried down the corridors together, Abby's hard-soled shoes echoing their clump in the forlorn halls, revealing the absence of happy laughter and raucous wildlife.

When they came to the fork to Netty's old kitchen, Abby stopped. Tobi slowed and turned, her trunk searching the air.

"You go on, girl. I know you have places to go. Your herd is waiting somewhere." She kissed Tobi and motioned her on. "I hope I see you again, Tobi, wherever life will bring us. I love you, girl."

Tobi snorted, her head waggling and ears flapping as she swiftly moved off down the corridor.

Her emotions on edge, Abby walked slowly toward Netty's kitchen, reluctant to view the location of so many fond memories, now picked over like a carcass that had been worked over by African vultures.

She stood slumped at the entrance to the kitchen, sweeping her eyes from wall to wall. All furniture, fixtures, and decorations had been removed. Even the fireplace mocked her with its disfigured maw, now unrecognizable having been stripped of every brick and piece of mortar they could salvage to reassemble in Dezi's new kitchen.

She ran her hands lightly over the membrane that still clung to the walls, forever doing its job until the Womb gave last call.

Standing in the center of the room, she shut her eyes, letting the flood of happy memories with her brother overtake her. She felt a lingering tear dampen her cheek.

Scotty had lived more than a full life. And she would always have her memories of the sad, beaten-down, sickly child who had grown into a handsome, mature, loving man with the woman of his dreams at his side. Who are we to ask for more than that?

"Abby?"

Whirling around, she came face to face with the man who haunted her dreams. "Cobby."

His happy grin lit up his face. "What are you doing here?"

She swept her hand around the room. "I thought I'd say goodbye. It's just not the same anymore."

"Nothing's the same any more. You . . ." Cobby stopped and bowed his head. "You're leaving."

Abby felt her body tingle and her blood rush as she stepped close to lift his face.

"I needed to see you, Cobby." She had a flash of Karen, wild and crazy with a gun in her hand. *No, I can't tell him now.* She deserved to have this goodbye. She needed to have it. Just once in her life, she was going to choose a precious moment for herself.

She smiled softly, soaking up every detail of his familiar, dear face as her heart raced and her breath came in short gasps. She watched a shift in his eyes. Hope?

"I need to say goodbye to your dear, handsome, wonderful face that I have loved for so, so long."

Cobby looked stunned. "Sweetheart . . . I." His voice broke as he stepped forward to crush her in his arms, her lips devouring his with her passion as she threw caution over the cliff.

He lifted her up and she wrapped her long legs around his waist, the strength of his urgency pressed against her pelvis.

"Oh God, Abby, I don't believe this." His lips crashed down on her with a deep groan.

Grinding into him, she shifted her weight to free her wings, pulling back to peer into his eyes. "Are you sure, Cobby?"

His eyes full of joy, he nodded his head. "I have never had any doubts. Are *you* sure, Abby?"

Before he could change his mind, she opened her wings to their full span. "This will protect us. I'll take us to one of the sleeping caves." Her wings enclosed them completely. But not before a tiny descendant of Gloria's original mice heard the soft tremulous words of the beautiful Elder tell the handsome sea captain how much she had always loved him.

Then they vanished.

Cobby nursed his doctored tea in Dezi's kitchen, trying to pull himself out of his unexpected let-down after the Elders' departure.

Kane and Kenya had left their baby with him while they ran off to the Hive for a dip in the bathing cave. No one knew for sure if they would still have access to the Hive when the portal closed.

It had been a difficult parting for everyone except Abby and Cobby. They alone had made their peace with the departure in the passion they had found in one other's arms during the long night. They both felt safe pledging their love through bitter tears over the realities of their responsibilities toward others.

It had been daylight when he returned to his dwelling; an early daylight, stark without the simple pleasure of songbirds. Returning from the Hive, he had encountered more animals, but hardly the profusion of the day before.

Cobby scratched his itchy stubble. He had been unable to find the time to shave in the morning, startled to find Karen already up and out.

Wondering how he would answer Karen's questions, he changed and hurried to Dezi's, where everyone was gathered to say goodbye.

Hugs, handshakes and tears . . . No obligatory promises to visit. This was to be a one-way trip. The departing Elders expressed their surprise that Baby and Echo had still failed to return, but felt confident they would join them in the portal eventually.

Abby and Cobby tried to keep it relaxed when they said goodbye in front of the crowd. She wore her infernal sunglasses, but her trembling shoulders when he hugged her told him her eyes were probably red and swollen. He sure as hell felt like crap himself.

But he had what he needed as he watched her turn away and walk up the hill with Wil, Netty and Jose. He knew she loved him. The pressure of the constant ache inside was gone.

They accepted that they could never be together; it had never been in the cards. Their night of passionate exploration of one another's bodies, and whispered entreaties for more, left them complete and ready to accept the future.

Parting from their temporary love nest had been as bittersweet as they had expected; his hunger for her even more powerful now that he knew she loved him.

But it was now a healthy hunger. Gone were the bitter recriminations he had used to torture himself with over the decades. Maybe now, in time, her memory would fade and he could try to concentrate on Karen and the baby.

Everyone had been surprised when Karen failed to show. Asking around quietly, it became clear that no one had seen her that morning. Missing the send-off was just not like her. She was a very controlled and responsible individual.

Kicking back in his seat, he watched Dezi turn a page in the book he was reading. His grandbaby lay next to him in her crib he and Kane had built from odds and ends they had found in the Hive. It might look like a butcher job, but to him it looked like pure love.

Chloe rested in a chair, smiling at him over her tea, Teddy trying hard to find a spot on her lap to curl up in.

"I hope it pleases you to know we took good care of Teddy while you were gone."

"Thanks, Cobby. I knew Kane and Kenya wouldn't forget about him."

"So what are you up to today, young lady?"

She sobered as she explained. "Father Garcia and Maddy are moving my things into Abby and Jose's dwelling. I think it would be better for me and the baby for now. I'll spend the day with the babies until they're done. I might as well get used to what babies do, right?"

"You sure are taking this pregnancy a might better than Kenya did."

"It's much easier to do when you know the baby's coming out on schedule, Cobby. She sure was funny though, wasn't she?" They were sharing a laugh when Kane burst through the door, Kenya right behind him.

They stood before Cobby, white faced and breathless, their eyes odd and unreadable.

"What, you don't trust the old man with his grandbaby?"

Kane swallowed and reached for his father hand. "Dad, we found Karen. She's dead." The room did a spin, Kane's words not sinking in.

"What did you say?"

Kenya knelt on the floor, her head in his lap as she tearfully relayed how they had found Karen's body floating at the water's edge in the bathing cave. She had been face down and clearly dead.

Cobby removed Kenya from his lap in a trance. He stood up and walked in an aimless circle.

"What the heck was she doing there?" He looked up quickly. "Did she have any clothes on?" he asked in a whisper, his eyes pleaded for the right answer. "No wait, don't tell me. I don't want to know."

"It's okay, Dad. She was fully dressed," he said gently.

Kane held out his arms to his father. Cobby let himself be comforted as his shock turned to anger.

At that moment, the kitchen door opened. All eyes turned to discover Baby and Echo standing in the doorway, their arms held in front of them as their fingers worked spasmodically in agitation.

Auras bombarded them at the same time. "We must go. We must go now. There is no time to waste, Brothers. It is almost too late, my Sisters."

"Sister Chloe, where is my Brother Scotty? I have tried for days to find our connection. Has he left for Oolaha without us?"

"What is wrong with your abdomen, Sister?"

"No time for questions, Brother Baby. We must all go now. The danger comes."

Chloe struggled to get up from her chair. Dezi snapped his book closed, sliding it into his apron.

"Where we gunna go, dudes? It's pretty safe in here."

Auras slammed them again. "No, there is no safety. We must return to the Hive now. We have saved our family for last. The animals have been implanted and are safe."

Kenya's eyes bugged out. "You guys are responsible for this migration? What the heck is going on, Echo?" She stood with her hands wrapped protectively around her infant.

"There is no heck going on, Sister Kenya. There is only danger."

Kenya turned to the others in the room. "What do you think's goin on, chickeys?"

Chloe snapped her fingers and Teddy jumped into her arms.

"I don't know what you guys think, but when Echo says to boogie, I boogie. I'm not messing with my baby's life. Kane . . . Cobby . . . grab the other babies. We can't leave them here. Dezi . . . you too. Grab a baby. We're getting the heck outta here."

The scramble up the hill took longer than it should, although the pathway was now clear with not an animal in sight. The rest of the survivors were all off doing chores, necessitating the men to shout for help all the way up, setting the infants to screaming and the wayward Barney, happy to be by Echo's side again, joining in with his sharp barking. Not to be outdone, Teddy threw his head back to sing, fraying everyone's nerves with his remarkably awful song.

No one heard. No one came.

At the top of the hill, they turned to look down at the settlement. They could see Johno and his men in the new growing field bent over at their tasks in the distance. No amount of screaming and waving got their attention. Baby and Echo took to the air.

"The time has come. We must run now." And they disappeared into the woods.

"Chloe," shouted Cobby. "Put Teddy down. He can run faster than you can. Kane can you grab Chloe? Help her . . . drag her if you have to."

White faced, Cobby took the infant Kane was carrying to free up his arms. Now he carried two squalling infants.

"Dad, where's the rest of the dogs? We can't leave them behind."

"There's no time, Son. Move it." There was no doubt in Cobby's mind that something catastrophic was coming. Fleetingly, he wondered what the scene was like for the tribe at the Franklin Mines. He cringed as he thought of all those unwary people who didn't have the benefit of a warning. Poor Lorna and Seth.

His heart shuddered with guilt and fear for his comrades in the settlement, blissfully unaware. *Could the minions be wrong? How bad could it be?* He prayed some would survive the danger as they made it to the granite rock. He turned to face the trail, strewn with organic evidence of the migration.

"Kane, move it. Come on, come, on," he cried as he watched his son struggle with Chloe a good twenty four yards down the trail. Her face was drained of blood and her breathing sounded hoarse and ragged.

"Go, Dad. Don't wait for us. Get the babies to safety. We'll be right behind you."

Cobby ran back to Kane.

"Dad . . . no."

"Take the babies," Cobby commanded. "Now get out of here." He passed the infants to Kane, giving him a push, as Chloe collapsed on the trail.

"The baby . . . my baby." Her face contracted in agony as she fought for breath.

Cobby bent down and slid his arms under Chloe's body, lifting her high and staggered toward the granite rock as Chloe's face turned blue.

"Oh, dear God. Give us the strength." Sucking in a deep gulp of air, he stilled his chattering arm muscles and pushed past his endurance. Lurching heavily, they continued on, his arms burning and Chloe silent.

Plunging into the Hive, he looked for Kane. The corridor was empty.

Eying the cavern wall, he discovered it bare and dry. No membrane, no welcoming light. He plunged into darkness as they left the mouth of the Hive.

Where was everyone? Agonizing streaks of pain ran up his legs as he stumbled on by memory. He could no longer feel his arms, numbness threatening his grip on the now unconscious Chloe.

He could feel the corridor expand into the cavern of their arrival so long ago, filled with memories happy and sad. He plunged on.

As he reached the end of the cavern, he fought the darkness to find the next corridor. From behind them, he heard a sound. Halting, he gulped air as he sensed a presence.

"Kane . . . Dezi?" The heart-stopping familiar roar of a great tiger froze him to the spot. He felt the tiger move in front of him to block his path. From the rear, he heard a sharp bark. Turning toward the bark, Caesar leaned into the back of his legs, urging him forward. The bark sounded again as Cobby followed the sound. Caesar kept the pressure on the back of his legs, abruptly thrusting him into an obstacle he sensed in the dark.

As he fell forward, his protesting arms released Chloe and she tumbled forward ahead of him. Down he went, breaking through the membrane portal with Caesar still exerting pressure from behind.

He fought, but consciousness deserted him.

Cobby stretched in the darkness, feeling better than he had in a long time. He tried to open his eyes and discovered they were already open. A twinge of nausea brought his hand to his stomach. He panicked as his hand floundered in the darkness, unable to feel his abdomen.

His breath increased, shallow and rapid as he fought unconsciousness again.

Where am I? How long have I been out? Where is everyone? His debilitating terror threatened to swamp him.

Without warning, a feeling of goodwill and warmth flooded his nerves, relaxing him completely. Light began to fill his senses. He jerked as something touched his face, tracing the contours down his cheek.

"It is me, Brother Cobby. Sister Echo. I am here for you."

"Echo? I can't see you. Where are we? Is everyone here? Are we safe?"

"Yes, Brother we are safe. We are on the pathway."

"What? What pathway?"

"The only pathway. The only one left. I will be here to calm you."

Cobby could hear sobbing in the distance. The sound got louder . . . a woman's sobbing drifting closer.

"Who's there? Is that you, Kenya? Are you okay? Kenya?"

"No. Is that you, Cobby? Can you help me find my way out of here?" Bonnie asked. "I need to find Peter." Her sobbing began again.

Echo's aura dimmed. "Brother Peter is already gone. They are all gone. We have traveled far, Sister Bonnie. This path has taken us many light years away. For you it has been momentary, but for the Earth it has been a lifetime."

Her sobbing stopped. "Are you effing kidding me, Echo? You take me back right this very minute!"

"That is impossible, Sister. The pathway is dissolving behind us. It will not be needed again. Please excuse me. My Barney needs me." Echo's voice floated away, his last words fuzzy in Cobby's mind. "We will be home soon."

"Are you still there, Bonnie?"

"Yes, Cobby, I'm here. I can't see you and I can't feel myself. But I'm not scared. Just confused. The light is so . . . calming. Why can't I see you?"

"I don't know, hon. Have you heard from anyone else?"

"No. Who's with you?"

"Kenya and Kane. Chloe and Dezi. I was carrying Chloe and I dropped her. We got separated. She needs help."

The sobbing began again.

"How did you get here? Bonnie . . .?"

"After the Elders left, I decided to look for Tobi in the Hive. I found elephant dung on the hill. I figured she might have taken the herd to the mineral lick where my sister . . ." Silence.

"Bonnie? You still there?"

"Yes, Cobby. Sorry. It's just . . . hard. Tobi wasn't there. It took me a long time to get back. As I walked the tunnels, the lights went out. The membranes were contracting. I ran, trying to keep up. I made it to the first cavern. Caesar was there. I thought it was strange that he wasn't with Chloe. He backed me up against the wall and pushed me into the membrane. That's all I can remember until Echo. I heard a voice in the distance. I tried to find the voice, but couldn't until I felt Echo touch my face. Then I recognized it was you."

"Can you reach out, Bonnie? See if you can find my hand." He flailed into the light with his arm, still unable to distinguish anything.

"Sorry, Cobby. I can't feel anything." Her voice sounded small and weak. Cobby flailed around some more, his hand striking something.

"Oh. I hope that's you, Cobby," Bonnie cried fearfully.

"Yes. Yes. Reach out, hon. Try again." His hand struck her again. She didn't pull away and he was able to wrap his hand around hers, pulling until he felt her next to him.

"I can feel you, Bonnie. But I can't see you."

"Yes. Me too. Feel better now."

Their minds erupted with auras as Baby and Echo rejoiced. A lone message of pure joy from Echo broke through to Cobby, saddening him deeply.

'We are almost home, family. My Brother Scotty will be so happy to see me."

The light dimmed as Cobby and Bonnie encountered a flexible barrier.

"Can you help me push against this thing, Bonnie?"

Together, they leaned into the barrier, stepping out into their new home. Stomach spasms forced them to cover their mouths, a movement duplicated by Kane, Kenya, Chloe and Dezi in various stages of sprawl.

Cobby lost his battle as he vomited all over the clay depression they stood in. As the sounds of his defeat carried to the others, a chain reaction set off a host of retching.

Cobby looked up as the clatter of tiny wheels flew down the sides of the clear dome that covered the clay depression. What looked like a twelve-inch furry robot, with the same shimmering eyes as the minions, swept toward him. In a matter of seconds, all signs of his upset stomach had been removed from the clay floor.

As he followed its path back up the curved side of the dome, it disappeared into a box that hung down over him, firmly anchored in place. Within a second, another popped out to make a trip to clean up another nasty effect of their journey.

"This only happens with first timers."

Cobby turned to see Wil, Netty and Jose standing with the dogs.

A heavy organic stench emanated from the portal. Cobby tuned to watch as the Kreyven emerged, trailing the precious membrane attached to its tail. As he watched, the Kreyven sucked the membrane through the portal, enveloping it into its mass as the portal dissolved. The Kreyven then exited the dome, leaving the survivors stunned.

Behind them, as far as the eye could see, the animals of the migration stood milling around. To his astonishment, he recognized other dome structures in the distance containing figures. The Kreyven hurried toward one of the domes, entered, then vanished into another portal.

Golden minions fluttered at all the dome openings. Lowering his eyes, he was taken aback as hundreds of minion eyes stared back at him from outside their dome. They lined up all the way around, faces pressed against the structure like wide-eyed children.

"The animals are waiting for Echo to release their implants. We'll let them take their places in our ecosystem until we can sort out those who may need relocating to other environments."

Cobby stood, speechless. Wil threw out his arms as Netty and Jose looked on. "Well . . . does an old friend deserve a hug?"

He felt Wil's arms go around him. He held on tight, trying to resist bawling like a babe. He straightened up to ask, "Are the babies all right?"

Netty shook her head, sadness evident in the droop of her wings.

"Yes. They had to be removed quickly, though. They left with some minions and might need medical attention. We must check the oxygen level of their blood. Adults are usually fine. You'll all get a thorough check-up later this evening."

She swept her hand toward the excited faces outside the dome. "As you can see, you already have fans. They are very excited to see the creation of the original Elders in the flesh after so many millions of years. They will want to examine your evolution."

"Our evolution?" Cobby spoke weakly, visibly cringing. He shut his eyes, repressing his questions. Then his heart fluttered as he casually asked for Abby.

Netty pointed to where she sat with Echo and Chloe, their arms wrapped around one another and sobbing. Caesar sat stoically in the distance.

Cobby approached slowly, the others following, afraid to disturb the emotional scene.

"Abby?"

Detaching herself from Echo, Abby turned at the sound of Cobby's voice. She flew into his arms without thinking. "Thank the Womb, you made it. I thought I'd die when we got here and discovered the Womb's plans," she whispered. Quickly detaching, she patted his arm in a friendly fashion to cover her emotions. "I'm so pleased you made it, Cobby. Thank you for all you have done for Chloe," she proclaimed loudly. Standing to the side, she let Cobby through to Chloe.

"Why all the tears, champ? We made it."

Chloe's eyes widened as she signaled silence. Echo lay on her lap, looking off into space, his arm wrapped around Barney's neck, who lay panting at her side.

Chloe turned back to Cobby, her voice choked, and whispered, "We just told Echo. She didn't know about Scotty. That's why you were all in the dark about the migration and the reason for it. Echo kept sending word to Scotty, but her auras couldn't find him. She couldn't return until she finished her mission. The Womb had sent the nooglets to help get it started."

Abby interrupted, Netty, Wil and Jose at her side, "Yes, Baby and Echo finally got to fulfill what was left of their mission. They were busy implanting all the wildlife so they would be saved before the Womb stepped in."

"But why? Cobby pounded his fist in frustration. "What about the others? Hud and Ginger Mae . . . Salina . . . Johno . . . all the others . . . Oh God . . ." He hung his head. "They deserved to live. We all did everything *right*. We did *exactly* as the Womb demanded."

Netty approached, reaching out to clasp Cobby's hand. "Don't you understand, Cobby? The Womb gave up on the human race long ago. An accommodation was made as Abby unexpectedly rescued humans with the wildlife. But that was all it was . . . an accommodation.

"With the discovery of the tribe at the Franklin Mines, the benevolent Womb granted them access to their own growing field so the cannibalism of their infants would stop. Babies, like the wildlife, are the innocent.

"The Womb decided to give humans a true second chance when Chloe proved we *can* respect life, despite our evil and venal inclinations."

Abby hung her head in disappointment. "It just wasn't to be. The evilness in humans cannot be restrained. On the one hand the Womb giveth and on the other taketh. There was just no time to warn the others. You had split seconds."

Cobby wiped tears from his eyes.

Kenya and Kane joined the group, giving hugs all round. Dezi hung back as Daisy looked from face to face, tears hovering in her eye. "Where's my mother? Where's Hud?"

As the silence from the survivors answered her question, Dezi stepped up to put his arms around her. "I loved her, Daisy. You know that?"

Daisy shook her head, speechless in the arms of her mother's best friend as they cried together.

"Can someone please tell me why? Why did the Womb decide Baby and Echo needed to complete their mission now? I thought we were through all that. We did everything right . . . for so darn long," cried Kenya.

Abby returned to Echo and Chloe, her hands upraised. Bitterness rang out in her voice, loud and true. "It was Seth and Lorna. Clyde's grandchildren. Seth couldn't suppress the evilness inside him. He murdered Lorna a few days ago, cutting off her hand like a trophy. He was planning a coup to take over their tribe. Barney had followed Lorna's trail when he ran away and came upon the murder scene. Seth decided to hold Barney for ransom until Baby showed up to rescue Barney for Echo. In the confusion of it all, they shot Baby with a harpoon gun, almost killing him and compounding Echo's difficulty of passing a message. She couldn't get through to anyone. She was too far away to send her aura to anyone but Scotty or another minion. She did manage to lock in on Baby's position before he went into a coma. Eventually, Echo rescued Baby—you don't need the details. It's safe to say Seth got what he deserved."

Echo sat up her aura pronouncing, "We can create more life, Brothers and Sisters. We will improve on Homo sapiens with the next generation. We have the babies. And we have my Brother Scotty's offspring here." Echo placed her leather hand on Chloe's bulging stomach, then turned to Abby to place her other hand on her stomach. "Life begins again."

Abby laughed nervously. "Don't joke like that, Echo."

Echo's aura privately stroked Cobby's mind. "Do not worry, Brother. Sister's journey through the portal did not hurt the young seed."

What the heck? Abby's pregnant? That can't be, can it? he asked himself, thunderstruck at the possibility.

Netty stood before them, her sadness more pronounced. "I'm sure you don't realize that millions of light years have passed as you spent mere minutes in the portal. The time is drawing near. Can I ask you all for a moment of your time as we say goodbye?"

The perplexed survivors looked to the sky, following the direction of Netty's hand. A large radiant light sat in the sky, dwarfing the surrounding stars. It appeared to grow larger, its radiance burning brighter, then abruptly winked out.

Shocked faces met terror-stricken eyes as Netty walked away with Wil to stand at the door to the dome that would lead them to their new life.

Earth . . . gone?

A sobbing Bonnie looked up as a herd of elephants rushed toward the dome, the indomitable Tobi in the lead, scattering the watching minions as Tobi thumped her trunk against the barrier.

No one said a word as they helped Chloe and Abby to their feet, the shocked silence a eulogy for their vanished homeland. Abby glanced back at Cobby, her expression unreadable.

No matter what, we'll work this out. Our baby . . . *ours,* thought Cobby.

They quietly stepped out on a grassy plain that shimmered with colorful buildings on the horizon. The setting sun began its winking goodbye, presenting the survivors with three bright red moons, iconic and ever watching, just as their own Earthly moon used to do.

Tobi trumpeted, the herd's confused displacement quelled with the familiar sound of their now happy matriarch having been reunited with her Bonnie.

Life goes on, no matter the heartbreak.

Trudging on, the silence was finally broken again by Daisy's plaintive sigh. "All those books. My books. What a loss . . . just heartbreaking."

"I think we might have one book for you, Daisy," said Kane. He gazed back at Dezi, who still wore his kitchen apron.

"You still have that book you've been reading forever, Dez?"

"Yeah . . . why?"

Kane held out his hand. "Pass it on up here."

Dezi pulled the book from his apron pocket. Kane looked at the title then held it up for all to see, his expression rueful.

The lettering was beautiful, gold leaf with prominent flourishes. It said simply, *The Holy Bible.*

The End

'Heaven is by favor; if it were by merit your dog would go in and you would stay out. Of all the creatures ever made [man] is the most detestable. Of the entire brood, he is the only one . . . that possesses malice. He is the only creature that inflicts pain for sport, knowing it to be pain.'
— Mark Twain

'We must fight against the spirit of unconscious cruelty with which we treat the animals. Animals suffer as much as we do. True humanity does not allow us to impose such sufferings on them. It is our duty to make the whole world recognize it. Until we extend our circle of compassion to all living things, humanity will not find peace.'
— Albert Schweitzer

Introduction to:

Species Intervention #6609 Book 7

When Aliens Weep,

Pre-orders now available on Amazon. Soon to be released!

Synopsis

As our survivors recover from the effects of travelling through the portal to Oolaha and the shock of losing their loved ones and planet Earth, the Kreyven closes the pathway and quickly scurries over to another portal to disappear. To where? A new task for the Womb? Or have other survivors become lost on another pathway?

Meet I-V, the minion navigator who will become entranced with Bonnie as she mourns the heart-rending loss of her Peter. What will the reaction be of the population of Oolaha to the introduction of humans into their life-creating culture? Does the Womb have plans of its own for the survivors?

Will Jose's slow realization that his relationship with Abby is waning as she quietly turns to Cobby and awaits the birth of their baby wreak havoc with the peace on Oolaha?

As Kenya finally has everything she has ever wanted: a good man and a healthy baby, she is forced to assess who she really is and where she fits in the rhythm of the new world.

Bonus Chapters 1-3

Earth—Eleven Hours before the End

Chapter 1

Seth lay prostrate in the dust of the red earth, snot from his exhausted crying jag dried on his face and congealed in the dirt.

It had been hours since the golden creatures and their flying entourage had left with the infernal dog. He'd miserably failed to recover from the shock of his glorious crumbled dreams and fallen asleep while the detritus of his fallen comrades mocked him with the unexplainable evidence of their rag-festooned skeletons.

The clicking sound of a beast slowly awakened him; a foreign noise that penetrated his consciousness, a dark awareness blossoming like a macabre pustule, throbbing and ready to burst its bacterial poisons.

Pain radiated from his clawed hand that lay jammed uncomfortably under his body, screaming for release. Slow to open his gummy eyes, he felt the hot breath of an ursine beast at his neck, forcing him to freeze as it investigated the stench that clung to him; the myriad of odors enticing to the bear, even as the siren call of the Hive tugged at it like a magnet.

The bear clawed once, turning Seth over and forcing him to look straight into the curious face, its breath smelling of berries and grubs. Finding the pull of the Hive irresistible, the bear chuffed in his face then wandered off down the road, leaving Seth to his ignoble fate.

And what a miserable fate that was. He curled into a fetal position, unwilling to lay eyes on what was left of his lover and his men. Their fatal images had been burned indelibly in his mind as they'd taken their last breaths and collapsed in the dirt, the miniscule black and red projectiles returning to the split antlers of the evil and vicious creature known as Echo. *Has that creature enslaved the Others with its diabolical power?* he wondered.

Tired of self-pity and with no appreciative audience, Seth began to take stock. The effort expended to force himself into a sitting position wore him down. No matter how hard he tried, his strength ebbed from the emotional distress his efforts were causing. Try as he might, he continued to flounder, unable to invent a plausible way to spin this hideous outcome to his grandiose plans.

The last thing he wanted was to become a laughing stock instead of the conquering hero he'd originally intended. Pathetically, the realization was just sinking in that the only thing conquered was him and his band of misfits and toadies.

He'd been made to look like a fool by two oversized *flying cats . . . no, deer . . . no . . . well, whatever the fuck they are . . .*

The next time I see those abominations, I'll show them just who they're toying with. If they hadn't caught me off guard . . .

Seth wiped the traces of his blubbering off his face with the ragged end of his sleeve. He scrambled to his feet and listened for sounds, the pre-dawn wrapping him in its silent awaiting. The absence of further rustlings from the edge of the road told him it must be safe to start his journey back to the tribe's settlement. Alone . . .

Every time he remembered he was on his own, depression returned. How would he explain the loss of his men? He remembered the confused reaction of the tribe as he and his men returned victoriously from the first meeting with the Others, waving Lorna's severed hand and declaring himself the new leader. The quiet covert whispers and tight faces of the women had not escaped his notice. *Who knows what havoc the nasties were working on behind my back while I bravely set out to negotiate with the Others? I did all this for them, the ungrateful bitches.*

Hitching up his pants, Seth stretched, his aching limbs testifying to the many hours he'd lain sleeping on the ground. Turning his back on what was left of his men, he began the long hike back to the settlement, watching as the moon began to disappear, soon to be rendered invisible by the sun's infant rays greedy to claim their rightful turn in the sky.

Hours later, the dawn long vanished, he knew he neared the tribe. His heartbeat ratcheted up with stress. Every possible lie long discarded, he knew it was time to face the music.

As he ascended the last rise, smoke from multiple breakfast fires rose to greet the late morning sun. From his vantage point, he saw various tribesmen and women still scurrying around with the chores of the morning. Carefree children were chasing each other while older teenagers egged them on.

The ramshackle nature of their dwellings appeared pleasantly blurred from his position, allowing the settlement to take on the appearance of an actual village. In the distance he could see the groves of fruit and nut trees they'd painstakingly transplanted from deep in the mine, a monumental task. The seedlings had thrived in the open under the watchful glare of the sun and the now skilled farming members of the tribe.

To the left, he spied figures in the fields, already at work tending their lush vegetable crops. They appeared to grow wherever they found a spot to plant them. The damage done by hungry roving creatures bothered them little.

A couple wandered away from the children toward an outcrop of rocks, closer to his vantage point. Young lovers? As he watched them kiss, he guessed it wouldn't be long before the young girl claimed her man and started a home of her own.

He tore his gaze away from the young lovers, jealousy an emotion that plagued him forcefully, reminding him of all that he no longer had.

It appeared quite clear that the tribe flourished well under the leadership of his dispatched sister. Did they even need him?

He vainly considered turning around and throwing himself on the mercy of the Others rather than face the certain wrath and scorn of his own people. Seth wiped his beaded brow, the sun making him sweat. Crouched with his back to the encampment, absorbed in his own self-pity, he failed to see members of the tribe stop their chores and stand speechless as the late morning air began to sizzle, the sun rising over the eastern horizon blinding them.

Seth's discomfort from the sun began to sink in. But not in time to witness the first of the monumental solar flares that lit the sky, making the forty-five-mile-wide chunk of metallic space debris glow as it fought with the flare to be the first to reach the vulnerable planet.

Two Hours Before The End

Chapter 2

Johno directed the keepers with a heavy heart. The men were ever flexible but he could see their broken spirits in the cant of their shoulders and the pain in their eyes.

"No, my friend. You're pulling up plants. We need to rid the field of the weeds. Like this." Johno demonstrated with a quick slash into the red dirt with his shovel, severing the roots and flipping the plant clear of the soil. He bent his timeworn back to retrieve the weed and stuff it into the sling hanging from his back like the other men.

A hand grasped his shoulder. Johno turned to see one of his men shading his other hand over his eyes and looking toward the hill that led to the woods and the path to the Hive. He just caught a glimpse of some of the other survivors disappearing into the trees. What was that glimmer in the air? *If I didn't know better, I'd say that Baby and Echo were back.*

"Boss, I think they were trying to get our attention."

Johno squinted back up at the hill, evidence of the migration to the Hive littering the ground. "Are you sure?"

He turned back to his trusted men. "I'd better see what's happening. I'll go see if I can find Hud, maybe stop by the kitchen and see what Dezi knows. You boys want to take a break? I'll wait and see what Dezi has for us for lunch while I'm at it."

Watching Johno give the hill another quick glance told his men that the concern in Johno's dark expressive African eyes was more for the loss of their beloved Tobi and her herd than anything else.

Johno started his trek out of the fields amidst the uneasy whispers and mumbling of his men as they took refuge under a huge walnut tree. It served as a welcome respite from an unusually hot late morning sun, a grateful balm to their overheated bodies.

Johno hurried, wiping his perspiring brow with a rag, his shirt plastered to his sleek knotted muscles even as sweat continued to pour down his underarms. He felt an uncoiling in the pit of his stomach, a viper he tried to quell with sheer willpower.

He tried unsuccessfully to shake off his emotional paralysis, served to him by the realization that he no longer shared the planet with the creatures he loved with every fiber of his being. Elephant-tender no more, he would tend crops until, by the grace of the Womb, Tobi and her herd would be allowed to return home. He nurtured the tiny flare of hope, refusing to relinquish his fiercely held aspiration.

Reaching the edge of the field, he raced to the kitchen. From his left, he could see Hud and Ginger Mae at the base of the road leading to the woods.

"Hey there, Hud . . . Ginger Mae. Wait up!"

The couple turned and waited, the smiles on their welcoming faces slowly melting as Johno's dripping condition and obvious state caused them to tense.

Johno caught up, heaving breath cutting off his words. "Hey . . . ah . . . You guys . . . you guys see anything unusual?"

"Like what, Johno? Something wrong?" They eyed him with concern.

Johno gulped a deep breath, calming down. "We thought we saw something on the hill. It looked like Echo or Baby to me . . . I'm not sure." He stared at the large box that hung from Hud's side. "Where are you going with that, my friend?"

Ginger Mae tugged on Hud's arm. "We need to get going, Hud, no telling how long we're going to have access to the Hive. Johno, we have no idea what you're talking about. You want to come with us? We could use some help." Turning, she waved at Peter returning to the kitchen, motioning for him to join them. Jogging up to the base of the hill, he asked. "What's up, guys?"

"Johno thinks he saw Baby and Echo on the hill."

Johno raised his hand, "No, not on the hill . . . at the top. My men thought they saw Cobby and Bonnie."

Peter screwed up his face. "No, not Bonnie. She's in the kitchen. I'm on my way there now."

"Can you spare another half hour or so?" Hud asked.

"Yeah," interjected Ginger Mae. "We could use the extra hand to carry some of the last of the good stuff from storage. I know it'll be needed eventually. Why waste it?" She turned her charm on Peter. "Please . . . Bonnie won't mind waiting with the babies."

He dismissed Johno's concerns, "Wish we could help you." Looping her arm through Hud and Peter's, she proceeded to tug them up the hill.

Peter cranked his sweaty neck back to Johno. "Can you stop by the kitchen, Johno? Let Bonnie know?"

"Sure. You guys go on. I'm headed for the kitchen anyway, got to feed the crew. You be off now. Keep your eyes open." He waved at the chummy threesome but they'd already turned their backs to him, deep in conversation, their laughter carrying back down the hill.

Johno watched quietly, his wise eyes scanning the quiet woods. Ginger Mae's voice was now a distant musical note fleeting and fading as they moved among the trees. The viper in his stomach twitched a warning. *Yeah, yeah, I hear you, my friend. Please . . . just settle down for me. I pray you're wrong and it's just my imagination.*

Johno hurriedly made his way back to the kitchen, Crystal now weighing heavily on his mind. He needed to find her and get her up to the Hive. Just on the off-chance that the viper in his stomach was correct.

Rounding the side of the kitchen, he observed the door closing behind someone. He heard voices inside as the door swung back open to admit him.

"Johno, what are you doing here?" Crystal approached her husband to give him a resounding kiss then turned back to the other survivors, who watched with stupefied faces.

Clyde, Salina and Jennifer stood examining the empty kitchen; there was no sign of Dezi or the lunch fixings that would normally be apparent. Dezi's counters sparkled clean and clear. Not a crumb in sight.

Clyde escorted his two women to a table, leaning in to be extra solicitous toward Jennifer who had yet to recover fully from her mental breakdown suffered the night they'd met the members of the tribe from the Franklin Mines. It was forbidden to mention the names Lorna and Seth around her even as Lorna's revelation about her parentage brought great bittersweet joy to them all. All the survivors had great hopes for the future and the uniting of Lorna's tribe with their group.

Father Garcia and Maddy approached from the confines of the nursery, worried expressions now shared by all.

"I don't understand. Where are the babies? Where's Cobby? And Chloe? They were here when we left." The blank looks on everyone's faces told Johno everything he feared.

"We need to leave now." All traces of the wise man they loved now vanished as Johno's face sagged, looking chalky and threatening panic.

From their table, Clyde's voice boomed out. "Settle down, everyone. Salina, why don't you go rustle up some grub? Dezi won't mind." He slapped her on the rump as she rose to obey. "You can still cook up some fine vittles, can't you?"

She gave him a quick glance of annoyance. "Try that again and the only vittles I cook up will be the ones I rip from your big belly." Salina huffed her way to Dezi's kitchen and grabbed some bowls amid the laughter from Father Garcia and Maddy.

"No, no . . . you don't understand. Something's going to happen. Something *bad*. That's why the kitchen's empty. We thought we saw them on the hill to the Hive. My men thought they were trying to get our attention. We need to *run*. Now!"

Clyde stood with his hand raised. "Now just a gosh darn minute."

Johno shook his head sadly and grabbed Crystal's hand. "Good luck, everyone." He dragged her out the door.

Ginger Mae stood with her husband and Peter in the old supply room surveying the shambles left from their effort to salvage what they could. The beam of her flashlight lit up what was left: long discarded shelves broken by the Kreyven when it had brought the contents of a department store to the Hive in preparation for their arrival so many decades ago.

"I think I saw the box of penlights under that junk." Ginger Mae lifted a piece of metal off a smashed box.

Hud hurried to her side. "Let us handle that, hon. If you're right, we could sure use some more light right now."

Peter knelt at the other end of the pile. "I wonder when the membranes disappeared. It never occurred to me that we'd no longer be able to see in here."

"Do you think they'll just leave what's at the mouth of the Hive and in the big cavern?' Ginger Mae asked.

"I don't think so, hon. Wil said it's the Kreyven's job to secure the Hive. They can't have anyone accidentally getting into the portal. They'd never find their way back. Even though there are now only two paths, one to Oolaha and one to . . . hmmm . . . I don't think he told me. I wonder where the other path goes to? Oh well . . . doesn't matter now. We better just concentrate on grabbing anything useful that's left and get out of here."

The threesome went to work, Ginger Mae with her flashlight and the men with the tiny pocket lights. It didn't take long to fill their big box. Hud managed to find a pile of work boots sitting on a heap of fabric as if someone else had readied them and promptly left them behind. Ginger Mae found a small cookbook in the rubble and slipped it into her pocket to hand over to Dezi. She was pleased with the tiny treat she could take to surprise him.

"I think we'd better head back now, Hud. The box is full."

Hud bent over to heft the box onto his broad shoulders. "Wait, what about some of this broken metal shelving? We could find a handy use for this someday. We might be grateful we grabbed some of it while we had the chance."

Ginger Mae bent down to gather it in her arms. She glanced up to see Hud heaving the box. "Come on, Peter. Gather some of this up with me. It's too heavy for me to carry more than a couple pieces by myself."

"Let me tie a few pieces together for you. Hand me that twine. It'll be easier to carry that way." After tying two bunches of the metal together, Peter slipped one bundle under Ginger Mae's arms. "How's that feel?"

Ginger Mae gave it a test. "Good. Not too heavy."

Hud nodded in their direction. "We gotta move. Peter, can you tuck in the tail of that twine? I don't want her to trip on it."

Peter wrapped the tail of the twine around her hand, securing it tightly then bent to do the same for his bunch. "Okay. We're set."

The three of them headed back down the lonely winding corridors, the shuffle of their feet on the rock floor the only sound as they conserved their strength for their burdens. Ginger Mae took the lead since she still carried the only flashlight, tucked into her breast pocket and sending most of the light straight up. Still, it was enough. She honestly thought she could traverse the corridors blindfolded anyway.

Before long, they arrived in the main cavern; the cavern of hellos and goodbyes, wedding and funerals, joy and sadness. Setting down her burden, she complained, "I need a rest, Hud. This thing is killing my arm."

The men halted, Peter moving over to Ginger Mae to examine the twine wrapped around her wrist. "Too tight?" he asked.

"Yeah, but I don't want to redo it now. Let's just get out of here." She bent to pick up the metal rods again. The beam of her flashlight moved with her, now focused on the cavern wall near the portal.

"Wait," Hud commanded. Setting down his heavy box, he walked to the wall. "Ginger Mae, can you train the light back over here?" With her free hand she removed the flashlight from her pocket to illuminate the wall.

Hud ran his hand over the wall. *The membrane was gone.*

"It looks like the portal has closed too." Peter's voice trembled.

"Wow, we really *are* alone now. Hud? Come on. I just want to get out of here.' Ginger Mae sniffed while Hud turned his back to the wall and hoisted his box.

"Okay, babe. I hear you. Let's go see what Dezi's cooking up for lun—"

With a terrific rendering, the wall exploded and the Kreyven burst into the cavern, lighting it up with its flashing iridescent streaks of illumination. It descended down on Hud, crashing his box to the rock floor. Ginger Mae screamed as her husband was sucked into the gelatinous mass without a sound.

Before she had a second to finish her scream, the Kreyven was on her, wrapping its sinuous mass around her, metal burden and all.

As Ginger Mae fought with the shock and surprise, she heard Peter scream and felt the beast move, carrying them along with it.

Hud, where's Hud? She found she was unable to speak as she felt an unfamiliar constriction at the same time as her light dropped from her hand and she was engulfed in a moving darkness.

Johno and Crystal ran through the woods. If Crystal stumbled, he simply yanked her back on her feet and ignored her protests. The heat from the sun intensified, drenching them thoroughly with their sweat. The urgency of their run forced them to look ahead and miss the dynamics of the solar flares headed to Earth and illuminating the gargantuan metal chunk of meteor that engulfed the sky from the west.

The comforting granite rock that marked the entrance to their salvation loomed in his eyesight, but he didn't slow down. The safety of the Hive lay yards away. Finally, plunging into the cooler darkness, he let Crystal catch her breath, his anxiety slowly abating.

"We made it, my love." He held his wife close, searching for moisture to loosen his parched and gummy tongue from the roof of his mouth. For once in her life, Crystal kept her smart mouth closed; only gently begging him to explain.

"Johnny . . . please. What in tarnation's going on?" Her brows knitted into a furrow.

"Not now, Crystal." He held her tightly in his arms, averting his terror-filled face. The viper in his stomach uncurled as his senses shrieked that his ordeal was not over. "I think . . . I think we need to keep moving."

They stumbled on, the darkness their friend as its slight coolness revived them. Johno moved on, the cavern of the portal dead ahead.

As they plunged into the cavern, they heard a muffled scream. Staring ahead, they were greeted by the stunning sight of the Kreyven in all its iridescent glory. Before they had a chance to call out, it plummeted into the rock wall to disappear, plunging them back into darkness.

Like zombies in a frenzy, the pair rushed to the cavern wall. Crystal tripped over Hud's fallen box, dumping the scavenged treasures. She bent down, her searching fingers discovering the tiny penlights. When she clicked one on, she was met with the sight of her husband pounding on the solid rock wall; there was no membrane, no portal . . . just unbroken rock. Tears flowed down his ebony face, freezing her to the spot.

"*Quick*, woman. Bring that light here." His fingers moved more frantically, nails splitting and bleeding. "We need to find it, Crystal. *Help me.*"

She rushed to her husband's side in a daze. Her stalwart rock, her love, the calmest man she had ever known . . . was ungluing in front of her eyes.

It was their good fortune that, when the blast came, the shockwave swept through the tunnels of the Hive, blowing them apart with such force that Johno and Crystal never knew what hit them.

Ginger Mae felt herself surrounded and compressed by the undulating mass of the Kreyven; the motion much like the beating of a giant heart. She tried to remove the twine from her hand but it now dug painfully into her skin and she couldn't locate the end that Peter had so carefully tucked away.

Instead, she wrapped herself around her metal bundle, hoping to stabilize herself. Her senses registered a strange pull exerting pressure on her body.

She tried to scream but to no avail. Where were Hud and Peter? *Please save me now, Hud, I need you so.* She felt herself moving through the mass of the Kreyven, its constrictions slowing her movement but not stopping it. She felt safe with the Kreyven, absorbing a calmness from the beast yet unable to negate her growing panic from her slipping-away sensation. She scrambled to hold on to something; her hands and feet unable to find purchase. Instinctively she knew she must stay with the Kreyven. It would take her to Hud. *It's in the service of the Womb, isn't it? Perhaps it's been sent by Netty or Daisy to take us somewhere.*

The darkness burst suddenly with agonizing light as she was pulled free of the comforting embrace of the Kreyven. She clung tightly to her metal bundle as she felt herself in a freefall, the pulling sensation growing stronger. She landed with a hard crash after what felt like an eternity, the light still blinding and her captive wrist now in pain so intense that she fainted.

Oolaha

Day One AE (After Earth)

Chapter 3

The survivors stared as Kenya marched up to Kane and ripped the Good Book from his hands. Shaking it in her fists, her fingers trembling with anger, she lashed out.

"*This* book . . . of *all* books? Why are you even reading it? It should be called *The Great Lie*. If we'd known the truth, we would still be on Earth." Bitter tears flowed from her desolate eyes as she threw imploring looks to them all.

"I don't want to be here. I want my baby to have a home. I want to be part of my community. I want Kane to go to work and come home to help me change diapers and eat my lousy dinner and tell me he loves it. I want a normal life. No more monsters, no more things that fly and read my mind, no more secrets and surprises. If I find out someone is holding out on us again . . . believe me, chickey, you ain't *never* seen the kind of hell I'm gonna raise . . ." Kenya's voice tailed off into a pitiful squeak. She tossed the offending Bible to the side where it landed in a heap, forlornly discarded.

Kane took her in his arms and her sobbing increased. "I just want to go home," she blubbered. "They don't really want us here anyway. We're nothing to this Womb thing. I don't want to be an *accommodation*."

Abby piped up, Chloe's strength beginning to flag. "It'll be okay, Kenya. Just hold on until we get settled in before you freak out. We need to get Chloe some care and check on the babies. At least we're alive and safe. I'm sure we'd all like to have a breakdown, but I don't think any of us have that kind of energy to waste. I know I don't. We can deal with our past later. Right now we'd better concentrate on the here and now." She panned the crowd with her golden eyes, assessing their blood-drained complexions, heavy with deeply etched loss and grief.

"Please . . . Netty . . . can you just get us to where we need to go . . . ?"

Netty opened her mouth to speak when the Kreyven suddenly burst from the dome and portal where it had disappeared. The survivors shrank back as the Kreyven moved toward them, its mass sending its telltale stench of ozone before it.

Kenya clenched Kane in a death grip. "Oh no . . . not more, please . . ."

The Kreyven stopped before them, the gelatinous mass rippling with striating flashes of light and a bulge deep in what appeared to be its throat. From high up, it lowered its head, the bulge moving forward to be vomited onto the ground.

A collective gasp from the crowd failed to wake an unconscious Hud. Seconds ticked by as the Kreyven hovered over the survivors, then hastened off to the distant dwellings, their fairy-tale colors advertising the survivors' eventual destination.

Bonnie was the first to break the silence, her face radiant with hope. Excited, she rushed to Hud's side, announcing to the crowd, "We're *all* saved. The Kreyven came to the rescue again." Her head swiveled back to follow the path of the Kreyven's retreat as she knelt on the ground to take Hud's hand. "Where's it going? Where's Peter? *Where's my husband?*" she shrieked.

Revolting sounds of vomiting drew their attention back to Hud, and Daisy knelt to join Bonnie. Hud threw off their hands as he rolled to the side, vomiting again.

A tiny robot cleaner emerged from the dome, this one on flat legs that slid over the grass on which Hud lay. He stared bleary-eyed at the strange sight of the creature as it cleaned the mess he'd left in the grass. As if sensing Hud's scrutiny, the creature cocked its head and leaned forward toward Hud. It gave him a thorough once-over with its minion-like eyes before retreating back into the dome.

Hud coughed and wiped his mouth with the back of his hand.

Daisy slipped her small hand back into Hud's, her voice betraying her emotion. "Where's Mom, Hud?"

"And Peter? Did he come with you?" asked Bonnie's quavering voice.

Wil stepped forward to pull the women away. He whispered gently into their confused and hopeful faces. "Give him a few minutes, ladies . . . please."

Hud gratefully nodded his head in Wil's direction and cleared his throat. "I sure am happy to see you guys." He looked around. "Peter and Ginger Mae aren't here. Where are we?" He looked through the legs crowded around him to catch glimpses of the milling wildlife and the thousands of minions that vibrated in the air above their heads like an upside-down sea of golden shimmering waves. He tore his eyes from the improbable sight above and looked back to Wil, a dawning of truth written all over him.

"Oolaha? We're on Oolaha?"

Wil carefully nodded his head. "Yes, Hud. The others were warned by Baby and Echo in time to save themselves. We have no idea how many were saved. You're the only one we've seen emerge from a portal since Cobby arrived with Chloe, Kenya, Kane, Dezi and Bonnie. And the babies." He pointed to the now closed portal in their dome. "The Kreyven sealed this portal off a while ago. We thought we were the last ones. How did you wind up in the portal over there?" He pointed to the other dome in the distance.

"I . . . I don't know," he said haltingly. "We were in the storage room and heading back to the settlement with a few things when the Kreyven burst through the wall and grabbed us."

"Us? Who is *us*, Hud? Tell me . . . tell me," Bonnie beseeched.

His fingers to the bridge of his nose, Hud massaged slowly. "Ah . . . well . . . Ginger Mae of course. And Peter."

Grateful tears slid down Bonnie's face. She threw herself at Hud, clasping him in a desperate embrace. "Oh Lord. Thank you, Hud. Thank you . . ."

Hud extricated himself from her grasp. "But where are they?" he demanded.

Bonnie sat up with a startled blink. "You don't *know?*" she asked.

Wil shook his head, his wings drooping in sympathy. "They aren't here, Hud."

Silence hung over the crowd. The only sounds were the fluttering of wings, the restless milling of elephants, and the collective sobbing heartbreak of the survivors as they realized their unrelenting pain had no limits.

It wasn't the pain that woke Ginger Mae. It was the cold and the smell. Even though she could feel herself shiver, her nose told her something burned nearby.

She had no idea how long she'd been out, but the hot-poker pain and swelling from her wrist told her it was broken.

Glancing out of the corner of her eye, she was confronted with a filmy image of an empty room. *How can this be?* She shook her head to clear her eyes, setting off a firestorm in her head. Her eyes squinted and blinked but she was unable to clear her vision. A burning sensation in her eyes told her something was wrong.

"Ugh." Ginger Mae stopped moving to assess her situation and relieve her headache. Even if she couldn't see clearly, she knew she lay on her back on a hard floor. She slowly scrunched her body together into a fetal position as her stomach boiled, threatening to erupt. "Ugh." Her mouth tasted like metal and a sensation of grease clung to the air, further exacerbating her rebelling stomach.

A new sound pierced her consciousness. A buzzing. Like a thousand crickets firing over one another.

Vomiting onto the floor, she heard a different sound. A prickling gave her hope she wasn't alone.

Choking through the vomit she called out, "Hello? Hello? *Anybody there?*"

Suddenly, the burning smell intensified. Wiping her hand across her mouth, she shrank back as two shapes materialized and weaved their way toward her. Ginger Mae blinked hard, her vision stubbornly refusing to clear.

"Hello? Who are you? Where am I?" The figures hovered over her. She felt something on her neck and all went black.

Ginger Mae awoke strapped to a hard surface. No matter how hard she twisted, she felt trapped. She could feel her metal burden had been removed, but her broken wrist felt weighed down with a brick. At least the pain had abated.

Blinking furiously, she tried desperately to clear her sight. As she gave up, her eyes were finally able to make out a shadowy object that appeared to be throwing off sparks, the tiny lights rising and falling like a delicate waterfall . . . disappearing with the limitations of her vision. She had no way to gauge how close it was; her vision was now almost useless.

She sniffed the air, redolent of the same hot burning smell from her room. Rocking her head back and forth, she felt obstacles on each side of her head. Softly rubbing her head against one, she discovered hard metal with only a tiny clearance between it and her body. Her fight or flight reflex paralyzed her with fear. The sound of her rushing blood flooded her ears.

The burning smell became more intense. Ginger Mae started with panic as strange, nebulous figures hovered over her helpless body, the sparkling waterfalls becoming clearer. Her terror rocketed through the roof as the metal alongside her head snapped and clamped down on her forehead. She was fully immobile, only her eyelids dancing with anxiety as she continued to try to clear her sight.

Thankfully for Ginger Mae, as one of the hovering figures reached behind her neck, the dark came rushing in like a long-lost lover, embracing her with its own benign anesthetic to which she gratefully surrendered.

Ginger Mae regained consciousness slowly, the darkness threatening to overwhelm her with its perilous mystery. She realized the hard floor of her enclosure had been softened by a pad of some sort on which she lay. Trying to reach up to her face, she found the weight on her wrist still oppressed her. Her tongue stuck to the roof of her mouth, swollen and dry along with her throat. She knew she must have water soon. Her stomach growled with a fervor that caused her to question how long she'd been out.

She fumbled around, raising her good arm to her face and discovered an obstruction covering her eyes.

"Oh . . . erm . . ." Her tongue floundered; a feeble lump in her mouth. She patted the obstruction down then tried to find some slack to gain purchase with which to rip it off. The material clung to her like plastic; there wasn't a single seam or slack spot to give her a chance to slip a finger under. Her fright increased as she realized she must be a captive somewhere and was clearly not alone. But where was she? And where were Hud and Peter?

Her fear so paralyzed her that she couldn't call out, even if she'd been able to make her useless tongue function. She tried to swallow; her mouth was parched and her throat raw and abused.

The helplessness of her situation hit her like a locomotive. Who had put the infernal blockage over her eyes and why? What didn't they want her to see? *I need information and now.* Rocking her body to and fro, she found no aches and pains. The nausea she remembered upon her first awakening was gone, *thank the Womb. Womb . . . now where the heck did that come from?*

Reaching out with her good arm, she felt around the floor of her enclosure, smashing her hand against something hard that tipped over and leaked moisture over her arm. She raised her arm to her nose and sniffed. She tentatively brought it to her mouth and sucked. *Water.* At least she thought it was water but then realized it had a chalky aftertaste.

Scrambling as best as she could, she maneuvered her body over to the spot where the spilt water lay on the floor. She powered through a wave of dizziness and managed to lower her mouth to the floor to lap up the remaining moisture.

Convulsively, she searched for the container with her good arm. In her scramble to get to the water, it must have rolled away. The longer her questing hand roamed over the floor, the more frightened she became. Locating the water container had become a representation of control. She *must* regain a semblance of control if she was going to survive this. She tried to push away the thought of breaking down completely. She could feel tears slipping from her bound eyes.

Suddenly exhausted, she rolled back to her pad and huddled, her tears now coming in sobs that soaked into the obstruction across her eyes.

Not being able to tell if her eyelids were open or closed was maddening. Overwhelmed with worry about Hud and Peter, she fell into an exhausted sleep, only to be awakened by a pervasive burning smell that signaled terror.

She feigned sleep as the smell became stronger. She thought she heard a yelp but, as she strained to hear more, the only sound she identified was the sound of bees buzzing; louder then softer, rising in pitch then fading.

She froze at the sound of something being dragged across the floor. She felt it pass in front of her then stop. She heard no more as the buzzing of bees faded in the distance, and then she was left again in complete silence.

As her heart continued its frenetic beating, she took a deep breath, hoping it would slow her respiration to a more normal level. Absently, she ran her hands through her hair. *What the . . . ?* Perplexed over a strange sensation, she withdrew her hand. Shaking it to rid herself of the softness that had clung to her fingers, she was unable to see the clumps of her hair as they fell from her scalp and fingers to land in her lap like spent tufts of gossamer.

What the heck was that? Gathering courage, she reached up to her face again and ran her hand over her head, swatting at imaginary bugs. Finding nothing in the air around her head, she relaxed, breathing in relief as more of her hair silently detached from her head to lie unseen about her shoulders.

The minutes ticked by. Before long they piled up as hours. Ginger Mae's stomach ached with a relentless acknowledgment of hunger and thirst. Her psyche begged for the darkness to go away. She needed light. It was only in the light that she could begin her hunt for . . . *for* . . . *for what?* she wondered. Her mind searched, confusion wearing her down. *I have to find it.* It was only then that she could begin to figure out how to get back home. She didn't know where she was but she knew instinctively that this wasn't her beloved Earth. *But what? What do I need to find?*

Before long, her tears stopped. Her strength taxed to its limits, she slept.

Crash— Ginger Mae snapped out of her sleep and sat up. *What was that?* Sniffing the air, she recognized the unmistakable dreaded burning smell. Huddled tightly on her pad she drew herself into a ball, hoping to be overlooked, if only she could make herself small enough.

She strained her ears, desperate to catch the sound of something familiar. She sensed the presence of others: movements and a thump. The darkness pressed in on her. She clamped her hand over her mouth to prevent herself from screaming out in fear. The sounds stopped as suddenly as they'd begun, the burning smell receding. The darkness froze her in place as her tears welled up again.

From out of the silence and the darkness, she heard a scrape.

"Hello," she ventured, her voice timid and tremulous. She was greeted by nothing more than silence. "Is anyone there?" The silence slapped her in the face again. Frightened yet mollified, she curled back into a ball to return to sleep. Who knew what trouble the singular sound would bring her? Maybe it was just her imagination or wishful thinking. Her mind eventually switched off to suck her deeper into the blackness.

The black void now her constant companion, her only escape became sleep: The sleep of the innocent that promised temporary oblivion yet insidiously and unknowingly robbed her of her memory. For it was during her sleep that the residue of the minute toxic substance contained in the hot burning smell—the odor that terrorized her so—was fractionally destroying the cells in her brain. In the part of the brain that stored memory; the essence of who we are and who Ginger Mae had been.

When Aliens Weep is now available

Due Late 2015

Alli Sun

An interracial thriller in 1940's Charleston South Carolina featuring the wanderings of a young orphan who takes to the streets with an unusual set of pups rescued from a deliberate drowning to solve one of the South's biggest and most horrifying crimes as she begins the overwhelming journey to discover who her parents are.

Author's Page

J. K. Accinni was born and raised in Sussex County before moving to Randolph, New Jersey, where she lived with her husband, five dogs and eight rabbits, all rescued, and currently resides in Sarasota, Florida. Mrs. Accinni's passion for wildlife conservation has led her all over the world, including three trips to Africa, where ten years ago she and her husband fell in love with a baby elephant named Wendi who had been rescued by a wildlife group. That baby is the inspiration for the character Tobi, the elephant featured in her fourth book titled *Hive*.

The character of Caesar is inspired by a real life iconic tiger from Big Cat Habitat and Gulf Coast Sanctuary in Sarasota. A portion of the proceeds from her third book, *Armageddon Cometh*, will be donated to the sanctuary in support of the enormous expense required to house and feed the displaced wildlife in their care. Mrs. Accinni invites her readers to visit *bigcathabitat.org* to view the astounding facility and plan a visit with your family.

Mrs. Accinni also invites you to visit her webpage at www.SpeciesIntervention.com, where information on The Big Cat Habitat and Gulf Coast Sanctuary can also be viewed. Readers are encouraged to comment about the book or your own creature experiences.